A

Suitable

Arrangement

A
SUITABLE
ARRANGEMENT

Castles & Courtship
Series

MARTHA KEYES

To all of us who have given a less-than-stellar first impression.
As for the rest of you, don't fret. Your time will come.

CHAPTER ONE

JULIANA

Equipages of all sorts rumbled down Princes Street in a display of organized chaos. From my place on the pavement, I gazed past the carts and on to each carriage.

It was a futile exercise, for Papa had written just this morning to inform me he was yet again delayed. Despite the news, I could not help hoping to see him, for I would feel a great deal calmer making the final part of the journey in his presence. But my cousin and I had already delayed two days, and there was no telling when the officials at the port would release Papa's long-awaited shipment of textiles, just arrived from the East Indies.

"Come along, my dear Juliana," Augusta said. My cousin was dressed for travel, and her blond hair, shifting toward gray now, peeked from beneath her bonnet before her head disappeared into the carriage awaiting us. The carriage was loaded high with my belongings and hers—in my case, *all* my belongings, for I might never return home to Newcastle.

I took one last look at New Town, intrigued by how the

stately, clean buildings contrasted with the ones in Old Town across the bridge. Would I have occasion to come to Edinburgh regularly in my new life? I hoped so. This town was to Scotland what London was to England, after all, attracting all of Scotland's peers. And as the future Countess of Lismore, doors would be open to me here that, despite Papa's wealth, had never been so in Newcastle.

Augusta's head emerged from the carriage door, and she smiled sympathetically. "He shall meet us at Lochlarren soon enough, Juliana."

"Of course," I said as brightly as I could, stepping into the carriage. I settled onto the squabs across from my cousin, arranging my skirts in a way that might prevent wrinkling. I could only hope Augusta had been right to choose this particular dress. It seemed a bit too fine for travel, with its embellished bodice, large epaulets, and embroidered hems, but Augusta knew far better than I did what would be expected of a future countess.

My own experience of Society was limited to the sort of assemblies and engagements a wealthy tradesman's daughter would be invited to frequent, and those events had simply not included peers of the realm. Of course, in our less exalted domain, Papa's significant wealth had made us some of the most sought-after attendees, but at Lochlarren Castle, things would be different. I would be below everyone rather than above.

Augusta regarded me as the carriage pulled forward. "I am certain your father wishes he could be with us, but it is the sort of hard work he is now engaged in which has made this match possible."

"I know it well," I replied. "No one works more tirelessly." And neither was anyone more deserving of the elevation my impending marriage would bring. It was Papa's dearest wish to see me established amongst the highest echelons of society. I, too, was eager for the opportunities such a life would bring—the mere thought of being looked toward as an arbiter of fashion or an example of the best Society made my heart flutter with anticipation. But equally, I wished to please Papa —to repay him for all he had done for me through his indefatigable work. My marriage to Lord Lismore would connect him with the wealthiest investors and consumers of fine goods in the country, and he was already planning how to expand his ventures.

Town soon gave way to country, and I stared through the window, watching it all pass by. I wondered what my new home would be like—and what to expect of the people within.

"It is my understanding that the earl's three brothers will be present at Lochlarren," Augusta said. "You remember their names and how to address them?"

I nodded, for these things had been drummed into me for the past fortnight. "Mr. Magnus Duncan, Mr. Blair Duncan, and Mr. Iain Duncan."

"Very good. And the earl?"

"Alexander Duncan, known by those nearest him as Sandy." I met her look with my own mischievous one. "I prefer Sandy."

Augusta cocked a brow at me, a stern look belied by the twitch at the corner of her mouth.

"However," I said with impish reluctance, "I shall endeavor to remember to call him by his title."

"I certainly hope so. If you are to marry into the aristocracy, my dear, you must play by their rules or risk being ostracized."

My humor dissipated slightly. I had no wish for such a fate. Indeed, it was quite opposite my goal. I would continue to call the earl Sandy in my thoughts, for it made him less intimidating. He had only recently come into the earldom, for his father's illness and subsequent death had been abrupt and unexpected. Almost as abrupt and unexpected as the arrangements for a match between us.

"I assure you, you have nothing to fear from me, cousin," I said.

Augusta did not travel well, for she hadn't a strong stomach, and she spent the majority of the time falling in and out of sleep. In the meantime, my mind strayed to Lochlarren Castle —or rather, to the picture my imagination had created—and to my future husband. What would he be like? Father had only ever met the *late* earl and could give me no descriptors of the new one but for unhelpful words like "sharp," "reasonable," and "business minded."

Not that it mattered much. This was a marriage of convenience, and I was content that it be so. I had never imagined for myself a love match, but instead had been raised with a mind to furthering our family prospects. I had hoped for a title, but marrying an earl was beyond even *my* dreams. My head still reeled at the title I would hold: Countess of Lismore.

After hours in the carriage, we broke our journey for the night in Stirling, continuing in the morning toward our final destination: the coast of Inverness-shire. The rolling green landscape slowly gave way to dense forests and bumpy roads that jolted us from side to side. I had spent my life in town and wondered with both eagerness and anxiety how I would find the wilds of the Scottish Highlands.

We beguiled the time by reviewing the more pertinent lessons Augusta had taught me over the years—proper meal etiquette, curtsies, and matters of precedence. "You must act the part of a countess, my dear," Augusta said, "from the moment you arrive. If they are not persuaded you are fit for the title, there is no telling how they will treat you. These aristocratic families can be quite ruthless."

I searched her face but saw no sign of hurt or resentment there. Cousin Augusta was the illegitimate daughter of an English baron. The man had been kind enough to provide generously for both her mother and her, and Augusta had thus been brought up in Society. When she was seventeen, however, her mother died, and the baron's support dwindled before failing altogether, leaving her in such circumstances that she was obliged to accept help from far less exalted quarters than she was accustomed to: my parents.

With no other options, she had come to live with us and, upon my mother's death, had come to act as a governess to me at the age of five. Since achieving my majority a few years ago, Augusta had become a companion, a guide, and a sort of mother figure, even. I owed her much, and I was grateful to have her with me on this of all days, especially with Papa's absence.

As we persevered into the depths of the Highlands and drew nearer Lochlarren, the roads became too pocked and uneven for Augusta to rest any longer. One particularly large jolt sent us both into the side of the carriage, and we assisted one another in getting resettled.

"I confess myself surprised at the state of these roads," I said over the din.

"I fear it is destined not to be the only surprise ahead of you, my dear." There was a grim note to her voice as I assisted her to the middle of the seat again. "The training I have provided may not have prepared you for the circumstances you will confront at Lochlarren Castle."

I nodded, feeling a wave of nerves and anticipation wash through me. "It is true that I have never met a peer nor been in a castle, but you have prepared me well, cousin."

She reached for my hand and squeezed it. "I do not doubt you, my dear, for you are exemplary—when you wish to be."

She cocked a teasing brow. "But Scotland is an altogether different place than England. And the Highlands?" She looked at me significantly. "A different world."

"But Sandy—forgive me, Lord Lismore is still an earl."

"A Scottish earl," she corrected.

"Are they so different from English ones?"

"They certainly can be. Lord Lismore was raised in the wild Highlands. Growing up in a place left untamed for so long, its occupants will exhibit behaviors you and I may find . . . strange. A bit barbaric, even. And with the sudden death of the late earl, too, it is entirely possible there have been or will yet be struggles for power—remnants of a less civilized time when brute strength rather than impeccable lineage determined who led the clans here."

My eyes widened. It sounded like something from King Arthur's days, not modern times.

"And while a castle may sound grand, you should prepare yourself for a place without many of the conveniences you are accustomed to at home."

I thought over her words for a moment, finding in them both reason for hope and anxiety. I chose to focus on the former. "Perhaps the Duncans will be less likely to look down on me for any blunders or lapses in propriety, then." The thought of being on my very best behavior all day, every day was a weighty one. I could comport myself admirably at a dinner party or ball, but such things always came to an end. Not so at Lochlarren Castle.

"They should *not* look down on you," Augusta said. "You are their salvation, after all. Perhaps they will be all kindness and consideration—I certainly hope so—but I feel it behooves me to warn you of all possibilities. Believe me, my dear, the arrogance and entitlement of some of these old families knows no bounds. An earl and his family are allowed more leniency in their behavior because of their title, while you and I must prove ourselves again and again through our conduct and bearing. Your behavior must be unimpeachable, Juliana. Otherwise, after you are wed and your money is theirs, they may no longer see your value to them."

I sat straighter in my seat. Augusta knew better than most what high society was capable of. She had been discarded as a young woman and naturally did not wish the same for me. Surely, she was acting overly cautious, though.

The carriage bumped and rumbled over holes and mounds, jostling every bone inside my body as we made our way down a narrow road. Finally, the trees gave way, revealing a wide-open expanse: a glistening gray lake surrounded by dense forest, and in the middle of it all, a fortress.

"Lochlarren Castle," Augusta said softly.

I took in the view hungrily. This was to be my home. It was foreboding—tall, gray, and hard—and I prayed those within would be warmer and more inviting. Lochlarren was nothing like the home I had known. I was trading the bustle and smells of town for a secluded, stone castle almost entirely surrounded by water. Augusta's talk of clan struggles and barbarism felt far more likely with this view before me.

"The family and servants will be outside to welcome you," Augusta said, her tone more pressing now that the time was at hand. "Remember your curtsies and to adjust them according to the person to whom you are being introduced. Meet the earl's eye with your chin held high."

Leaning over, I peered through the window as the castle and my curiosity loomed larger. How many servants would they have? Would Lord Lismore's brothers be kind? I had never had any siblings of my own, and I feared I might treat them with too much familiarity—or not enough.

"Come, my dear." Augusta pulled me away from the

window and closed the curtains. "A countess would not be too eager nor too quick to be impressed. Starting now, you must act like a Lady Lismore, Juliana, for in just over a week, you shall become her."

I lifted my chin and pressed my shoulders down as Augusta looked on with approval. There would be plenty of time to explore the castle and take stock of my new surroundings. For now, I had a part to play, an audience to convince, and an opportunity to make both Augusta and Papa proud.

Augusta was right. I needed to look not like Juliana Godfrey but like the woman meant to be Lady Lismore. The woman I saw in my mind's eye was refined. She was accorded the greatest of respect and deference, for that was her due.

If I could manage to portray such a person, the Duncans would welcome my arrival with open arms. Their desperation may have led them to make this match, but I had to ensure they had no cause to regret it.

CHAPTER TWO

SANDY

Billiard balls clattered behind me as I compared the most recent payment request with the ledgers before me. I rubbed at my eyes, everything blurring together.

"Come away from it, Sandy." My brother Blair stood straight, resting the billiard cue on the faded rug which covered the floor. Magnus took his shot, which was no small feat, for his left arm was in a sling.

"You've been staring at those ledgers for hours," Blair pressed.

So I had. But far from distracting me from my growing annoyance, the ledgers were only adding to it. It had taken the better part of the past few weeks to sort through the mess, and I was nowhere near being finished. The estate accounts were entirely dissatisfactory. Worse, even, than Father had given me to believe, and that was saying something.

My jaw tightened instinctively at the thought of those last moments with Father. As though his sudden death hadn't been enough to shoulder, he had thrown on my back a host of hitherto unknown debts, along with the injunction to marry a tradesman's daughter in order to save our family from ruin.

The long-anticipated match between my friend Nelly Cochrane and myself was no longer an option. Our family needed money too desperately. My pride was to be sacrificed on the altar of the earldom. The title that was meant to raise me in everyone's esteem would now come by the debasing act of marrying far beneath me.

My gaze flicked to the window, covered by threadbare curtains but for a small gap, but there was no sound yet to indicate my intended's arrival.

Iain, noticed the direction of my gaze. "Worrying she thought better of the match?" At two and twenty, Iain was the youngest of the four of us, though taller than Magnus and Blair. All of them wore black, but only Magnus, with his ever-furrowed brow, looked severe. Iain and Blair were both too good-natured to appear anything but pleasant, whatever their clothing.

Iain's mouth quirked up at one edge as he looked at Blair. "Or perhaps she cannot read and mistook the date."

The two of them laughed, drawing the ghost of a smile from Magnus. They had no such reaction from me. I found it difficult to laugh at such a real possibility.

"Or," Blair added, "she decided she would rather have a duke than a measly earl. Her father could certainly afford it, and I hear Banff's wife is ill."

I snapped the ledger shut and stood. "You had better hope that is not the reason for their absence."

Blair and Iain shared another look. I knew what it was: commiseration over my short temper. It had been thus since Father died. I missed joining in the antics of my brothers. Even two months ago, I might have played at billiards with them and laughed and teased, but those times were past.

Now, I was saddled with the cares and burdens of the estate, including the weight of my brothers' futures. Both theirs and mine relied on the wife I was to take in a matter of a week. If she ever arrived. She was already two days late.

I could not decide whether to hope for her arrival or dread it. Part of me hoped there might still be another way to tow ourselves out of the River Tick—a way that didn't force us to demean the Duncan legacy with this unfortunate match. Allying ourselves with a tradesman, no matter how wealthy he was, seemed unwise.

But our predicament was not the fault of my brothers.

"Forgive me." I sighed and rubbed my eyes again as I walked over to the billiards table. Iain leaned over for his shot, and I rested my weight on a corner edge of the table to watch. There was a creak, then a sudden clatter as the table gave way under me.

The balls all rolled, falling toward and then into the pocket nearest me, while a light snowing of plaster fell from the ceiling.

The four of us looked at the off-kilter table, the side nearest me now drooping lower than the other three.

A burst of pent-up laughter erupted from Blair, and the other two soon joined in. I covered my own mouth with a hand. I should not laugh, but it was such a perfect demonstration of the state of things at Lochlarren. The once renowned plastered ceiling was chipped so that the original design was hardly recognizable. It sagged in places from water damage. Stomping too hard was enough to bring bits of it down.

As for the floors, they creaked and groaned like a witch being burned at the stake. The billiard table itself was a relic, with old ivory balls that bulged in some places from so many years in the damp. In short, the castle had seen better days.

"Better lay off the puddings, Sandy," Iain teased.

"Or marry an heiress?" I bent down to look at the leg which had buckled under my weight. "You see how we need her."

"Who *is* she, though?" asked Iain.

"My guess?" Blair said. "A short, freckled thing with four missing teeth and a lisp."

"Or a forty-year-old spinster with bad breath," Iain said.

Jaw tight, I knocked on the leg of the table with vain hope to straighten it. They were only teasing, but I truly had no idea what to expect of Miss Godfrey. She had a wealthy, successful father who was willing to part with a great deal of money for me to take her as a wife. That was all Father had needed to know, but it opened up frightening possibilities about what she might be like. I didn't need Blair and Iain's assistance imagining such grim possibilities.

She might be a vulgar, outspoken young woman, or perhaps she would shake in her slippers and barely say a word. I didn't *think* she was older than me, but suddenly, I wasn't at all sure. Had her father even mentioned her age in our letters?

Not that it mattered much. I was not hanging out for a beautiful wife. This was purely a business arrangement, and the greater our differences, the easier it would be to see it as such. I hadn't any time to cater to romantic notions of marriage when we were drowning in letters from Father's creditors.

Perhaps my brothers were right, though, and Miss Godfrey would not come at all. She and her father had informed us they would arrive two days ago. Yet here we were, another day passed, and no bride in sight, blushing or otherwise.

The only thing more humiliating than marrying so far beneath my station would be to be *jilted* by someone so far beneath it.

If Miss Godfrey was to come, I would rather have the whole ordeal over and done with. She could have her title, and I could have my money. There need be no great level of intimacy between us. Indeed, I would not be opposed if she wished to live in town, which I gathered she was accustomed to doing. I had enough on my plate without having to attend to the vagaries of a wife. As one of four sons, I wouldn't even know *how* to do so. My mother had died shortly after Iain's birth, and since then, the only female presence in the castle had been the housekeeper, Mrs. Boyle, and the maids.

Of course, the estate would require an heir at some point, but for now, my only desire was to prevent the need to sell every last thing within Lochlarren's walls—not that they would fetch much money in their present state. And even absent an heir, I had three brothers able to take on the title. There were options.

There was a knock on the door, and Mrs. Boyle appeared in the doorway. She was a crabby but loyal woman who had been with the family for two decades. "Good day, my lord. I've come ta see how many places ye wish to be laid for dinner."

We were still a few hours from the meal, but I saw her question for what it was: an attempt to draw attention to the continued absence of Miss Godfrey and her father. Mrs. Boyle had strict notions of what was due a Duncan of Lochlarren, and marrying a tradesman's daughter, no matter how wealthy, was not one of them. "Just the usual number. I will inform you if plans change."

Her lips pinched together, but she curtsied and left.

"I would have thought Boyle would be overjoyed the girl hasn't arrived yet," Blair said. "No one to challenge her ruling the roost."

"Her greater concern is for Sandy's pride," Iain said. "Heaven help Miss Godfrey if she *does* arrive, for Boyle shan't take the slight lying down. Come, let us see if we can fix the table."

Blair and Iain lifted it, and I gave the leg a smack until it stood upright again, the crack in the wood barely visible. Slowly, they lowered the table, and all of us braced ourselves for it to break again. But it didn't.

Iain set to pulling balls out of the pockets and setting them back on the faded green cloth. I had seen paintings of this room from yesteryear, and the table had once been a fine, grand thing. Its glory days were past, however, just like many of the once-fine furnishings in the castle.

The sound of carriage wheels brought my head around, and my brothers' gazes all shifted to me.

Iain walked to the nearest window and pulled back the curtain. After a moment, he nodded.

My heart thudded, the future pounding against my chest.

Blair and Magnus joined Iain at the window, but I couldn't bring myself to move. It was too soon, and yet the tardiness— with no word of excuse—was unforgivably rude. A slight with heaven only knew how many more to come.

"Should we go out to meet them?" Blair asked.

I hesitated a moment. But the Godfreys had made me wait; they couldn't possibly expect to arrive two days late, without notice, and have the household ready to receive them.

When I did not respond, Blair turned back toward the gap in the curtains, going up on his toes to see over Iain's shoulder.

The sound of the carriage wheels ceased, replaced by a muffled opening of a door.

Iain and Blair's heads whipped toward each other, their eyes wide.

"What?" I asked, more impatient than ever.

Blair cleared his throat, then pulled his lips between his teeth to stop a smile.

Magnus looked at me, his face sober. "Iain was right."

"Right about what?"

"The spinster with bad breath," Iain said, looking half-gleeful, half-apologetic.

I hurried over to the window, determined to know whether they were having a laugh at my expense, as they so often did.

But the woman stepping down from the carriage did indeed look the spinster. She was well- if somewhat gaudily dressed, but the little I could see of her hair and face certainly proclaimed a more advanced age than my thirty years. She must be forty at least.

So, this was to be my wife. The new countess. It was her portrait that would hang on the old walls near mine.

I sucked in a breath, and Blair looked back at me, grasping my shoulder as the woman turned her head toward the castle window—and us.

I snapped the curtain shut.

"Enough ogling," I said testily. "For pity's sake, at least give the appearance of doing something useful when she is announced, or we shall seem as vulgar as they are."

Hands not terribly steady, I returned to my ledgers, awaiting my bride and her father.

CHAPTER THREE

JULIANA

With all the elegance I could muster, I stepped down from the carriage, my gloved hand in Cousin Augusta's. Once my feet were planted firmly on the ground, I lifted my gaze, bringing my chin up high to look on the audience awaiting our arrival.

There was none. Only a squirrel took note of my grand entrance, its bushy ears on the alert, its paws grasping some morsel. After a moment, it skittered away, disappearing behind the wall of the castle, apparently underwhelmed.

I looked to Augusta, whose furrowed brow made clear how troubled she was at the silence greeting us. My heart pattered more heavily in my chest. She had been so certain we would be welcomed by Duncans and servants alike. We *were* late, of course, but Papa had assured us he sent word to apprise the earl of the circumstances.

"What are we to do?" I asked Augusta in an undervoice.

"Keep your head high, my dear," she said, leading by example. "Who knows but what they may be observing us even now. This may be a test."

The large, wooden door creaked as it opened, and a middle-aged woman emerged, a set of keys jangling at her waist. The housekeeper, then. She looked in no hurry, though, which I would have assumed if our arrival was indeed unexpected.

Her eyes roved over me, unsmiling as they took me in leisurely, from head to foot. My cheeks burned, and I lifted my chin a bit higher.

"Miss Godfrey, I presume?" In Edinburgh and Stirling, I had heard plenty of Scottish accents, but hers was different—stronger and more pronounced. It was a small thing, perhaps, but it made me suddenly conscious of what Augusta had said: things would be even more different here than I had imagined.

I inclined my head in acknowledgement. "And this is my cousin, Miss Augusta Lowe."

The housekeeper's brows drew together as she looked to the carriage behind. "And your father?"

"Was detained by urgent business," I replied.

Her lips pursed, and she nodded curtly as two more servants appeared. She directed them to begin unloading the trunks and valises from the carriage.

"This way, miss," the woman said, turning back toward the castle.

I glanced again at Cousin Augusta, hoping for some indication whether such brusque treatment was normal. The pinched look on her face told me what I needed to know. Perhaps the housekeeper was merely an ornery type of woman, though. It was premature to despair just yet.

"I am Mrs. Boyle, the housekeeper," she said as we followed her to the door. "Ye'll have ta excuse our lack of readiness. We expected ye days ago." The censure in her tone was unmistakable. Had they not received Papa's letter informing them of the delay?

We entered a dim entry hall. One grand, stone staircase, nearly ten-feet wide faced us in the center. In the corners sat two narrow, winding ones.

"I will inform his lordship of yer arrival," Mrs. Boyle said. "Please remain here while I do so." Without waiting for confirmation, she continued to the main staircase that wound up and around, taking her from our view.

Without moving my head, I let my eyes explore the room around me. It was dark, lit by a few scant, flickering candles, with a low, stone ceiling and very few furnishings. A family crest hung over the fireplace, which was empty of the glow that might have otherwise brightened and warmed the room.

"Do not let yourself be intimidated, Juliana," Cousin Augusta said in a low voice. "Show them you belong—that you are comfortable becoming mistress of such a place."

I took in a deep breath as the sound of footsteps descending the stairway grew closer. *Was* I comfortable becoming mistress of this grand but dark castle?

Papa's face came to my mind, and I reaffirmed my determination to become Lady Lismore, however foreign she now seemed to me.

Augusta sneezed violently just as Mrs. Boyle appeared again, remaining on the second step from the bottom and watching her as if the interruption might be repeated. "His lordship will see ye now." She turned back the way she had come. "Follow me, if ye please."

Dabbing her nose with a handkerchief, Augusta nodded at me, as if to remind me of my aim. I gathered my skirts in hand and followed the housekeeper up the dark stairway, my cousin trailing just behind me.

My heart fluttered, and I tried to convince myself it was nothing but the exertion of the steep, winding steps. I would not allow myself to be intimidated. The Duncans needed me. Both I and they would do well to remember that.

Of course, I did not need them nearly as much. Becoming a countess and helping the growth of Papa's business was not a necessity, but they were both things I dearly wanted.

We came to a landing, with a door to the left and one to the right. While the stairs continued to climb, disappearing around another twisting bend, I directed my gaze to the door on the left—the one thing standing between me and the people I would call my family.

My nerves leaped and whirled, and I took in a deep, fortifying breath just as Mrs. Boyle turned toward me. The way her keen eyes rested on me told me she sensed my anxieties. Perhaps she could smell my fear with that upturned nose of hers.

Hoping to throw her off the scent, I inhaled and exhaled twice in rapid succession, fanning my face. "I must accustom myself to steep stairs and dark corridors."

"I'd have thought ye had such experience already, miss," she replied with a stony face. "Are no' the tenements in yer town similar?"

Before I could answer or even decide whether she meant offense—which seemed quite likely, for we had not lived in poor, tenement-style housing since my childhood—she opened the door and stepped to the side. "Miss Godfrey, my lord."

Augusta made a noise at the housekeeper's choice not to also announce her, and my jaw tightened. It was one thing for her to be short toward *me*; I could not allow her to be unkind to my cousin. Augusta had already experienced enough disrespect in her life. Did Mrs. Boyle know Augusta was the daughter of a baron? And an English one—a proper one.

I stepped into the room, trying my best to stand as I

thought a countess might. And though my eyes itched to explore, I kept them straight ahead. There were four men in the room, and my gaze tripped between them. All of them were dark in aspect, and not only because of their mourning clothing. Their hair varied in its shades of brown like coffee grounds.

A man with a deep frown on his brow and an arm in a sling stared at me with piercing eyes. Was this the earl? He was certainly foreboding enough to be one. How had he come by his injury? Augusta's talk of clan loyalty struggles pressed itself upon me.

More importantly, though, all four of the men were seated, their surprised eyes upon us as though we were a spectacle rather than welcome guests. Not one had risen at my entrance, despite being engaged in what appeared to be leisurely pursuits—the billiards table seemed to have been recently in use. When they had not appeared outside to greet us, I had chosen to assume our arrival had perhaps coincided with urgent business. But no.

Did they think me unaware of what was my due?

One of the men finally rose from his chair. He was tall and broad, holding himself with the sort of authority that told me *this* was Lord Lismore—or Sandy Duncan, rather. His frowning gaze jumped from me to Augusta and back. "You are Miss Godfrey?"

"I am," I replied evenly, though his critical eye made me feel anything but calm.

His frown deepened. Was he underwhelmed? He certainly did not look pleased. Might he run off as the squirrel had done outside? Whatever he was thinking, I did not like the way it led him to look at me. With every second, my pride became more ruffled.

"You are . . . alone," he said.

"Not alone, Sandy," said one of his brothers. "She has her maid."

Beside him, the last of the brothers leaned over, speaking in an undervoice that carried in the room. "But does she have bad breath?"

My teeth clenched until I thought they might break. I suppressed the urge to look at Augusta to see what she made of this. I could no longer defer to her without giving these people to think me unfit for the role I would step into. "This is not my maid," I said tightly. "This is my cousin and companion, Miss Augusta Lowe."

Augusta sneezed as she dipped into a curtsy. Unfortunate timing, for it made it less elegant than I knew she was capable of.

"Stand, you fools," the earl said to his brothers through clenched teeth.

They all hurried to their feet, and my cheeks burned, my pride smarting. If they imagined themselves so far above me that they needn't accord me the barest civility of standing, I would teach them a much-needed lesson. "I take it you are Sandy?"

He blinked at me, and one of his brothers coughed.

"Lord Lismore, ma'am," he said with a tight jaw and a shallow bow. "Forgive my brothers. When I said you were alone, I merely meant that your father is not with you. We were expecting him to accompany you."

Given how Mrs. Boyle had reacted, I gathered Papa's absence did not add to our consequence—assuming we had any such thing in the eyes of the Duncan family. "He had urgent and unexpected business," I said icily, "but he shall arrive as soon as he is able."

The looks shared between the brothers told me they doubted the veracity of my statement—or perhaps they thought Papa apathetic enough not to feel it necessary to accompany me.

I bristled like a cat. "I imagine you can appreciate that creating vast wealth these days requires more than simply having the undeserved fortune of being born into an old family name." I looked around the room with as much bland curiosity as I could muster. "How very quaint is your castle!" I smiled the way a mother might when offered a wilted flower by her child.

The earl's gaze fixed on me, and I met it unflinchingly, though my heart bounced about violently in my chest.

"The *quaintness* you see," he said with a smile that didn't reach his eyes, "is the result of hundreds of years of existence under the ownership of the Earls of Lismore, of which I am the eighth." His smile grew, as did the intentness of his gaze. "I imagine you can appreciate that a castle with the history and prestige of Lochlarren cannot simply be bought up with a newly acquired fortune, however large that fortune may be."

Heat rushed into my neck and cheeks, but I forced a serene smile to match the one he wore. "Can it not? I was under the impression that was the precise reason I was here."

A muscle in his jaw jumped. "I assure you, Miss Godfrey, that it is only the direst of circumstances which have led to your presence here."

Above the smile plastered on my lips, my nostrils flared at the sheer nerve of the man, while all his brothers looked on silently, their eyes wide.

There was a sudden clatter, and the billiard table shifted, collapsing at the corner nearest Lord Lismore. Balls rolled in his direction, settling into the pocket above the broken leg.

"Dire, indeed," I said. "No matter. However, far from civilization we may be, with enough money, a billiard table is easy enough to procure." I hardly believed my own audacity, but the man absolutely must be put in his place—or else he would continue to put me in what he saw as mine. "Polished manners, on the other hand, are an entirely different matter. Those must be difficult indeed to come by in such remote parts as these."

The earl's brown eyes lit at my words. "Och, ye're no' wrong there, lass. But, o' course, we canna do anythin' but our best with the scant materials and company we have access to in these backwoods."

I blinked at the sudden strength of his accent—and at being called *lass* for the first time in my life. Had I not noticed his accent before? Or was he doing it intentionally?

"Perhaps ye'd like ta see the rest of the castle ye're buyin'," he said. "I'm certain Mrs. Boyle is eager ta give ye the tour of our humble abode."

I had no desire to rejoin the company of Mrs. Boyle. She terrified me, and I needed time to assess the situation in which I found myself. Augusta would know how to proceed, but that conversation required privacy.

"While it would be wise to know at the outset just how much money shall be required to make the place habitable, I am rather tired from being jostled about in the carriage on the mottled mud you call roads here."

"Aye," he said, his gaze going to my hair. "It looks as though Scotland has given ye a proper and bonnie welcome."

I put my hand to my hair in spite of myself, wondering what sort of image I presented that he would say such a thing. Cousin Augusta would never have let me show my face unless I was looking my best, though, surely.

The earl was merely trying to discomfit me. I would not give him the pleasure.

He approached me, and I found it difficult to maintain the regality of my bearing, for as he drew nearer, I was obliged to tip my head back to meet his eye. He was a handsome man, with dark eyes and hair that curled. Unfortunately, any physical attraction he held was eclipsed by his disagreeableness.

He held my gaze, then took my gloved hand in his. "A tour tomorrow, then, perhaps. Scotland is no' a place for the fragile, but with yer *vast wealth*, perhaps we can make it more hospitable for ye." He brought my hand to his lips, holding my gaze as he kissed the back of my hand in a way that felt more like a slap on the cheek.

He thought me fragile. *Me.* I had spent the early days of my life running about dirty streets with the children of shopkeepers and laborers. And though I wished to tell him just that, Augusta would have spasms if I did so. The only reason the earl could even begin to think me fragile was because I was at pains to appear like the coddled sort of woman a peer might wish to marry. He was testing me, but it was not the test I had anticipated. Augusta was right: I had not been prepared for this.

But I would pretend to be.

"I certainly hope that is the case," I said.

"Mrs. Boyle will show ye ta yer room that ye may gather yer strength for dinner," he said, going to pull the bell.

I said nothing, though I felt the eyes of all the Duncan brothers upon me. I had not even been introduced to any of them. I was being shuffled away as soon as could be managed —precisely what Augusta had warned me of, and it was happening after only five minutes at the castle.

But though I followed Mrs. Boyle out of the room, I determined to make it abundantly clear to Lord Lismore that I would not be swept aside so easily. If I was to be mistress of Lochlarren Castle, I would be so not only in name but in deed.

CHAPTER FOUR

SANDY

The door closed behind Miss Godfrey and her companion, the click of the latch echoing like a gunshot in the silent room.

A soft whistle from Iain interrupted the quiet, and all eyes turned to me.

"What?" I said testily.

No one spoke for a moment. Blair looked from Iain to Magnus and back. "Very well. I will say it if no one else will. Is Lochlarren truly worth keeping if its mistress will be *that* woman? Better be poor and have you marry Nelly Cochrane than to be saddled with her."

"Nelly has made it clear a marriage between us is not an option," I said, trying to conceal my annoyance.

"If only she were an heiress!" Iain said.

I didn't deign to reply, for my pride still smarted over the whole ordeal. A long-anticipated match between neighbors and friends had crumbled once the weight of Father's debts became clear to the Cochranes. Even *they* had been primarily concerned with the ways I could further their aspirations. I was and always had been a means to an end.

"Perhaps Miss Godfrey will change her mind about the match now that she has arrived," Iain said. "She seems to think little enough of the castle."

"And of Sandy," Blair said.

"And of Scotland," Magnus added.

"Well, I cannot blame her for the latter two," Blair said with a smile at me. "Not after your wild brogue."

"Or lack of manners," Iain said. "You did not even introduce us, Sandy."

"She did not seem particularly interested in any of you," I said, irritated to have my lapse mentioned. I had been too focused on winning the battle with Miss Godfrey to spare a thought for anything else.

"Nor in you," Iain joked.

"A higher compliment I can hardly imagine," I said frostily. My initial surprise at Mrs. Boyle announcing Miss Godfrey as not the forty-year-old spinster I had seen descend from the carriage but the young, beautiful woman, holding herself with all the confidence of a queen had indeed made me forget my manners. But after the astounding arrogance Miss Godfrey had demonstrated, I couldn't bring myself to regret it. The woman desperately needed a set-down.

My father might have hand-picked her as a blow to my pride.

Blair came over and clapped me on the back. "Take heart, brother. After seeing you and your *quaint* castle, perhaps she will choose Banff after all."

I chewed the inside of my lip. Was he right? Was Lochlarren so below what she was accustomed to that she might truly cry off? It was true the castle furnishings were not in the first stare of fashion, but they were of fine quality despite their age.

I shook my head. "Her father has made it abundantly clear, by her marriage portion if nothing else, how much he wishes for the match. Or how much he wishes to be rid of her."

"We could *make* her cry off," Iain said with a mischievous smile. "Give her *a proper Scottish welcome*." He said the last words in a thick accent like the one I had used.

The idea was more tempting than it deserved to be. I glanced down at the sheaf of papers I had been looking over—physical evidence of the poor choices my father and *his* father had made. Debt upon debt upon debt. They had been so concerned with their own comforts and copying the ways of their English counterparts, they had ceased to think what the estate could bear.

I would not be that way, though. I was determined to make more of Lochlarren and the earldom than it had been when I had come into it, even if it meant marrying a woman with overinflated self-importance. I didn't need—indeed, didn't *want*—any warmth of feeling to grow up between us. I merely needed her money and, eventually, an heir. Though, after these last few minutes, simply allowing the title to devolve to Magnus had become significantly more palatable an option.

In any case, Lochlarren was large enough we could avoid one another with near ease. Or perhaps I could rent a townhouse for her in Edinburgh or London. Something told me she would have a great deal to say about how things were managed here, and I would far rather be left to my own devices.

For now, though, Miss Godfrey needed to understand her place here. I needed her money, yes, but I wasn't fool enough to be ignorant of the attraction a match with an earl held—even a Scottish one.

"We have far too many pressing debts for me to wish her to cry off," I said. Heiresses were not exactly jumping out of the loch to marry into a heavily indebted Scottish family living so far from town. Too many other families had managed their finances better than we and could offer both title and fortune.

Both Blair's and Iain's shoulders dropped with disappointment. I couldn't blame them. The prospect of adding Miss Godfrey to our family was bitter on my tongue.

"However," I said significantly, "she seems to hold a number of interesting ideas about what sort of earldom she is marrying into, and I would hate to disappoint her expectations."

My brothers' eyes lit up with anticipation as I thought back on her words. Miss Godfrey seemed to think this marriage was essentially a purchase of my title and castle. The nerve of it was astonishing, particularly given how low an opinion she held of the things she had come to claim.

"If it is a Scottish earldom she has come for," I said determinedly, "a Scottish earldom she shall have."

Ignoring the questions my brothers pelted at me, I strode from the room, ascending the stairs to the next landing, where my own quarters were. It was strange for me to call them *my* quarters, for they had belonged to my father just a few short weeks ago. His portrait hung just outside the room, and I stopped in front of it for a moment, letting my gaze travel over the likeness.

It was ugly—there was no denying that, for it had been done by an obscure, traveling artist, and the likeness was hardly recognizable. I had been there the day the painter had brought in a dozen half-finished paintings. The neck, shoulders, and torso were already completed; Father had but to choose the one he liked best and sit for the painter to paint the head. The result was as seamless as a pair of thrice-patched breeches.

"Well, Father. Are you happy?" I challenged the uneven eyes.

Mrs. Boyle appeared down the corridor, emerging from the bedchamber set aside for Miss Godfrey.

"Ah," I said, turning from the portrait. "How fares Miss Godfrey?"

Her lips pinched together. "I'd like ta give her a fine lashin', my lord."

I couldn't stop a smile. Mrs. Boyle would likely not have taken to my intended bride no matter how agreeable she had been, but Miss Godfrey gave her more than ample reason to dislike the match. "I beg you will refrain. For now, at least."

"I'll do my best, my lord, but if she makes another comment about how clearly the castle wears its centuries of wear, I willna be able ta restrain meself."

I took in a large breath. "I quite sympathize. Lashings, however, must not make up part of her welcome to Lochlarren. But I do have a few instructions for you in regards to her arrival —and dinner."

"Aye, my lord. What are they?"

"Have a peat fire made up in her bedchamber, and then—"

"A peat fire?" She looked at me as though I was mad.

"A peat fire," I repeated.

"But, my lord, where do ye imagine I'll find peat?"

"I haven't any idea, Mrs. Boyle, but your ingenuity knows no bounds." Peat was a common source of fuel in much of Scotland, particularly the more barren moorlands, where not a single tree would grow for miles. Lochlarren, however, was surrounded by a loch and thick trees, providing plenty of wood for fires. "Miss Godfrey has come expecting a true Highlands experience. She should not be deprived of something so entirely Scottish merely because she happens to have the misfortune of being at Lochlarren. She should experience our country fully—including its smells. Do you not agree?"

Mrs. Boyle narrowed her eyes at me, and I couldn't help the way my lip trembled at one side, for the thought of Miss Godfrey's fine clothes saturated with the smell of peat was an irresistible one.

Mrs. Boyle seemed to understand my request, for her eyes lit with anticipation. "My lord, I shall find peat even if I have ta dig it up meself."

"I trust that will not be necessary, but I appreciate your vigor. I think some changes to tonight's menu are warranted, as well."

She looked at me warily. "What sort of changes?"

I thought for a moment. "Let us welcome Miss Godfrey and Miss Lowe with something more . . . traditional. I should like to present her with a spread that will help her appreciate the tastes of our fine country."

Mrs. Boyle's expression morphed into a smile. "Gladly, my lord. I reckon I ken just the thing." She curtsied, looking more glad than I had seen her in weeks, then walked toward the stairs I had just scaled.

"Oh, and Mrs. Boyle?"

She stopped and turned back toward me. "Aye, my lord?"

"Perhaps the forks can be given an extra polishing tonight."

Her brows went up. "But . . ."

"We shan't require them at the dinner table tonight."

She smiled conspiratorially and gave a nod.

I was not usually one to be late, but tonight, I was making an exception. Miss Godfrey clearly thought I had barbarous manners, and I wasn't in a particular hurry to disabuse her of such a notion. She seemed to think she was the one sacrificing by making this match; I intended to make her acknowledge just how much she wished for the title she would gain—and that required pushing her to her limits.

Everyone was already seated when I strode into the dining hall, but rather than making my way directly to my seat, I stopped at the threshold, waiting for all eyes to turn to me and behold me in all my glory.

"Forgive my tardiness," I said, speaking in the strongest accent I felt able to sustain without too great an effort.

No one responded, for their attention was on my clothing. My valet, Gillies, had stared, too, when I had instructed him to have my great kilt ironed and prepared for wearing. He had obeyed me without a word, but when I had asked him to bring my saber, too, he had been unable to contain himself any longer.

"To dinner, my lord?" he had protested.

I put my hand to its hilt, pressing it gently so that the candlelight caught upon its blade.

A sudden snort came from Blair, followed by an immediate hacking cough. Iain obligingly slapped him on the back, though the smile on his face told me he was just as near to losing his composure.

Satisfied that the three times I had been obliged to re-pleat my kilt had not been wasted, I took my seat at the head of the table, with Miss Godfrey to my left. She sent a wary, sidelong glance at my saber, as though it might jump out of its place and harm her. The flicker of fear was the first indication I had from her that she was capable of feeling any emotion besides superiority. It was gone as soon as it had appeared, but I couldn't help wondering if my choice to drive home her prejudices against Scotland might be an unkind one or an overreaction on my part. I needed to ensure she realized the advantages she was gaining without pushing her so far she no longer wished for them.

"It willna harm ye, lass," I said with a hint of amusement.

She forced a smile in return. "I am not accustomed to weapons at the dinner table, Sandy. I suppose in these parts, though, precautionary measures must be taken to ensure our safety."

I repented of my thought. My choice had *not* been unkind or an overreaction. It was entirely merited. Again, she used my given name, a wholly presumptuous familiarity.

And then there was her comment about safety. Did she imagine our dinner might be interrupted at any moment by ruffians? Where had she come by such notions of Scotland?

My gaze shifted to Blair, whose brows were raised at her comment. For good reason. Miss Godfrey was far safer at Lochlarren Castle than she was in a town like Newcastle, full of vagrants and the desperate poor.

"I trust the power struggles within the clan have not been too violent since your father's death?" Her gaze shifted to Magnus's broken arm, and for a moment, I was speechless, unsure whether to laugh or take offense. She thought his injury a result of struggle for power amongst the Duncans?

"Och," Iain chimed in, "if only that were true. Poor Magnus here"—he set a hand on his shoulder—"is a prime example of what happens when ye attempt to take power that doesna belong ta ye."

I shot Iain a look, then met Miss Godfrey's gaze, which flitted from me to Magnus and back. "*You* broke his arm? Your own brother?"

I cleared my throat, torn between amusement at Iain's unprompted assistance and wondering if it would alert Miss Godfrey to the fact that we were purposely trying to shock her. "Order must be preserved, whatever the cost."

She raised her brows, looking unsure what to believe.

"We dinna regard a wee skirmish, miss," Magnus said in his low, emotionless voice. "'Tis merely the way of things."

"I see," she said as she was served a generous helping of haggis. "So, this sword of yours is not simply protection against foes outside of Lochlarren, but against your own family?"

"I dinna think Magnus unwise enough ta attempt such a thing a second time," I said, glaring at him in an exaggerated manner. "But 'tis best no' ta take any chances." Pulling the small dagger from the side of my belt opposite my saber, I held Magnus's gaze, trusting he at least would manage to keep from collapsing into fits of laughter. Iain and Blair could not be relied upon for such a thing.

Miss Godfrey was proving more difficult to rattle than I had anticipated.

An idea occurred to me, and using the dagger, I split open the casing around the haggis on my plate.

Miss Godfrey's eyes went wide, and I felt a flash of satisfaction. Beside the haggis were potatoes and turnips, and I made a mental note to compliment Cook on managing the meal on such short notice.

Miss Godfrey cleared her throat, peering at the haggis on her own plate. "And what, if I may ask, is this . . . interesting creation?"

"Haggis, neeps, and tatties, lass," I said, using the edge of my blade to pick up some haggis and put it in my mouth. I let the blade scrape between my teeth as I pulled it out, studiously ignoring the way Iain covered his mouth. If I let mine even begin to turn up into a smile, I would lose my poise entirely.

Miss Godfrey swallowed. "I see." She looked on either side of her plate. "Forgive me, but it seems my fork has been mislaid."

"Fork?" Blair said, picking up his knife. "What need have ye for such a thing?" He stabbed a potato and brought it to his mouth.

After a moment of hesitation, Miss Godfrey took her knife in hand, peering it as though trying to decide how to best utilize it while preserving her poise and dignity. I was certainly eager to see how she would accomplish it.

"Where is yer cousin?" I asked, for Miss Lowe was absent.

"She is feeling unwell and preferred to rest." She poked at the haggis with the edge of her knife. "And what, if you please, *is* haggis?"

This was the moment I had been waiting for. I scooped up as much as I could with my dagger. "Ye've never had haggis afore?"

"I have not had that"—her lips turned down at the sides as she watched me clean the dagger—"pleasure."

"'Tis sheep, lass."

"Ah," she said, apparently taking heart.

"That is ta say," I continued, "'tis the entrails and organs of a sheep, mixed with a few other things"—I left to her mind the mystery of what those things might be—"cooked inside the sheep's own stomach." I reached over to her plate and pierced the casing around the haggis. It split open, letting out steam as a hundred of the little granules cascaded over the side and onto her plate.

CHAPTER FIVE

JULIANA

It was all I could do not to retch right then and there. But Lady Lismore—that hazy figure I was meant to become —would do no such thing. Somehow, she would manage to maintain her composure.

Or would she make her disgust known?

This was becoming far more complicated than I had anticipated. Was I meant to act superior? Or to show that I had a place here, eating sheep innards with a knife?

Even more importantly, I had a persistent fear I was being mocked somehow. Augusta had urged me to expect some degree of barbarism, however, and without her, it was hard to know for certain.

I cursed the fact that she was laid up. Her sneezing had only become more frequent since our arrival, and added to it a headache and coughing. She had been determined to be present, but after seeing how pulled and pale she had looked, I had insisted she rest.

I was regretting such compassion heartily. If ever I had

needed her direction, now was that time, for stabbing my food with a knife went against everything she had taught me.

The eyes of all the Duncans were upon me, waiting to see whether I would appreciate the food. Surely, the most important thing was for them to see I was up to whatever task I was put to.

I looked around at each one, and I saw it in their eyes and in the tilt of Iain's mouth: this was a test. Could I eat the less savory parts of a sheep and keep my dignity intact? Perhaps if I had been marrying an earl in Somerset, the trial would have been whether I could converse easily with a duke or perform a quadrille with no warning.

I was in Scotland, though, and, like it or not, *this* was my lot.

Well, if that was the case, I would show them I was equal to anything they lay before me, even sheep guts. This was for Papa. It was for Cousin Augusta. All their work would not— could not—be in vain.

Head held high, I scooped up the pellets of sheep offal— better not to think on that too much—and brought the knife to my mouth. Even if it tasted like rancid milk, I would not betray my dislike of it.

As long as I ignored the true origin of what was in my mouth, the taste was surprisingly enjoyable. But as Augusta had said, a countess would not be overly eager to heap praise upon the food. She would take everything in stride. I chewed a few moments, then set down my knife gently on my plate, keeping my expression calm and neutral.

As it became clear I did not mean to make a scene at the table, the others directed their attention to their own plates.

Satisfied I had passed this test, at least, I glanced at Lord Lismore. He was a striking figure in his double-breasted coat, with the tartan great kilt slung over his shoulder. The saber at his waist glinted as he shifted to eat from his plate or drink from his cup of ale.

For the first time, it occurred to me that he was the only one thus attired. Was it because of his title? He had been wearing an ordinary tailcoat and pantaloons when I had first met him.

My brow furrowed as I thought on the meeting, for his clothing was not the only difference between those first moments and now. Had his accent not grown stronger—far stronger—in the past few hours?

Something was not sitting right.

"My lord," I said, stabbing a turnip with my knife as elegantly as could be managed, "do explain something to me, if you will. When we first met, I detected a slight accent. Perhaps my memory fails me, though, for it has since become quite strong. Does it come and go like the tide?"

"Nay, lass," he said with a smile that might make a heart flutter if the voice hadn't belonged to a haughty oaf. "When ye first arrived, I thought ta impress ye. But seeing as we'll soon be married, I realized 'twas useless ta pretend. How can I be anythin' but what I am?"

"I see," I replied, unconvinced. "And the clothing you now wear, is that the expected dining attire? I couldn't help but notice your brothers are not similarly dressed."

"A keen observation," the earl said, sliding the dagger between his teeth another time. "That is—"

"Because our kilts were soiled in the most recent scuffle," Blair interrupted. "A neighboring clan stormed the castle Sunday last, and we were obliged ta defend it. I hope ye're no' offended by our inadequate dress this evening, Miss Godfrey. We mean no disrespect ta ye by it."

Lord Lismore cleared his throat. "How do ye find yer room, Miss Godfrey?"

"Colder than expected," I said truthfully. It was nigh on summer, but the castle seemed to function like an ice house, keeping out the warmth. I could only imagine what it would feel like in the winter months.

"I'll have more blankets sent up," he replied, "and the fire lit."

"Thank you. Though, it will require cleaning, for it seems someone mistakenly placed some mud bricks in the grate." I directed my attention to my plate as I pierced a potato with my knife. It was soft enough to break in two pieces, forcing me to try again and again to stab it. In the end, I had to scoop it onto the knife as best I could.

"Peat bricks, ye mean?"

My brow wrinkled. "Peat bricks?"

He smiled again. "Aye, lass. 'Tis Scotland's greatest treasure. Our proud source of fuel."

I stared at him, trying to determine whether he was teasing me. But his smile seemed rather to be at my ignorance.

"It burns bright and hot, not ta mention its . . . distinctive smell. Scotland is fair covered with it."

"How fortunate for you," I said, wondering what smell I should expect once the fire was lit. I used my knife to scoop more haggis into my mouth. How was one to look like a countess when one was trying not to stab oneself with the knife one held, and all the while sheep innards tumbled off of either side, evading ingestion?

Lord Lismore's dark eyes glinted playfully. "And for you now as well, lass. Ye're ta become one of us. A proper Scottish countess."

I forced a smile and avoided his eye. The teasing glint there and the way he called me *lass* were meant to make me forget just how intolerable he had been—an impossible task.

By the time dessert was placed before us—oatcakes and

preserves—I was anxious to see how Augusta was faring, and even more than that, I desired solitude. Everything was new at Lochlarren: the people, the food, the manners. More than once, the earl's brothers had dispensed with knives entirely and brought the plates to their mouths for easier access. Iain, as I understood him to be called, had actually licked his plate clean like a dog.

I couldn't blame them. It was easier than trying to make the knife serve the functions of a fork and spoon.

But for all that, Iain and Blair seemed kind enough. Magnus, on the other hand, was reserved and somber, and I rather suspected he did not think highly of me. Or perhaps he did not think of me at all. It was possible that I was overly concerned that he—indeed *everyone*—could see through me immediately, that just by looking at me, they might know that I had never spoken with a countess, let alone seen one. What would they think if they knew I had spent my first years of life in the cramped and dilapidated tenements of Newcastle?

"Well," Blair said, rising from his place before I had even left them to their drink, "I'll be retirin' now. I dinna wish ta be too fatigued for clan feuding practice in the morning."

My head shot up. "Clan feuding practice?"

"Aye," Iain confirmed as he stretched his arms up and yawned. "Bright and early at six o'clock on the lawn. We canna allow enemy clans ta gain the advantage over us."

Lord Lismore coughed, pounding on his chest with a fist. "Forgive me. I inhaled a wee breath of dry bannock."

That, or the idea of *clan feuding practice* was as novel to him as it was to me. It seemed entirely too ridiculous to be real.

"Ye'll be joinin' us in the morning of course, Sandy." Blair rose from his seat. "We canna practice properly without the Duncan clan chief ta guide us."

I looked at the earl, seeing him with new eyes, for he

wasn't only an earl; he was a clan chief. Not that I knew what that meant, but it sounded both important and intimidating—much like the saber at his side. Perhaps that *was* the reason he wore something different than his brothers: a statement of status rather than a means of discomposing me as I had come to suspect.

I truly did have a great deal to learn.

Lord Lismore held his brothers' eyes, something passing between them—something that put me even more on alert. Somehow, I needed to determine which parts of what they were saying were real and which were simply meant to tease me.

"Unless, that is," Iain said with a challenging smile, "ye're afraid."

The earl scoffed. "Afraid of hearing yer girlish screams when I wrestle ye ta the ground, perhaps."

Looking at the broadness of his chest and shoulders compared to Iain's taller, lankier form, I couldn't help but share the opinion that he would emerge victor from such an encounter.

Augusta was asleep when I reached her bedchamber, and after a moment's hesitation, I declined to wake her. I was impatient to speak with her, to ask whether she had ever known Scotsmen to forgo the use of forks or to participate in clan feuding practice, but such questions could wait for the morrow. I hoped she would be better then, for I desperately needed not only her guidance but her company.

It was possible, of course, that Augusta's limited knowledge of Scotland would not provide the answers to my questions, and I entered my bedchamber with a furrowed brow.

There was a pile of extra blankets at the end of my bed, and I coughed lightly at the smell and smoke that permeated the room. I hurried across the stone floor and opened the window latch to release some of the potent scent.

So, this was the peat the earl had spoken of. I wasn't certain what I thought of its smell yet, except that it was unlike anything I had ever encountered—earthy and mossy.

Despite the extra blankets, I found sleep difficult to achieve. It was exhausting to be ever-conscious of what people thought of my actions, but rather than being able to find oblivion in sleep, I seemed doomed to review those actions over and over again.

Should I have sent the food back to the kitchens, demanding pheasant and jellies? Should I have accused the Duncans of trying to torment me with their stories of clan struggles and their insistence I eat with a knife?

I had no wish to let them make a May game of me. That would hardly serve my goal of appearing capable enough to become Lady Lismore.

Heavier still on my mind and heart, though, was the prospect of continuing as I was, of facing a future full of the exhaustion and disappointment I felt reflecting on the day. What other horrors lay in wait for me—and how would I meet them in a way that inspired approbation?

I had spent hours and hours learning from Augusta, but I was still at a loss to know how to behave at Lochlarren. I was ignorant enough of Scottish customs that I could not tell for certain whether the earl and his brothers were in earnest or playing me for a fool.

Being able to determine truth from fiction was absolutely essential—almost as essential as ensuring they never received the satisfaction of ruffling me.

A small smile crept across my lips as a thought presented itself. One thing, at least, I could determine as truth or fiction. All it would require was rising early.

After all, it would only be proper to show my support for my future husband and signal my interest in estate dealings by observing clan feuding practice in the morning—if such a thing was truly to take place.

That was something I sincerely doubted.

CHAPTER SIX

SANDY

After dinner, I found my brothers not in the beds they had claimed they would be seeking, but rather in the small study just off the drawing room. The three of them were partaking of their after-dinner spirits there, undoubtedly to avoid having to rejoin Miss Godfrey in the drawing room once they were finished.

They might have saved themselves the trouble, for she had retired to see how her cousin was getting on. Apparently, she *did* care for someone other than herself.

"So much for retiring early." I shut the door behind me.

"Sandy," Blair said jovially, getting up to pour me a glass of the whisky they had pilfered from the liquor cabinet.

I took the glass from him but declined to drink it just yet. "I'd like a word with the three of you."

"Of course you would," Iain said, setting a foot on the small table in front of his chair. "But what *I'd* like to know is whether we're speaking to our brother Sandy"—he paused for effect— "or the boorish clan chief we dined with."

Blair laughed, and Magnus smiled reluctantly, sipping from his glass and leaning against the wall.

"That is precisely the subject on which I wish to speak." I undid the pin that clasped my great kilt in place at my chest, and the fabric fell, leaving me in my shirtsleeves. It was a relief, for the fabric was weighty. "Firstly, what in the name of all that is good and bonnie is *clan feuding practice*?"

Iain's grin grew. "That's the beauty of it. It is whatever we want it to be."

"An excuse to get out of doors—and away from *her*—whenever we need it," Blair added.

I couldn't help but sympathize. "Be that as it may, it is taking things too far."

Blair scoffed. "You were the one who began it all, coming down to dinner in your kilt, saber hanging at your waist, for all the world as though we were sitting down to dine before the battle of Stirling Bridge. And eating with your dagger." He smiled at me with amused admiration. "We thought you had decided you wished to be rid of her, so we thought to help you along."

"You thought wrong," I said. "I merely wished to teach her a lesson. One that *you*"—I poked my fingers at Iain and Blair—"have taken too far." I looked at Iain. "Licking your plate clean?"

He snorted in an effort to contain his mirth, and though I tried to suppress it, my own responsive smile emerged despite my efforts.

"You may as well have brought in the pigs to dine with us," I said.

"What has she against pigs?" Blair protested. "I happen to appreciate them very much. An obliging one provided me with breakfast this morning. Besides, what of Magnus? He is not without fault, for he confirmed his injury had come at your hands."

"The woman needs a set-down," Magnus replied, "but once she becomes better acquainted with us, she will inevitably learn how improbable it is that Sandy would be able to break my arm." The comment was delivered in a sober tone, but the glint of mischief in his eye told me he was intentionally provoking me.

"Improbable, is it?" I asked, stepping toward him threateningly, though I couldn't hide my smile entirely. "Perhaps you think yourself safe to say such things—that I will have mercy on you due to your injury."

He matched my gesture with a step toward me, lifting his chin to meet my eyes. "Perhaps you think *yourself* safe for that reason."

"Resolve it at clan feuding practice in the morning," Blair suggested.

I turned to him. "I would be glad for an opportunity to pummel the three of you."

"Highly unlikely outcome," he said. "Shall we lay wagers?"

"Oh, you mean to rise at six, do you?" I asked with feigned curiosity. "I'm not aware when you have *ever* risen at such a time—or even two hours after, for that matter." I paused and looked around at my brothers. "There will be no clan feuding practice."

"You will make liars of us," Iain said.

"Yes, we have set an expectation," Blair said. "What happens when Miss Godfrey notes we have not done as we said we would?"

I took a seat. "We must hope she does not. Besides, Miss Godfrey abhors violence. I doubt she is eager to observe, much less take part in, your ridiculous practice. We must hope she will forget it was ever mentioned—heaven knows we gave her plenty of other things to think on over the course of the meal." I squared them all with a stern gaze. "All of you will desist from teasing her."

"Oh, come, Sandy," Iain said, sounding ten years younger for a moment. "There's no harm in it. It is only a bit of fun."

"Until she realizes you are trying to make a fool of her," I said, "something I imagine *she* already suspects."

"Are you not doing the same?" He nodded at my clothing. "Only look at you! Why do you get to have all the fun?"

"I am not doing the same," I said sternly, though my conscience wriggled a bit. "I merely wish for her to acknowledge, if only to herself, that she stands to gain as much as we do from this arrangement. She looks down upon us, but would she be here if she did not see value in the match?"

My brothers said nothing, and I pressed my point. "If we push her too far, however, she may cry off, and spouting nonsense about clan feuding practice or the castle being recently breached is likely to lead to such a thing."

There was silence as the three of them pondered my words. "Do you all agree to cease the charades, then?"

My brothers shared glances with one another.

"What happens when she inevitably says something insufferable?" Blair asked.

I thought back on last night's conversations and the number of insufferable things she had *already* said. I would have liked to think myself well enough in control to simply hold my tongue, but so far, I had not been successful. I couldn't very well expect my brothers to do better than I could.

"Some comments simply cannot be ignored," Iain pressed, pouring himself another glass.

"Perhaps not," I replied, "but your reaction should be somewhat measured. Can we at least agree on that?"

They all gave reluctant nods.

"You had better tell Mrs. Boyle of your wishes, Sandy," Magnus said. "She regards Miss Godfrey like a cat regards a mouse."

I sighed. I couldn't blame the woman. Indeed, I bore much of the fault for that, for my requests for dinner had encouraged her to view Miss Godfrey in such a way. I would have a word with her, though. It was one thing to have *me* teaching Miss Godfrey a lesson; having the entire Duncan family and all those employed by us engaged in such a thing was bound to drive her away. And, much as I hated to admit it, I needed her to remain. Lochlarren needed her. But if we could have a humbler version, I would feel far more reconciled to the match.

"Sandy. *Sandy.*"

I rolled away from the sound of Blair's voice, taking refuge in the blanket.

He jostled my arm. "Wake up!"

I sent a drowsy throw in his general direction.

"She's waiting outside!" Blair hissed. "Miss Godfrey is waiting for clan feuding practice."

My eyes flew open.

"Hurry, Sandy! Iain and Magnus are already dressing."

I swore and threw the covers from my body, going over to the window that looked out over the lawn and pulling the curtain aside.

Sure enough, Miss Godfrey sat on the stone wall that surrounded the lawn, separating it from the loch beyond.

"You fools!" I whispered as Blair took refuge by the door. "You had better pray you do not end practice face down in the loch!"

Apparently, I had been wrong about Miss Godfrey abhorring violence. Well, she had picked the right day to observe, for I was ready to throttle my brothers.

Satisfied I meant to come, Blair made his escape as I pulled on my breeches, socks, and boots, then threw on a waistcoat, not even bothering with the buttons.

It was still early enough that the sun hadn't fully risen over the tree-filled hills in the distance, but the sounds of the servants in the kitchen could be heard in the stairwell. I hurried out into the brisk morning air, glancing at the sight of the loch glistening in the early morning light.

"Over here!" Iain called to me, his head peeking around the corner of the castle.

I clenched my teeth. Despite the early hour, he looked particularly energetic. All thoughts of sleep had fled me, and I, too, was left with energy, though mine was less jovial than his.

I turned the corner, my gaze flitting to Miss Godfrey still seated at the wall. All three of my brothers were present, each looking as hastily awakened and dressed as myself.

Miss Godfrey took out a timepiece and displayed it to me. "Six-thirty-three. You might have told me I would be left waiting in the cold for more than half an hour. I almost thought you weren't coming."

"Forgive me," I said brusquely, yanking a saber from Blair's hands. I had no patience for Miss Godfrey's insults and barbed comments at the moment. "I hadna thought a woman as delicate as yerself would take interest in such an activity."

She smiled, the expression full of false sweetness. "It has been made abundantly clear that delicacy is not a Scottish priority."

"Nay, ye're right about that," I said, striding over to Iain and raising my saber over my head. He realized my intent just in time, stumbled back a few steps, and parried my thrust with his own weapon.

He looked at me as though I was a madman, and I smiled, breathing heavily as the familiar anticipation of action coursed through me. It had been an age since I had engaged in sport with my brothers, and I was eager for it—eager to take out my frustrations on them through the means they had forced me into.

CHAPTER SEVEN

JULIANA

I blinked at the force of Lord Lismore's blow against his brother. Iain had attempted to block it, and he had saved himself, certainly, but the tip of his saber sank three inches into the grass, his brother's holding it down.

Iain looked at Lord Lismore with wide eyes, while the earl smiled wickedly back at him, visibly satisfied by the reaction.

Iain's apparent fear was replaced by a gritting of the teeth and a building, chesty roar as he yanked his saber from the ground. Blades clashed, and their feet danced back and forth.

"How did ye sleep, Miss Godfrey?" Lord Lismore asked, his words punctured by the collision of the blades.

Was he truly engaging in polite conversation as he attempted to maim his own brother?

"Passably," I said, raising my voice slightly over the din. I had slept quite well, in truth, but I was reluctant to admit such a thing.

Iain was no match for his brother, and soon surrendered, breathless and perspiring.

"I'm glad ta hear it, lass," Lord Lismore said with a perfunctory smile in my direction.

He was glad I had only slept passably? The insufferable brute. I was tempted to steal Iain's saber to show the earl what I truly felt. I wasn't unwise enough for such an action, however. Lord Lismore was twice as broad as me, a fact fully on display by his unbuttoned waistcoat and shirt. I wasn't certain whether the Duncans had been in earnest about the castle's recent breach, but Lord Lismore's frame alone would certainly give *me* reason to rethink challenging him in any physical bout.

Blair went up against the earl next, and while he held his ground better than Iain, it was only a matter of time until he gave in. It was difficult not to be impressed with the earl's strength and endurance.

His forehead was glistening, his eyes bright with energy even as his chest heaved. He picked up a second saber from the ground. "Well, Magnus?"

Magnus went to accept the saber with his right hand, for his left was in its sling.

"Surely not," I blurted.

Magnus stopped in his tracks, his hand shy of the saber. They both turned to look at me, and Lord Lismore raised his brows.

"That is hardly a fair match," I complained. I had no particular liking for Magnus, indeed, I hardly knew him, but one's sense of justice recoiled at such an unequal pairing. Even without his injury, Magnus would not have a chance. He was built well, but not as well as the earl, besides being a few inches shorter.

Lord Lismore chuckled softly, touching the tip of one blade to the grass. "If ye're too delicate ta watch, lass, perhaps ye should consider returnin' ta yer room."

"It has nothing to do with delicacy, Sandy. Does it make you feel mighty to attack the weak? Do you take pride in beating down your inferiors?"

All three brothers scoffed in annoyance at the implication of my words, but the earl's mouth pulled up at one side in amusement as he took a few steps toward me, two sabers still in hand. "Nay, lass, but ye should ken somethin' about me." He stopped and faced me, his eyes holding mine from mere inches away. "I never back down from a challenge when 'tis offered, be the challenger inferior or superior."

I held his gaze, my nostrils flaring. "And, pray, how do you classify *me*?"

His eyes narrowed slightly, then his mouth stretched in a smile I itched to slap from his face. "Och, lass. I may seem a barbarian ta ye, but I'll no' offer ye an insult ta yer face."

Outrage rose through my chest and into my throat. I wrenched one of the sabers from his hand, and he stumbled backward in surprise. His eyes grew wide and wary, flitting from my face to the saber I held.

"What're ye doin', lass?"

"Offering you a challenge," I said, stepping toward him and taking a swipe at his saber.

He parried it, stepping backward. I pursued him, my body infused with energy and determination, and thrust the blade toward him again and again.

With each clash, he stepped backward toward the castle, his brows pulled together in focus, as though I might make some sudden, unanticipated move. His retreat simultaneously emboldened and bothered me. He wasn't even trying.

"You said you never back down from a challenge," I said through clenched teeth that shook with each harsh clash. I raised my blade and brought it down, meeting his in a clang that reverberated through my entire body.

My breath came in gusts as I held my blade ready to counter him at any second.

"You'd no' last ten seconds if I fought back, lass," he said.

"So you say, Sandy."

He met my eye, and there was a second of hesitation before he thrust his saber toward me.

I met it with my own, but the shock of the contact rang through my hand and up my arm. I gripped the hilt more tightly as the earl's blade came again.

Again and again, I parried just in time, but each hit forced me backward. I glanced to the side from the corner of my eye, aware that we were drawing nearer the stone wall that over-looked the dark loch waters below.

There was no time for me to mount an opposition, for all my concentration and energy were required to meet Lord Lismore's. Back and back I stepped, my determination begin-ning to give way to apprehension. Would he truly press me until I fell into the loch? I didn't know for certain how close we were, and I couldn't chance a glance at the stone wall for fear I would miss one of the earl's hits. His gaze was fixed on mine, dogged and unblinking.

I should surrender, but my pride resisted. Surely, he would stop before letting me fall to injury. His barbarism couldn't extend that far. He needed me.

The heel of my boot hit the wall, and I felt myself pitching backward. Lord Lismore dropped his saber and grabbed my arm, pulling me toward him and away from the loch.

His chest pressed against me, his eyes intent and fiery as they stared into mine. "Ye're in over yer head, lass," he said in a frustratingly even voice.

I had no retort to offer. My tongue was tied and my lungs desperate for air as his warm body pressed against mine. I swallowed, unsure what I was feeling as I met his gaze. Anger? Relief? Embarrassment? Admiration?

Under all of those was the annoyed realization that perhaps the earl was right. He had not even tried his hardest and had beat me handily despite it. I *was* in over my head.

But I would never admit such a thing.

I wrested his hand from my arm and dropped my saber to the ground. "Thankfully, I am a good swimmer."

CHAPTER EIGHT

SANDY

I didn't meet my brothers' eyes as I picked up the saber Miss Godfrey had left behind. My own lay on the ground nearby, dropped in haste to prevent her from falling into the loch.

The silence as she disappeared around the corner and out of view was deafening. I didn't need to look at them to know all three of my brothers were staring at me.

"What the devil, Sandy?" Iain said. "You nearly killed her."

"I assure you, I did not." I picked up my saber and set the two of them against the stone wall. "I was very much in control." It was true. I had been taken off guard by Miss Godfrey's intrepidity when she had taken the saber from my hand, and I had allowed her to goad me into fighting back, but I would never have harmed her.

I thought she would have surrendered well before she had, but once again, she had proven me wrong. She would have gone over the stone wall had I not stopped her, and I didn't know what to make of that. It was both admirable and entirely mad.

"Well," said Blair, "I'll give her this, the woman's got more pluck than any I know! Can't help being impressed." He paused. "With her, not you."

I shot him a look. "Are you happy with yourselves and the result of your madcap idea?"

Iain and Blair looked at one another, then nodded with fervor.

"I think we should do this every day," Iain said. "Come, Sandy. Tell me you didn't enjoy it."

"I certainly enjoyed making you look a fool," I replied. There had been enjoyment in the sparring with Miss Godfrey, as well, if I was being perfectly honest. And a flicker of something—perhaps animus—when I had held her against me.

"You only won because you caught me off guard," Iain said with a wave. "Perhaps tomorrow we can forego the sabers and combat with only our bare hands. What do you say, Sandy? Clan feuding practice may have begun as a figment of our imagination, but I'm of the opinion we should make it tradition."

I kicked at a loose stone in the wall. I did miss this sort of thing. So much of my time had been spent behind the desk, staring at ledgers and accounts, that I had forgotten the thrill of more active endeavors with my brothers.

Apart from that, I was tired of being the short-tempered one they had come to expect would put an end to any fun.

"Very well," I said. "But not at six. I cannot be responsible for the result if I am roused so early." I sent a playful punch at Blair's side, and he dodged it with a grin, then came back with his own.

Soon, we were tussling again, the air filled in turn by grunts and laughter.

For all my complaints about it, perhaps clan feuding practice had been precisely what my brothers and I needed. As for

Miss Godfrey, I had the feeling our spats had only just begun. She was infuriating and condescending, and she was to become my wife. How would I bear a wife who looked down upon everything I held dear?

I may have donned my kilt to teach her a lesson, but deep down, I was proud of my heritage, proud of the history contained in Lochlarren's solid walls. They had survived hundreds of years, some of which had included violent sieges and battles.

Lochlarren was worth saving. It was a quest far grander than any one person. I wanted to ensure it was restored to its proper state, its history preserved for generations to come. Such a goal required sacrifice. *Great* sacrifice, even. Men had given their lives for it; Miss Godfrey would only cost me my sanity.

CHAPTER NINE

JULIANA

My heart had hardly slowed when I reached my bedchamber. My body still hummed with the effects of my encounter with the earl. If I closed my eyes, I could still see his, staring down into mine with an intensity that stole what little breath I'd had left. I swore I could feel his chest pressing against mine, and my heart thumped at the memory.

I shut the door to my bedchamber, still thick with the smell of peat, and went straight to the window. For its large curtains of blue damask, the window was disappointingly small. Its pane was warped and difficult to see through, except for the blurred outline of deep green trees and the blue loch.

I lifted the latch and pushed it open, letting in a rush of glorious, fresh air. Such crisp, clear air was simply not to be had in Newcastle. There, carriages and carts kicked up dust, and all the smells of town accosted one the moment one stepped through the door.

I had never seen anything like the view at Lochlarren—the loch such a deep, vibrant blue, with little crests of white where the wind whipped its surface. The trees that skirted its edges were so textured and green, the blue sky filled with puffy clouds.

My gaze searched the lawn and landed on the four figures I had been searching for. The Duncan brothers walked at a leisurely pace toward the castle, their sabers in hand. Blair walked alongside the earl, and he bumped into him—intentionally, from what I could tell.

I braced myself for the inevitable retaliation. Instead, Lord Lismore slung an arm around Blair's shoulders, grinning just as his brother was. Lip-cracking, ear-splitting grins.

Iain and Magnus joined on either side of them, listening to something the earl said. A chorus of laughter followed.

All I could do was stare at my intended husband. He had smiled at dinner last night a few times, but this . . . this was different. This was joy unfettered. In this moment, all four of the men had it.

A little ache stabbed my chest. As the only child of my parents, the camaraderie between the Duncans was something I had never known. Foolishly, I had hoped I might come to know it here and that it would make me feel more at home in this strange place.

But the sight of them laughing together had the opposite effect, making me feel my foreignness more than ever.

Suddenly, all the sabers dropped, and the three younger brothers tackled Lord Lismore to the ground. The earl struggled mightily against them, but he was overpowered. I leaned forward in apprehension. Should I be worried for him?

Every attempt at escape was met with preventative measures by Iain and Blair. Magnus did what he could with only one arm at his disposal, holding one of the earl's wrists and tripping him the one time he was able to scramble to his feet.

My heart thumped as I tried to gauge whether the fighting was good-natured or in earnest.

Finally, I caught a better glimpse of the earl. Though he struggled to free himself, the smile never left his face. It was a stark contrast from the way he had looked at me when we had sparred. I sincerely doubted he would ever wear such a smile in my presence.

A knock on my door had me whipping around. I pulled the window shut, latched it, then yanked the curtains together.

"Come in," I said.

A maid stepped inside the room, demure and unwilling to meet my eyes.

I held my chin higher, considering for the first time what sort of gossip had likely been passed amongst the servants about me. I had not intended to come to Lochlarren acting like a shrew, but so far, that was precisely what I must have seemed.

"Mrs. Boyle wishes ta ken if ye're ready for a tour of the house, miss."

Had the maid been looking at me she would have known I had no desire to spend time with the housekeeper, no matter how curious I was to see the rest of the castle. The sooner I faced her, however, the sooner I could ensure she understood I would not tolerate her insolence.

I glanced down at the hem of my dress, which had become muddied outside. "Thank you. I shall need time to change first."

She nodded. "Would ye like my help, miss?"

What I would have liked was a bath to rid my hair and skin of the smell of peat. Something told me countesses were meant to smell like rosewater or lemon rather than burnt blocks of earth.

But there was no time for a bath just now. A tour of the

castle would at least help me feel less foreign here. I could bathe afterward.

"I would like that," I said.

Hopefully, Augusta would be feeling well enough to join the tour.

CHAPTER TEN

JULIANA

Augusta's health had not improved, but she insisted on joining the tour with Mrs. Boyle despite that fact. I did not try to dissuade her, for I was glad not to be alone with the housekeeper, even if it meant the tour was punctuated with constant sneezing and sniffling.

I assisted Augusta into her clothing, utilizing the time to ask her the questions burning within me. As I had begun to suspect, Augusta had never heard of clan feuding practice. On discovering I had eaten an entire dinner without the use of a fork, she was astounded—and then grim. "It is just as I feared, Juliana." She paused to wipe her red nose with a handkerchief. "They are testing you—testing your mettle. I am terribly sorry not to have been there."

I smiled and patted her hand. "It is of no account, cousin. I believe I managed well enough."

I declined to tell her about the morning's events, for I doubted she would approve of my actions. Fighting with sabers was not something she had required me to practice in my efforts to become accomplished.

We made our way to the entrance hall, where Mrs. Boyle was waiting.

Had there been ghosts living here, I would still have considered *her* the most frightening prospect in the castle. I was under no illusion she liked or approved of me.

I gathered she thought me unworthy of becoming the mistress of Lochlarren. But her comportment toward me only made me want to dig in my heels more. I had some idea that, if only I could force her to recognize my right to be there, my success would be assured.

Mrs. Boyle led us up another winding staircase—I had counted four so far, all in different towers. Augusta was miserable after the first two, and when we passed the corridor to our bedchambers, I finally insisted she rest again. I could manage Mrs. Boyle well enough now that I had spent more time in her company.

Augusta was feeling unwell enough to capitulate to my demand, and I was left alone with the housekeeper, who took me to the southernmost tower, starting at the ground floor and showing me each room that branched from the winding staircase. She had shown us or at least mentioned what purpose each room served, but she passed by one on our right without a word.

"What room is this, if you please?" I asked. I couldn't very well be mistress of a castle I did not know.

Mrs. Boyle turned, her lips pinched as they always were when her gaze rested upon me. "'Tis the royal apartments, miss. Far above the likes of you and I, of course, and no' a place ye'll ever need ta go."

"I should like to see them, all the same."

Our gazes held, a moment of challenge between us. Perhaps she realized it was the money from my dowry which would be paying her wages, for she finally relented, going to the door and turning the knob.

I followed her into the dim room, for the curtains were drawn.

Mrs. Boyle stopped just inside, hardly allowing me any space. "This is the royal bedchamber, and beyond it, a bedchamber for attending servants." She made quick, showy gesture around the dark room. "And now we can proceed with the tour."

Ignoring her, I strode over to the window and pulled the curtains open. Both of us blinked at the light that poured in, illuminating the fine furnishings around. It was nothing like the rest of the castle. Nothing was worn or tattered here. The bed was not four-poster as the others in the castle. Its hangings, a rich red with gold tassels and embroidery, seemed to float, hanging from the ceiling itself. The plush mattress and generous coverings appeared a soft crimson cloud.

Mrs. Boyle hurried over to the curtains and pulled them to, shrouding us again in darkness. "The light will damage the furnishin's."

"Have the apartments ever been used by royalty?"

"Nay," she said with a degree of reluctance, moving toward the door. "No' yet."

"By anyone else?"

She drew back with obvious offense. "Of course no'." Her eyes locked on me. "And if anyone tried, I'd have their hide!"

"It seems a great waste of a perfectly good bedchamber," I said, my indignation at her behavior growing by the minute. It was true, though. The fireplace sat against the west wall, neither too far nor too close to the bed, and the windows looked out on the side of the loch opposite my bedchamber. There were even fresh logs—not peat—in the fireplace.

"Ye dinna understand how things are done in ancient families, Miss Godfrey," Mrs. Boyle said. "These apartments are the pride of the family, *only* ta be used by those of royal blood." Her piercing gaze was enough to convey how very far from such a standard she considered me.

"If only half such care had been taken for the rest of the castle," I said as we left the room. "Apparently, the Duncans have found it more important to impress some imagined royal guest—one who has clearly no thought for the Lismore title—than to see to their own comfort or the comfort of their *actual* guests."

Mrs. Boyle continued down the stairs. "Most guests dinna consider themselves deservin' of better than the king himself."

By the time we made our way back down the staircase to the entry hall, my jaw ached from how tightly I had been clenching it.

The front door opened just as I reached the bottom of the stairs. The four Duncans entered, their breath coming fast, their mouths stretched in smiles, and their clothing tousled. Had they been outside all this time, enjoying one another's company?

How I envied them.

They stopped short at the sight of us, their smiles dimming considerably. The reaction made my cheeks warm. How had I been foolish enough to think I might find friendship and family here? I was not welcome. Papa's money was, but I was not.

I was simply the string attached to the money.

"Good day, Miss Godfrey," Lord Lismore said, inclining his head. His waistcoat dangled open, his dark hair was disordered, and his eyes were still bright with energy. The effect was to make him odiously handsome. Or handsomely odious.

"Good day," I replied.

"Were you coming in search of me?" he asked.

I stared at him for a moment, wondering if I was imagining it or if he had misplaced his accent again. When his brothers looked at one another, sharing conspiratorial looks, I was certain I had been right. So, the accent had been adopted for my benefit, had it?

Indignation filled my chest. What games did they think they could play with me?

"No," I replied. "Mrs. Boyle was good enough to give me a tour of the castle. The royal apartments in particular I found fascinating." I smiled. "I certainly hope not *all* of my money will be devoted to them. That seems to have been the custom until now."

Lord Lismore's mouth twitched. "Nay, lass, for how could we even spend the half of a fortune as grand as yers?"

I kept my expression pleasant, holding his gaze. "I wish for a warm bath to be drawn. I have no wish to smell like peat all day and all night. You *do* possess a bath, I assume?" I let my eyes trip from the earl to each of his three brothers by turn, then offered a condescending smile. "Perhaps not."

Lord Lismore watched me for a moment in silence, as though considering my words, while eyebrows inched up on the faces of the other three Duncans. Mrs. Boyle had retreated a few steps and was looking at the earl, her mouth drawn in a tight line. It was an uncomfortable moment, but I was determined to have the last laugh this morning. If mockery was the order of the day, I could participate just as easily as anyone.

"Och, lass, of course we're possessed of a bath," Lord Lismore said, his accent returning more pronounced than ever. He motioned to the door they had just come through. "What better bath than the loch? 'Tis large enough for all of us ta bathe at once, though I canna promise 'twill be warm."

"The loch?" I scoffed. Did he think I was stupid enough he could convince me to bathe in it?

He smiled. "There's naught like a refreshin' dip."

"In full view of the castle, no doubt," I said.

"Nay," Iain said, stepping forward, "there's a wee spot by the bushes with all the privacy ye could want. As for what ye're smellin', 'tis only Sandy. 'Tis nigh on three months since he last bathed."

"Is that all?" I asked. "I would have guessed six."

Iain snorted and tried to make it sound like a sneeze.

"And how often *is* it customary to bathe at Lochlarren?" I asked, pretending curiosity.

"Every month or two," Blair said. "I had one barely a month ago." He raised his arm and put his nose near his armpit, inhaling then grinning. "Fresh as a newborn lammie. Or a month-old lammie."

The door opened again behind them, and a manservant entered, a knapsack hanging across his body. Upon seeing us, he opened it and withdrew a handful of letters.

"The post, my lord." He handed the papers to the earl.

"Thank you," Lord Lismore said as the servant bowed and went on his way.

He rifled through the letters, his brow pursing further with each one. He paused halfway through the pile, then looked up at me.

"For you, Miss Godfrey." He handed me a letter.

My name in Papa's writing graced the front, and my heart skittered at the sight. I wanted to open it immediately, impatient to know whether the news was good or bad. I wanted him here to guide me, or, preferably, to see just how impossible this match was.

Surely, he did not wish me to put up with the sort of people and lifestyle expected of me here, even if the result *was* a title. What good was being a countess if I was to be stuck in a cold, half-ruined castle in the middle of a loch all year long?

"Will yer father be joinin' us anytime soon?" Lord Lismore asked. "In time for the weddin'? Or the engagement party?"

I looked up. "Engagement party?"

"Aye," the earl said, his brow furrowed. "He didna tell ye of it?"

I searched his face, trying to determine whether this was yet another trick of theirs. I found no such evidence, however. "He failed to mention it. It must have slipped his mind in the chaos of business affairs and preparing to leave."

Lord Lismore nodded. "Aye, that'll be it. Given the shortness of the engagement, 'twill be held the night afore the weddin'. The invitations were sent out nigh on a fortnight ago. 'Tis only fittin' that our acquaintances meet the future Lady Lismore."

"Of course," I said, though the instability of my voice sapped the words of their strength. Any hope I'd harbored that Papa might arrive and save me from this increasingly undesirable match flickered like a candle against a winter draft. An engagement party made everything seem so final—and invitations extended nearly two weeks ago.

Lord Lismore's gaze was on me, watching me carefully. "I'm sorry ye didna ken of it. Its purpose is ta honor ye, Miss Godfrey. I hoped ye'd be pleased."

Hoped I'd be judged and condemned by the entire county, more like.

All five sets of eyes were on me, and I straightened. The Duncans were holding an engagement party in honor of the future countess. I needed to show them I could handle such an affair with the grace it required. "Very pleased indeed, I thank you. I look forward to it. Now if you will excuse me, I would like to read my father's letter."

I waited until I was concealed from their view by the stairs, then broke the seal and opened the letter, consuming it in less than a minute.

Papa *had* known of the engagement party. His letter made that clear, for he promised to arrive in plenty of time for it. He spoke of it as though he assumed I, too, had known of it.

I sighed.

His head was so full of numbers and business, he often forgot to pass along critical pieces of information like this.

He expressed his eagerness to see me in my new home and spoke of three new business opportunities he had managed to find with acquaintances of Lord Lismore's in town.

I folded the short letter, debating whether I should respond and convey my fears to him. But I couldn't.

His excitement at the new business prospects was a splash of cold water over my peat-saturated hair, reminding me why I was here. This match was not just about me. It was about Papa, about showing him my gratitude for all he had done for me over the years. It was about ensuring his posterity and my posterity had better prospects than he had grown up with. They never need know true hunger or bone-chilling cold. I could sacrifice for them the way Papa had sacrificed for me.

And perhaps the sacrifice would not be as great as it now seemed. Once I was married and titled, I would have more freedom. There would be no need to stay at Lochlarren once I had produced an heir.

CHAPTER ELEVEN

SANDY

I shut the door to my bedchamber behind me and raised my arm to my nose. Did I smell? I didn't detect anything unpleasant, but perhaps I had become so accustomed to my own stench, I merely failed to recognize it.

Of course, it was entirely possible Miss Godfrey had merely said what she had to be disagreeable. She certainly had enough spirit for that. It was a pity she was not more amiable, for spirit was a trait I generally admired, and the woman becoming the Countess of Lismore would need a heavy dose of it. Despite the umbrage I had taken at Miss Godfrey's low opinion of Lochlarren, it *was* a remote place and the living conditions often difficult and inconvenient. Perhaps even malodorous?

I strode to the armoire and pulled both doors open. One by one, I smelled my shirts and coats. I frowned. Was I imagining it, or was there a hint of an objectionable smell there?

I yanked on the bell cord beside the fireplace. Better have them laundered again to be certain.

I waited for my valet to arrive, cringing at the thought of how close I had held Miss Godfrey this morning. Had she wrested her arm from my grasp due, at least in part, to the odor I was unconsciously emitting?

I shouldn't care what she thought of me—indeed, had I not been going out of my way to make myself unlikeable to her?—but I didn't wish to put *others* off by my smell. Besides, it would be one thing if I had intentionally made myself reek to be off-putting, but I had not, and that was embarrassing.

The door opened, and my valet stepped inside. "My lord?"

I took the clothes I had gathered into a pile in hand and offered them to him. "I would like these to be laundered immediately."

He frowned as he accepted the pile. He peered at the garments, then at me. "I reckon these are freshly laundered, my lord. Is there somethin' amiss?"

"No," I replied. "That is . . ." I paused. "Do I *smell*, Gillies?"

His frown deepened. "Smell, my lord?"

"Yes, smell. Stink. Reek." I waited for him to pronounce the verdict.

"Nay, sir. Ye dinna smell, stink, or reek. Are ye displeased with my work—or that of the maids??"

"No, certainly not." It was Miss Godfrey who was displeased. "But I would like those laundered despite that. And if the laundry maid has anything she might add to . . . enhance the smell of freshness, I would appreciate it."

"Verra good, sir." Perplexed, Gillies bowed and left the room.

I was acting strangely. I quite saw that. I was finding it difficult to know what to do with Miss Godfrey's insults and complaints. I should not have given into her taunting on the lawn that morning, and I should not be asking for my clothes to be washed, dried, and ironed again. But here I was.

I sighed and went over to the window, leaning on the sill to look at the blurry view it afforded. My goal to humble Miss

Godfrey was not working. If anything, she was more pompous and haughtier than ever. If we were to be married, we could not carry on in this way forever. Well, perhaps *she* could, but I could not. Yet, what *was* I to do? She was impossible to understand.

I stilled, my gaze fixing on movement on the lawns below —two figures, both women. I unlatched the window and opened it as quietly as possible. Miss Godfrey and Miss Lowe were walking the lawn, arm in arm.

I breathed carefully, as though they might hear me two stories above. I had not had the opportunity to study Miss Godfrey unobserved, and I could not forgo the chance now. Perhaps it would offer me some clue, some insight into her.

They stopped, and Miss Lowe sneezed violently. Miss Godfrey hurried to produce a handkerchief, offering it to her cousin and setting a hand on her back as a sequence of sneezes followed. It was a kind gesture—and certainly not noteworthy from anyone else—but I stared at Miss Godfrey's gentle hand pensively.

Was her cousin the only person she had any kindness for? My interaction with Miss Lowe had been admittedly limited so far, but she hardly seemed more pleasant than Miss Godfrey. What, then, did that say about Miss Godfrey's attention to her? Was kindness to a rude person another form of unpleasantness?

They carried on with their leisurely stroll, stopping at the lone bench on the Lochlarren lawns. The ground was uneven, making the seat sloped. Miss Godfrey saw that her cousin was safely settled before taking her own seat, where they sat conversing while they stared out at the loch.

Another movement caught my attention, farther off. It was one of the maids—Dolly, from what I could tell—coming toward the castle from the laundry. She carried a burden of three large and unwieldy baskets, full of what appeared to be sheets. It was a task for two people, something made evident by the difficulty she was having.

She fumbled for a moment, but it was no use. One basket fell to the ground, its contents spilling onto the grass. She carefully set down the other baskets, then began gathering up the laundry to return to the now-empty basket. Once it was all back in its place, she attempted to rebalance the two baskets on her hip, then pick up the third one in her free arm.

The top basket teetered dangerously, then toppled over, spilling its contents a second time. I winced. Perhaps this was why my clothing smelled less than satisfactory.

"Juliana!" Miss Lowe's call filled the air, and my gaze darted back to the bench.

Miss Godfrey was hurrying over to the maid, to scold her, I could only assume. We were not even married, and she was taking it upon herself to criticize how I ran the estate and instruct my servants. The poor maid—*my* poor maid—didn't deserve such a thing.

I opened my mouth to call down just as Miss Godfrey grabbed Dolly's baskets and set them on the grass. She must need a full view of the maid's face to properly chastise her.

But then she crouched, gathering the sheets which had hitherto been carefully folded and were now in disarray on the ground. I could hear the muffled sound of Dolly's apologies, and Miss Godfrey responded with a shaking of the head and . . . a smile?

Who was this woman? I hadn't even realized she was capable of a genuinely kind expression, to say nothing of exhibiting the sort of concern which would lead her to assist one of the servants. Her face was transformed by the expression, presenting a captivating picture.

I leaned forward as though, if only I could draw near

enough, I could hear the conversation being carried out between the two of them. Miss Godfrey was capable of saying harsh words through smiling lips.

Dolly set down one of her baskets and reached for the one in Miss Godfrey's hands, but Miss Godfrey shook her head and said something which made Dolly laugh.

Miss Lowe had left her place on the bench and joined the spectacle. She reached for the basket in Miss Godfrey's hands, addressing unintelligible remarks to her. Miss Godfrey drew away, keeping the basket in her arms. She was clearly intent on keeping it.

After a short exchange, Miss Lowe returned to her seat on the bench while Dolly and Miss Godfrey began walking side by side toward the servant entrance of the castle below my window, chatting happily.

I blinked, wondering if my skirmishes with my brothers had knocked something within me out of place. Surely, I was hallucinating. I leaned further out of the window as Dolly and Miss Godfrey drew nearer, straining for any snippet of sound from their conversation. I struggled to believe my eyes; perhaps my ears would be more convincing.

I gripped the edge of the sill as I leaned forward to see below, startling a pigeon roosting near the window's ledge. As it fluttered away, it knocked a small piece of broken stone from its place, which, to my horror, dropped below and directly onto Miss Godfrey's head.

I retreated hurriedly out of view as the conversation stopped abruptly. My heart beat wildly. Confound my curiosity! Dolly would recognize my window and see that it was open.

I did the only thing that occurred to me—attempted the call of a pigeon.

"Coo! Coo!"

I winced, for it was far from satisfactory, but as the conversation resumed, apparently it had been convincing enough.

I kept my place in the safety of the curtain folds as though one of the women might scale the walls at any moment and catch me.

The shutting of a door and the subsequent sound of retreating footsteps gave me enough courage to chance a glance through the window. Dolly was gone, and Miss Godfrey was retreating toward the bench, rubbing the spot on her head where the rock had fallen.

I sympathized with her; I, too, felt as though I had been knocked on the head with something. I hadn't the slightest idea what to make of what I had just observed. Was there a side of Miss Godfrey that was . . . normal? A lowly maid was the last person in the castle I would have expected her to treat with kindness—and not just kindness. She had gone out of her way to help her with a menial task. It was entirely contrary to everything I knew of my intended.

What, then, was I to make of her behavior toward *me*? Why did she despise me so heartily? Or feel herself so far above me?

Was I the problem?

One thing was certain: I hadn't given her as little reason to like me as she had given me reason to like *her*.

CHAPTER TWELVE

JULIANA

"Your kindness does you credit, Juliana," Augusta said when I came to sit again beside her, "but I am afraid it will not be seen that way by your betrothed or his family. It is unwise to debase yourself in such a way—anyone might have seen."

I let out a large sigh and slumped back in the chair in a way entirely contrary to everything she had taught me. "I am weary of being so starched up, cousin. And surely you see that it has done nothing but make the Duncans dislike me. I cannot even blame them."

"You are used to being well-liked, my dear, and for good reason." She grasped my hands warmly. "You are the kindest of women. But things are different in the world of the titled, Juliana, and to be accepted, one must play their game. It is all pomp and pride. I know it is difficult now and you feel a wretch, but all your work will stand you in good stead once you are married. You are laying the foundations to ensure you have the greatest liberty and respect in the future."

I nodded, but it seemed to me my behavior would only

ensure I was the most despised woman in Scotland. I had grown up liked and admired for my wealth but unable to reach the heights I wished to attain due to my low birth. I had no desire to reach those heights at the cost of amiability. Surely, there must be a way to have it all?

All I knew is I was tired of being so high in the instep. Though I valued Augusta's company, I desperately wanted a friend at Lochlarren. One person, at least, in whom I could confide, who would assure me I wasn't entirely hated by everyone I had met—and preferably, one who might help me ascertain what was truth and fiction.

"Me, miss? Yer lady's maid?" Dolly looked at me with wide eyes, my evening attire draped over her arm.

I nodded with a small smile, my heart pattering nervously in my chest. What if she said no? It would be humiliating—and understandable. I had not been unkind to her, but my reputation at Lochlarren could not be positive. I could only imagine what Mrs. Boyle had said to the maids about me.

Dolly blinked, momentarily speechless. "But . . . but . . . I dinna ken how ta be a lady's maid, miss."

"I am confident you can learn the necessary skills. You are young and bright."

"But would ye no' rather find someone who already *has* the skills?"

I shook my head. "You have been kind to me, Dolly, and that is something I value more highly than skill." I was not certain asking her to take on this role was wise or acceptable, but she was the only person at Lochlarren who had been kind to me, and I needed the friendship, however unsuitable Augusta or the Duncans might think it.

She looked touched. "'T'would be a great honor ta serve ye, miss. Though, I reckon I should ask Lord Lismore—ta make certain he doesna mind me leavin' my other duties ta assist ye."

"You needn't do that," I replied. "I shall inform him." This would be an opportunity to assert myself to the earl—and, if I judged the time right, see what his reaction would be if I acted less arrogantly.

Dolly was not particularly adept with hair, but with a bit of instruction, my coiffure was acceptable enough. It was not ideal, but she could be trained. She would learn quickly. Friendship and kindness, however, could not necessarily be taught or counted upon.

Already in the last three-quarters of an hour, she had warmed up to me considerably, losing much of her shyness. Her easy company made me feel more hopeful for the future than I had since arriving. Perhaps my marriage would be miserable, perhaps I would never have a true smile from Lord Lismore, but I would have one friend at least.

"May I ask you something?" I said as she folded my discarded daydress.

"Of course, my lady."

"I am not *my lady* yet, Dolly," I said, pausing in the act of dabbing perfume on my wrists. I was determined not to smell of peat tonight.

She sent me a smile with a bit of mischief in it. "No' yet, no. But soon enough, ye'll be married ta his lordship."

I shifted in my chair. The wedding day was drawing nearer, and I hardly knew the man but for the fact that he was disagreeable—except to his brothers. Although, what was one to think of a man who broke his brother's arm and then laughed with him so jovially as he had done this morning?

Dolly continued. "And the two of ye so verra handsome

together, if ye dinna mind me sayin' so. 'Tis a kind master he is, and I reckon he'll be an even kinder husband."

My cheeks warmed, and I busied myself with putting the stopper back in the perfume bottle. I hadn't assumed Lord Lismore would be a particularly kind master, neither did I know—or *want* to know—what Dolly anticipated his kindness as a husband would entail. Whatever it was, she was mistaken. He had no liking for me whatsoever.

Knowing that both his servants and his brothers were recipients of his kindness while he pointedly withheld it from me made me feel strange and alone all over again.

"Ye had a question, though, miss?"

I cleared my throat. "Yes. Does his lordship bathe in the loch?"

She frowned. "Perhaps on occasion. He would never do so in the winter, though, for 'tis cold even in the summer."

"So, in the winter, he simply uses a regular bath?"

"Aye, miss." She glanced at me curiously. "Why do ye ask?"

I hesitated for a moment. "I am afraid I was quite rude when I first arrived, Dolly, which has made your master and his brothers wish to put me in my place. They have been telling me all manner of tales about Lochlarren, and, not having experience anywhere but the town I grew up in, it is hard for me to know what is true and what is not. Today, they informed me everyone bathes in the loch here."

Dolly laughed, then covered her mouth with a hand. "Forgive me, miss. 'Twas unkind of them. But nay, we dinna bathe in the loch—no' unless we wish for a shock ta the heart. What else have they told ye?"

"Well, it is not simply what they have *told* me but what I have experienced since arriving. Will you tell me the truth, even if my questions seem ridiculous?"

"Aye, miss. I swear it."

I nodded. "No doubt you have smelled the peat in this bedchamber . . ." It hadn't escaped my notice that none of the bedchambers Mrs. Boyle had shown me had contained either the smell or the actual presence of peat.

Dolly's brows came together, and she closed the lid of the trunk at the base of my bed. "Aye, and I thought 'twas peculiar, for we never use peat here. There's plenty of wood nearby."

"Just as I thought," I said. "And last night's dinner . . . the haggis and turnips."

She scrunched her nose. "His lordship doesna like haggis, miss. I had assumed 'twas *you* who wished for it."

I let out an unladylike laugh. "Me? I had never even heard of such a thing. And I was forced to eat it with only a knife. I assume this was also done for my benefit?"

She tried not to smile. "We *do* have forks, miss."

"And have you ever heard or observed the Duncans participating in *clan feuding practice*?"

She grimaced and shook her head. "I'm afraid ye're right, Miss Godfrey, and they've been having a bit of fun at yer expense."

I sighed and rose from my chair. "I suspect so, Dolly. I hope you will help me avoid making a fool of myself from now on."

"Of course," she said with an eager nod. Suddenly, she inhaled, smiling slightly. "Ye smell of lemons, miss."

"Not of peat?"

"Just a bit, perhaps. But tomorrow, I'll draw ye a warm bath if ye'd like."

"I would. Very much." I smiled at her, feeling more hopeful than I had since arriving. "Thank you, Dolly. Now, if you will excuse me, I shall have that conversation with Lord Lismore regarding your new duties."

Lord Lismore's valet informed me the earl could be found in the study, and I made my way through corridors and winding stairways toward him. I declined to tell Augusta of my intent, for I wasn't certain she would approve of my seeking out a private audience with the earl—or stealing one of the maids as my own. But if the earl and I were to be married in less than a week, surely there was nothing wrong with spending time unchaperoned. The mere thought that something untoward might happen was laughable.

I wondered whether to confront him about his untruths or to go along with his game. I could find ways to have my own fun at his expense if I wanted, or I could challenge him outright with the things he had been doing to make a fool of me. Both were intriguing ideas in their own way.

I stopped and looked around me, trying to determine where in Lochlarren I was. Certainly not where I had meant to go. With a sigh, I retraced my steps.

Augusta's arguments in favor of continuing my imperious behavior toward the Duncans were difficult for me to agree with. They needed my wealth, yes, but I hadn't come into this match out of the goodness of my heart. I had come for a title and Papa's business prospects, and without them, I could not have those things. Ensuring they knew my value was one thing; antagonizing them was another thing, and that was certainly what I had been doing. The situation required a display of at least a measure of humility on my part. There was little sense in debasing the title I would be coming into.

Mrs. Boyle was another matter, however. She continued to treat me with shortness, and I could not tolerate it. What right had *she* to look down upon me? I was the daughter of a well-respected merchant; she was a housekeeper.

I would settle things with her later. Now, it was the earl I needed to confront.

I paused at the partially open door to the study. Lord Lismore sat behind a large desk covered in papers, an ornate but rusted inkstand standing front and center. His forehead rested in his palms, his hands threaded through his dark hair as he stared at the paper before him. The effect was a harassed sort of look, and I hesitated.

It couldn't be easy running such an ancient and grand estate as Lochlarren, and I had certainly not been making his lot any easier. Indeed, I had come even now to meddle with his servants.

I knew little of the Duncan situation beyond the fact that they were in dire need of money. Dire enough that Lord Lismore was willing to marry *me*, a woman he heartily disliked.

He glanced up, apparently sensing he was being observed. Though his hair was disheveled and his brow lined with worry, a sort of wary curiosity sparked in his eyes at the sight of me.

"Miss Godfrey." He stood. "How may I assist you?"

I nearly commented on the lack of heavy brogue. Did he think I was so stupid I would fail to note the constant shifts?

"Forgive me for interrupting," I said.

"Not at all. Please come in." His tone was welcoming enough, even if tinged with caution. Perhaps after looking over accounts, he was remembering just how much he needed me.

No, not me. My fortune.

He walked to the liquor cabinet. "Shall I call for tea?"

"No, thank you. I shan't keep you long. I merely wished to speak with you regarding one of your maids."

He glanced at me as he put the stopper in the decanter. "Is there a problem?"

"Not at all. That is, there is no problem as far as *I* am concerned, and I hope there will be none for you, either." I paused. "I would like to make Dolly my lady's maid."

His eyebrows crept up. "Dolly the housemaid?" Was he passing judgment upon my decision to employ a maid who wasn't trained in the capacity of a lady's maid? Augusta would likely have fainted to hear my request. A true countess would never use anything but a trained lady's maid.

"Do you have more than one maid named Dolly?"

He smiled slightly. "Just the one." He replaced the quill in the inkstand. "So, Miss Godfrey, you mean to steal one of my servants for your own." The words were accusatory, but the tone was almost playful. Was he trying to provoke me? Or simply engaging in a bit of the sort of teasing I had witnessed between him and his brothers?

I tried to strike the same ambiguous balance with my own response, smiling slightly to rob my words of their arrogance. "As it is to be my money paying them, I assumed there would be no issue with the arrangement."

"Your father's money," he corrected without malice.

"Which you are acquiring only by marriage to *me*."

He held my gaze for a moment, as though trying to determine my mood. "Yes. In exchange for the centuries-old title and prestige you can acquire only by marriage to *me*."

"Either way, you may hire another housemaid easily enough. Unless your reputation as a tyrannical master presents a barrier . . ."

He chuckled. "Very well, Miss Godfrey. You may have Dolly. May I leave you to inform Mrs. Boyle of the situation?"

I pressed my lips together. Arguing with him over Dolly's future was far more enticing a prospect than arguing with Mrs. Boyle.

Though he was hardly putting up a fight. He had shown himself so docile despite my presumption. I had done nothing to give him anything but a distaste for my company, and yet he spoke of our marriage and accepted my speaking of it with such calmness.

Was the desire for my money so strong that there was nothing I could do to vanquish it? The thought should perhaps have been empowering, but I found it lowering. Precisely how miserable could I make the earl before he decided I was not worth the trouble? I wanted to press up against those limits, if only for any indication that Lord Lismore thought of me as anything more than a bank to draw upon at need.

And yet, I was tired of the charade. I was tired of pretending to be someone I was not.

Lord Lismore's lip quirked up at my continued silence, as though he knew precisely what an undesirable task he was requiring. There was a playfulness about his expression that struck me with a strange feeling—like a shift in the air. It was subtle, but a shift nonetheless, a tipping of the scales from animosity to something more like banter.

"I shall speak to her when I next see her." I curtsied and left the room, uncertain what to make of the meeting.

Things might be changing between Lord Lismore and me, but that was not the case with Mrs. Boyle. At some point in the near future, she and I would have to cross swords, and I meant to come out victor in that skirmish.

CHAPTER THIRTEEN

SANDY

"My lord?"

I looked up from buttoning my sleeves, meeting the eyes of my valet. He was holding out two dinner coats.

"The blue one," I said, wondering how long he had been waiting for me to reply. My mind was elsewhere.

On Miss Godfrey, specifically, and our encounter in the study. If I hadn't such a vivid memory of the morning's combat or last night's dinner, I might have said I'd imagined her insufferableness. But the way she had spoken to me in the study had been—dare I say it?—a bit playful. Arrogant, still, but playful. It was not the same sort of arrogance she had shown thus far, though. It was almost as if she was teasing herself as much as she was teasing me.

Or perhaps I was reading too much into things.

Gillies helped me shrug into the blue coat, and I gazed at myself in the mirror. I was not wearing my kilt to dinner tonight, which would alert Miss Godfrey to the fact that last night's attire had not been the standard we kept here. I rather thought she might have guessed that already, and I was ready to do away with the pretense if she was.

Would her haughtiness make a return at dinner?

"That will be all, Gillies," I said.

He bowed, and I waited until he had shut the door behind him to sniff my coat. It smelled harmless enough. I hoped.

Both Miss Lowe and Miss Godfrey were in the drawing room when I arrived. I had little experience of Miss Lowe, but I thought she looked unwell even compared to yesterday. Her nose was pink and her eyes droopy and red. Miss Godfrey, on the other hand, looked very well indeed. She was a beautiful woman, with dark hair and lashes—and a dark heart, I had come to assume. Now I wasn't so certain.

Both of them turned at my entrance. Miss Godfrey's mouth smiled slightly as she curtsied, while Miss Lowe somber expression remained for her curtsy.

"Are you unwell, Miss Lowe?" I asked, walking toward them.

"Nothing but a cold," she replied in a plugged voice.

"Shall I call for a doctor?" I asked.

"Yes—"

"—No."

Miss Godfrey looked at her cousin, who wiped her nose with her handkerchief and said, "I will be well presently. No need for a doctor."

"As you wish," I said just as Iain and Blair arrived. Magnus came shortly after, and we made our way to the dining room.

With the night's course lying before us, Miss Godfrey picked up her fork. Her gaze flitted to me for a fraction of a second, and I thought I saw a twinkle there. But perhaps I was imagining it.

I had thought I would prefer cordial dislike between myself and my wife, but I was beginning to realize I had been wrong.

It would be better to be on civil terms. Nothing more, nothing less. Was such a thing possible with Miss Godfrey?

"Och, what is this?" Iain held up his fork, looking at it as though he had never seen such a thing before in his life.

"Iain," I said in a warning voice.

He met my eye and lowered the fork, sufficiently cowed.

"A modern wonder, is it not?" Miss Godfrey said in an amused voice.

"Miss Godfrey," I said, "you hail from Newcastle, isn't that right?"

"It is," she said. "I have lived there all my life."

"In an estate on the edge of town," Miss Lowe added. "A very fine home indeed."

"Ah," I said, trying to sound interested in this unsolicited fact. "And how do you find the countryside? Apart from our pocked roads and quaint castle, that is."

She stiffened in her chair but, noting the hint of a smile on my lips, seemed to relax. "I find it"—she took in a breath, searching for the words—"quiet. And beautiful, of course. Though there is a certain charm to rows and rows of slanted rooftops, I think."

I smiled. I had offered her the opportunity to say something cutting about Lochlarren, and she had not. She had called it quiet and beautiful. Did she miss the din of town?

"Have you visited Newcastle, my lord?" she asked.

My lord. Not Sandy. Not the icy *sir* she had used once or twice.

"Only once in passing," I replied. "We took refreshment at" —I thought for a moment—"the Bull and Bear, if memory serves?"

"Yes," she said with an eager smile, "just beside the haberdasher. I know it well, for I lived just a street away as a child."

Miss Lowe put her hand on Miss Godfrey's arm with a little

laugh. "That was before we moved to the edge of town. Long ago." I didn't miss the way she squeezed her cousin's hand. I had utilized that squeeze on more than one occasion for my brothers. It was the equivalent of kicking Iain under the table —a warning.

I began to suspect it was Miss Lowe who had put all the ideas into Miss Godfrey's head about Scotland and had encouraged her to act so impossibly pompous. Did she think to impress me by it?

My brothers seemed to take my lead, engaging in regular conversation which, for them, meant a number of silly jokes and insignificant topics. Rather than redirecting the conversation, I used it as an opportunity to observe Miss Godfrey. The warning squeeze seemed to have worked to some extent, for she was more subdued for the remainder of the meal, though once or twice, I caught sight of the way her lip twitched at comments from Iain and Blair.

When we joined her and Miss Lowe in the drawing room later, I tasked Magnus with engaging Miss Lowe in conversation with the hope I might pursue my suspicions about Miss Godfrey. There was more to her, I was sure. But Miss Lowe's sneezing, congested presence was difficult to escape. She hovered about her cousin almost doggedly. I couldn't blame her entirely—she *was* Miss Godfrey's companion. How she could assume I harbored any designs on her charge was a great mystery, for we were engaged—and barely on speaking terms.

It wasn't until the next morning that I had any opportunity for private conversation with Miss Godfrey. She was in the library, on her tiptoes, reaching for one of the higher shelves, to no avail.

"May I be of assistance?" I asked, stepping into the room.

Miss Godfrey's gaze whipped to me, and she lowered to her

feet again with a sigh. "Perhaps a ladder should be the first purchase after the wedding."

I chuckled and made my way toward her. It was small as far as libraries went, but not scarce. Every possible space had been filled with the books collected by Father, Grandfather, and the earls before them. "If you are an avid reader, perhaps so. I cannot say Iain or Magnus or Blair would even notice the addition, though." I came up beside her and searched the row of gold print titles. "Which one?"

She went on her tiptoes again, moving from side to side in search of the title she wished for. Her movement momentarily brought her shoulder against my arm, a fact she seemed not to notice. "Buchan's book," she said, pointing.

"Ah," I said, pulling it from its place. "Good choice. A Scottish physician, you know."

"One must make do," she said with a smiling glance up at me as she took the book.

"Is something amiss? Or have we bored you so terribly that you are reduced to reading *Domestic Medicine* for entertainment?"

She let the book fall open and shot me an arch look. "Might not both be true?"

I chuckled as she searched the table of contents, her finger stopping on the heading titled *Colds*.

"For your cousin?" I asked.

She nodded, turning to the desired page. "She insists on making light of her ailments, for she hates to be a burden and refuses to see a doctor, but I hoped I might find a remedy here she would accept."

I watched her, so intent on her task with hardly a care for me. I suppose that was better than hurling insults at my face. "You care deeply for her."

Her gaze flickered to me, then back to the book. "I do. She

has been much like a mother to me." Her finger traced each line on the page, her lips moving silently as she read.

That explained a great deal about Miss Lowe's demeanor and about Miss Godfrey's conceding to her guiding hand. It also made me wonder . . . Miss Godfrey and I had both lived most of our lives without our mothers. Had that bred any similarities between us? Yesterday, I would have thought such a thing impossible.

A twist of guilt tightened my chest. I had not given her the welcome she deserved. She had been very late and had arrived without the escort of her father, but perhaps things would have gone differently if *I* had set aside my pride and annoyance to welcome her. She had not acted well, of course. Neither of us had.

I owed her an apology.

"There," Miss Godfrey said, tapping a line near the bottom of the page. "Linseed sharpened with the juice of orange or lemon." She smiled up at me, slamming the book to a close. "Thank you for your assistance, my lord."

And just like that, she was gone.

CHAPTER FOURTEEN

JULIANA

D olly ensured Buchan's concoction was prepared for Augusta. To my relief, it seemed to relieve her congestion, making her voice less nasal and plugged. I hated to see her so miserable, particularly now that things with the Duncans were looking better than they had at first.

Within an hour, however, she was as nasal as ever—and sneezing more. She slept most of the afternoon, rising just in time to dress for dinner.

In comparison to my first night at Lochlarren, the two more recent dinners had been thoroughly enjoyable. There was still the slight awkwardness of dining with near-strangers, but it lessened with every smile or laugh—things Iain and Blair might have been born and bred to elicit.

Augusta only picked at her food, but my appetite seemed to have been whetted now that I felt less anxious about how I was being perceived. I tried to mirror Augusta's ladylike nibbling and avoid giving the impression that I wished to eat every last morsel on the table, but my patience wore thin after a time, and I surrendered to my appetite.

Augusta and I left the men to their port once the covers had been cleared, making our way to the drawing room.

"You seemed to enjoy the meal," she said as we took seats on the sofa.

I smiled at the implication of her words. Apparently, I had not done as well masking my hunger as I had thought. "And you seemed *not* to."

"It was well enough," she said, "but I thought we would be better served by feigning otherwise. I noticed more than once the eyes of the earl and his brothers upon you, my dear. I am sure they noted the eagerness with which you ate the peas. Perhaps tomorrow you can make a suggestion or two for the meals. Once you are married, you will be the one consulted about the dinner menu. They will expect you to take an interest in such matters." She wiped her nose with a handkerchief—a constant companion to her now.

"Certainly," I replied, though the thought made me cringe inwardly. If acting like a countess meant constantly presuming and interfering, I wasn't certain I would enjoy it. If it meant pretending not to like food I heartily enjoyed, I would like it even less.

The earl and his brothers joined us some thirty minutes later, and the youngest two played at cards while Augusta engaged the earl in conversation about how often he went to town and whether he owned or rented when he did so.

I shifted uncomfortably in my seat during the conversation, busying myself with a book I had no interest in. While Augusta was a capable conversationalist, it was hard not to feel as though she was putting Lord Lismore under the microscope with her questions. The earl took it in good part, seeming a bit amused by it, I thought. But he must have felt as fatigued by it as I, for he retired shortly after.

Augusta and I followed suit a few minutes later.

I saw Augusta to her room, ensuring she had everything she might need during the night, then bid her goodnight and closed the door. In the corridor, I found Mrs. Boyle and a maid approaching, a basket in the maid's arms.

A quick glance at the maid's basket brought me up short. It was full of peat bricks.

"Is that intended for my bedchamber?" I asked Mrs. Boyle.

"Aye, miss."

I smiled humorlessly. "I am sure you went to great trouble to acquire this"—I held her gaze to convey that I knew what she was doing—"but I have no need of it. Please return it and see that wood is brought instead."

Her jaw shifted, but she curtsied, and so did the maid. "Certainly, miss."

"There is one more thing, Mrs. Boyle," I said.

She raised a brow. "And what might that be?"

"I have employed Dolly as my lady's maid. As a result, she will no longer be available for housemaid duties."

She paused. "Dolly, miss?"

"Yes," I met her gaze. "Dolly." I had told Lord Lismore I would speak with her on the subject, but I did not require her permission.

The housekeeper stared at me, and I met her gaze unflinching.

"Dolly is a housemaid, no' a lady's maid."

"*Was* a housemaid," I corrected.

"But . . ."

"Yes?"

She pinched her lips together and straightened, as though

deciding to speak her mind after all. "'Tis simply no' how things are done. Perhaps ye dinna ken the expectations people have of the wife of an earl, and who could blame ye? Ye dinna come from this world, so no one could expect ye to. But a lady's maid should have the decorum and experience such a position requires."

I kept my smile, but my nostrils flared. *Expectation. Expect.* I was becoming tired of the words.

Sooner or later, Mrs. Boyle would need to learn that it was not her place to instruct or expect anything of me. "I am less concerned with what other people expect and more concerned with my own expectations of my lady's maid, but I thank you for your concern on my behalf."

She lifted her chin. "Verra well, miss. But as 'tis the earl's estate, he is—as ye no doubt understand—the only one with the authority ta make such a change. I will broach the topic with him and relay his response when I have it." She turned to go.

"I spoke with him already, so you need not trouble your-self. He agreed to Dolly's change in position."

She turned toward me again, her lips pressed together. "Ye've certainly made yerself comfortable here, Miss Godfrey." Her curtsy was stiff, her gaze penetrating and full of judgment, as she motioned for the maid to follow her back down the stairs.

Comfortable. She said I had made myself *comfortable*! I had hardly known a moment's comfort since arriving. All my efforts were directed toward trying to meet people's expecta-tions of me.

I was through with it. If Mrs. Boyle and others were intent on finding fault with me, they would do so no matter what I did. If she thought I had made myself comfortable already, she would soon see just how much more comfortable I would become.

Dolly arrived minutes later, looking harried.

"Dolly," I said. "Have you been doing your old duties belowstairs *and* attending to me today?"

She swallowed, then nodded. "I dinna wish ta anger Mrs. Boyle, miss."

I could certainly understand that. I sighed and turned toward her. "Dolly, you no longer answer to her. She cannot dismiss you, for I am your mistress now. I do not wish for a lady's maid who is worn to the bone from trying to do the work of two people. Do you understand?"

She smiled slightly. "Aye, miss."

"Good. Now, help me out of these clothes and into my dressing gown, if you please. You leave the curtains open, as well. I am not sleeping in here tonight."

Dolly's hands paused at the buttons of my dress. "Where *are* ye sleepin', Miss Godfrey?"

I squared my shoulders and smiled slightly. "In the royal apartments."

CHAPTER FIFTEEN

SANDY

Holding an engagement party for an arranged marriage had one challenge. The money I needed to pay for it would not be available to me until after the wedding. Given the family's embarrassing reputation for acquiring debt, many of those supplying us with food, decoration, and even music for the party were already insisting upon payment. I could not blame them, and I wished to return my family to esteem by providing it to them in a timely manner.

If Mr. Godfrey had arrived as expected, I would have been able to broach the matter with him in as delicate a way as possible, but unfortunately, that was not an option. Instead, I stayed awake until late that evening composing letters to assuage any concerns harbored by our suppliers.

When I made my way to partake of breakfast the next morning, I stopped in front of Father's portrait and straightened my cuffs. Even in his nearly unrecognizable likeness, I thought I saw a self-congratulatory glint in his eye, as though he had planned all of this. "Sins of the father indeed," I said.

I turned my head at the sound of footsteps nearby. Mrs. Boyle emerged from Miss Godfrey's room, her face dangerously near purple, and the vein in her forehead pulsating above the murderous expression she wore.

"I'll throttle her!" she said, her eyes forward as she made her way toward the stairs.

"Mrs. Boyle," I said, stopping her with a hand on her arm. "What is it?"

She set her hands on her ample hips. "Yer intended, my lord, fancied herself a queen last night and decided 'twas fittin' for her ta sleep in the king's own bed."

My brows shot up. Miss Godfrey had slept in the royal apartments? "Are you certain?"

"Aye, sir, for one of the maids went ta dust and nearly jumped out of her skin when she saw her in the bed."

I felt a strange desire to laugh. If Miss Godfrey was intent on making certain she was taken seriously at Lochlarren, she had hit upon a very effective way to do so. I couldn't but admire her pluck.

I suppressed my amusement, as Mrs. Boyle's temper was only being contained with great effort.

Her lips pressed together in a line so tight I thought they might disappear. "She's done it ta spite me!"

My brows shot up. "Has she?"

"Aye, my lord." She narrowed her eyes, looking past me at nothing in particular. "I saw the look in her eye last night."

"What occurred last night?"

"She informed me she'd made Dolly her own lady's maid. She claims ye agreed ta the change in position."

"I did. She must have a lady's maid, Mrs. Boyle, and the decision of who to employ should be hers." It occurred to me that I had not spoken to Mrs. Boyle about her treatment of

Miss Godfrey—and apparently, that had been a great mistake. It was clear the two had been quarreling.

"But ye didna give her permission ta sleep in the king's bed, did ye?"

"No," I conceded. "I did not."

Her chest rose in indignation, the fire reignited in her eyes. She stared ahead, as though she could see through the walls to where Miss Godfrey was sleeping.

"Stay, Mrs. Boyle," I said. "I shall speak to her. I appreciate your long-suffering with our guests. Of course, you must feel free to employ a replacement maid immediately. You had mentioned a niece of yours looking for work, had you not?"

She nodded. "Aye, sir. And a fine lass she is."

"Then let her be the one to take Dolly's place. As for Miss Godfrey's night in the state rooms, let us say nothing more of it. I cannot think the bed likely to host a truly royal guest in the near future—or distant future, if I am being frank—so the laundering of these linens should be the least pressing of your worries."

She looked down at her burden and sniffed. "'Tis the principle of the thing, my lord."

I suppressed a chuckle. "I quite understand, but unfortunately for us, principle does not pay the creditors."

"It *should* do." She shook her head. "Ta think of ye havin' ta marry so far below yerself, my lord. 'Tis almost more than I can bear."

I squeezed her hand, both amused and touched by her consideration for my pride. "I hope you will try, for I need you here. I would like to make Miss Godfrey as comfortable as possible going forward. I let my pride get the best of me upon her arrival, but I have repented and mean to be better. Will you help me?"

She met my gaze, her mouth twisting to the side. I was asking a great deal of her. But finally, she nodded.

I gave her a bracing smile and made my way to the tower that housed the royal apartments, the ghost of a smile on my lips as I planned how to approach the situation.

The door to the bedchamber was cracked, undoubtedly left so after the hurry in which the maid left. I stayed outside the door for a moment, listening for any movement within. There was none.

My smile grew as I imagined Miss Godfrey's surprise upon waking to find me staring over her in the bed. Gently, I urged the door open. Thanks to the care Mrs. Boyle took, it was one of the only doors in the castle that did not squeak. These apartments were her pride and joy, and she made sure everything was in perfect order in the event the Prince Regent or King George dropped in on us at any moment.

In short, Miss Godfrey could not have chosen a more certain way to infuriate the housekeeper.

I stepped into the room, preparing to clear my throat loudly. I stopped short, however, at the sight of Miss Godfrey asleep. She was nearly drowning in the voluptuous crimson bedcovers, one hand cradling her cheek, the other stretching above her head. Her expression was peaceful and pleasant, no fieriness, no arrogance, no teasing.

I don't know what I had expected. Had I thought she slept with a smirk?

I stared and stared, trying to make sense of what I was feeling. Rattled, perhaps? Uncertain? What was she dreaming about so peacefully? Perhaps it was her life in town. Had she left someone there she cared for?

I hardly knew anything about her, and what I had *thought* I knew had been called into question.

Whatever the case, I couldn't bring myself to wake her.

After a few more moments, I turned and left her to her slumber.

A clatter belowstairs interrupted my perusal of the latest payments approved by my steward, Cairnie. I paused, then returned to my work when no further disruption occurred. I had been here since breakfast and my legs were begging me to stand.

A second sound pierced the silence, and I rose, following the noise and laughter as it grew louder.

I came to a halt at the bottom of the narrow staircase. "What the devil?"

Miss Godfrey sat atop a bay mount, her riding habit flowing over the saddle and down the side. She looked majestic, as though she was riding the moors rather than inside my castle entry hall. Iain stood just beside her, his eyes pinned on the pocket watch he held.

Neither seemed to have heard me, and I couldn't blame them, for there was a great thundering of clopping hooves and unintelligible yelling in the wide, main staircase. Seconds later, Blair emerged from those stairs on horseback.

"Eighteen!" Iain shouted once he reached the bottom.

Both he and Miss Godfrey set to clapping and cheering. Blair grinned, bending at the waist in a half-bow to accept their congratulations as his horse huffed and sidled.

"Your turn, Miss Godfrey," Iain said. "If you are certain you are equal to it." He cocked a provocative brow.

Miss Godfrey let out a scoff. "Watch and learn, sir."

I stepped forward to stop her, but it was too late. She kicked at her horse's flanks, and he went charging up the stairs with her atop.

"What in heaven's name?"

Miss Lowe had joined me in slack-jawed, wide-eyed observation of the chaos. I hadn't a thought to spare for her, though, as I hurried over to the bottom of the staircase to see what madness was happening there—and to prepare to run after Miss Godfrey and prevent tragedy.

But Miss Godfrey had a fine seat, the likes of which I was only able to see for a moment before she rounded the bend in the stairs and disappeared.

My heart raced, and my ears strained for a sound to indicate anything was amiss. But soon enough, the clatter of hooves drew nearer again, and she reappeared, leaning back in her seat to counter the forces at work on the descent. Her brows were drawn in concentration, but she wore a smile.

If she had been the personification of slumbering peace in the royal apartments two hours ago, now she was that of bright-eyed adventure and daring.

Or perhaps utter disregard for safety and propriety.

"Sixteen!" Iain called out as she reached the bottom of the staircase.

He and Blair clapped and cheered raucously, their admiration evident in the way they looked at her. Following Blair's example, Miss Godfrey let go of the reins with one hand and dipped into a seated curtsy. Though meant to be amusing, it was as elegant as her riding had been adept.

"Would one of you care to explain this madness?" I turned my gaze on my brothers.

"The fault does not lie with them," Miss Godfrey said, her eyes bright, her cheeks flushed, and her mouth stretched in an energetic smile. "I insisted on being included in the bet."

"Juliana," Miss Lowe cried.

"Forgive me, cousin," she said without seeming the least bit apologetic. She rubbed at her mount's neck appreciatively as he clopped around the entry hall—to cool down, I could only assume. "You know I have been wishing for a chance to ride. I simply couldn't resist—particularly not when odds were offered."

"What is the bet?" I asked, my curiosity getting the best of me.

Iain grinned. "Who could race up and down the stairs most quickly, obviously. So far, Miss Godfrey is the winner at sixteen seconds. But I have yet to take my turn, so I think we can safely say the best is yet to be witnessed."

Miss Godfrey only laughed at this, and I was distracted for a moment. Though she raced horses inside Lochlarren, this was one of the few times since I met her that she seemed sane. Normal and natural in her behavior. Yesterday's behavior from her did not seem to be chance occurrences, then.

"Conveniently for you," Blair said to Iain as he dismounted, "your attempt is unlikely to be witnessed at all." He shifted his gaze to me. "Sandy disapproves."

"Of course I do," I replied as Miss Lowe nodded her agreement.

Iain and Blair shared grimacing looks. I glanced at Miss Godfrey, whose smile had been replaced by something more serene. Everyone was waiting for me to express further disapproval and put a stop to things.

"Fifteen seconds should be more than sufficient," I said.

Heads whipped around, eyes fixed upon me, none more astonished than Miss Lowe's. I purposely avoided her eye. I had spent the last few weeks drowning in accounts and creditor letters. I was ready for a bit of amusement—and to encourage the change in Miss Godfrey. If she could play so nicely with Iain and Blair, perhaps she could do so with me, as well.

"Very well, then," Miss Godfrey said, putting out a hand to

Iain, who assisted her down from her horse. She gave him the reins, then took the ones from the horse Blair had ridden and held them out to me, her eyes holding a challenge. "Show us the proper way, my lord."

Our gazes held for a moment, and I felt a flash of something new for the capable woman before me—a reluctance to look away from the roguish challenge in her eyes.

"Well?" Iain said impatiently.

I took the reins, put a foot in the stirrup, and swung my leg over the saddle.

"Miss Godfrey," I said, eyeing Iain's pocket watch. "Perhaps you will do me the service of ensuring my brother stays honest in his measurements."

Iain scoffed, but Miss Godfrey nodded. "Everything shall be above board, my lord."

"I thank you." I steered the horse toward the bottom of the stairs. "By the by, what does the winner of the wager receive?"

"You need not concern yourself with that," Miss Godfrey replied, smiling at me serenely as she stroked the neck of her horse. "It is highly unlikely to affect you."

"Juliana," Miss Lowe said in that same shocked tone.

I laughed, well able to appreciate a competitive spirit. Iain and Blair found it highly amusing as well, and both of them regarded her with admiration. How rapidly their opinions of her had changed. Apparently, all they had needed was a show of adventure from her. The saber fight alone had likely been sufficient.

"Ready," Iain said as my mount sidled anxiously, sensing my eagerness. "Steady. Go!"

With a kick, my horse shot forward, and I leaned my body toward his head. We raced up the broad stairs, veering with the bend of the stairway. An echo of hooves filled the space as I counted the seconds in my head. We climbed to the landing, pivoting to make our descent. With a little effort, I successfully maneuvered my mount around the old set of armor there. Blasted thing!

My horse lost his footing midway down the stairwell but recovered himself—and I my seat—quickly enough. We sailed over the last three steps and into the entry hall as Iain called out, "Sixteen and a half!"

"I measured sixteen even," Miss Godfrey said.

I shot a look at Iain.

"The extra half-second is penalty for Sandy's braggadocio. Either way, it matters not a jot." He handed the watch to Miss Godfrey and urged me out of the saddle with an impatient hand. "I shall beat all three of you now."

I dismounted to make way for him, then stepped to Miss Godfrey's side to supervise the timing of Iain's attempt. I shot a quick glance at Miss Lowe, who was standing at the far wall, her hands clasped and her lips pursed. I had no qualms relinquishing the role of the responsible party into her capable hands. I was tired of playing that part, at least for today.

Despite Iain's boastful predictions, the clattering of the suit of armor upstairs did not bode well for his effort. Blair, Miss Godfrey, and I were unanimous in declaring his time eighteen seconds.

"Eighteen and a half for your braggadocio," Miss Godfrey amended.

I glanced at her in amusement.

Iain's demands for a repeat fell on deaf ears. Even Miss Lowe declared everything had been done fairly, a statement she could hardly lay claim to, as she had arrived late, just as I had.

He finally surrendered, making Miss Godfrey and I both claimant to the prize, whatever that was.

"What do you say, my lord?" she asked. "Would you like to

make the attempt again to ensure a clear winner? Or would you prefer to split our winnings evenly?"

I furrowed my brow. "These winnings you speak of . . . are they the ones you said would not affect me?"

She inclined her head in apology. "An error of judgment on my part."

I copied her gesture, accepting her admission, then leaned in to speak in a low voice. "I fear Miss Lowe will faint if we make another attempt."

Miss Godfrey glanced at her cousin. "She is well-accustomed to my shocking behavior. Split the winnings, then?"

I tipped my head from side to side. "I am rather a selfish man, Miss Godfrey, and find myself reluctant to do so."

"Despite having no notion what the winnings are?" she said, diverted.

She was right, of course. I was making no sense. But having seen this side of her, I was reluctant to put an end to things. The woman beside me now was someone I could bear to marry much more easily than the stiff, arrogant one I had first met. "One cannot put a price on victory."

She considered me for a moment, her brown eyes fixed upon me. "What do you have in mind?"

"*Ghillie callum!*" Iain said from behind us, surprising us both with his proximity.

I shot him a look, and Miss Godfrey's brow wrinkled in confusion. "What was that?"

"*Ghillie callum,*" I repeated. "It is a traditional Highland dance, using two crossed swords. And not at all what I had in mind." I squared Iain with another look to let him know what I thought of his suggestion.

"A sword dance," Miss Godfrey said. "It sounds intriguing, though, forgive me, but I am unclear how one might *win* a sword dance."

"If the swords are touched, the dance ends," Iain explained.

"When they were done as war dances," Blair said, stepping toward us, with one of the horses following behind, "displacing a sword was thought to be a bad omen, foretelling loss or defeat. I heard of a chief who, when a dancer kicked a sword by accident the night before battle, took the sword and beheaded him."

"Thank you for that, Blair," I said, suppressing an eye roll. "Why don't you and Iain take the horses back to the stables?"

They grumbled but obeyed. I turned back to Miss Godfrey, who was speaking to her cousin. Miss Lowe nodded at her, then looked at me consideringly, as though she was loath to leave.

Did she think me untrustworthy? That I would force myself upon Miss Godfrey the moment she left?

I gave her a smiling nod, and she reluctantly left via the stairs that led to her bedchamber.

"So, *ghillie callum*?" Miss Godfrey said.

"Pay no heed to my brothers. Most of what they say is ridiculous."

She raised her brows. "You do not wish to challenge me at sword dancing, then?"

I paused, trying to read her expression. "Do you wish to challenge *me*?"

She shrugged her shoulders. "If I am to become the Countess of Lismore, I should be better acquainted with the traditions of the Highlands. So far, I have eaten a traditional meal without the use of a fork, slept in a peat-saturated room, and participated in clan feuding practice. Why not *Ghillie callum*?"

I gave a soft laugh, still unsure what to make of today's version of Miss Godfrey—or of the way she spoke of becoming my wife. I hadn't thought she would truly be interested in our traditions. I was finding myself wrong multiple times a day since her arrival.

"Though," she continued, "if you mean to behead me if I happen to nudge one of the swords, I may reconsider."

"There shall be no beheadings," I reassured her.

"And you will teach me how to perform the dance before we challenge one another?"

"To the best of my poor abilities, yes. If you wish for it."

"I do wish for it, if only for the prospect of seeing the esteemed Earl of Lismore dancing between swords. When shall the challenge take place?"

"I am entirely at your disposal, Miss Godfrey. Shall we say tomorrow?"

"Tomorrow," she agreed. With a small dip into a curtsy, she turned away.

"Oh, Miss Godfrey?"

She looked over her shoulder, waiting for me to continue.

"I trust you slept well last night? Like a queen, even?"

CHAPTER SIXTEEN

JULIANA

I stilled. In the excitement and novelty of riding horses indoors, I had forgotten my choice to sleep in the royal bedchamber. I hadn't even told Augusta of it.

"I slept quite well, I thank you," I said, unable to entirely hide my smile. The earl did not seem angry with me, merely amused.

"Surely you do not mean to leave me without more details. I have been wondering these thirty years what it would be like to sleep in that bed. I insist you satisfy my curiosity."

"Or you could simply try it yourself," I suggested. I had hardly expected him to accept the challenge of riding a horse up the grand stairs, but he had thoroughly surprised me. In no small part because of how well he looked astride a horse. Not that such a thing mattered. It was simply an observation.

When I had found Iain and Blair discussing the width of the central staircase at breakfast, an argument over whether one could comfortably ride a horse in the available space had morphed into a wager over how quickly it could be done.

In my efforts to be less unpleasant, and with an admitted

hope to be accepted by them, I had asked to join. The looks of surprise and approbation on their faces had confirmed my choice.

Lord Lismore cocked a brow. "I am not nearly as brave as you, Miss Godfrey. The ire of Mrs. Boyle is enough to keep me in my own bed."

"Should I expect more peat in my fireplace tonight? Or to be deprived of a fork again perhaps?"

His eyes wrinkled with amusement. "Neither, I assure you. Let us admit that our first impressions of one another were not what we might have wished."

"Nor, in your case, the second, third, or even fifth impressions," I retorted, though I was too relieved by the amiability he was demonstrating to be truly angry. After all, I had done my level best to be every bit as unlikable as I had found him.

He nodded, a humorous glint in his eye. "Whereas you were a specimen of perfect amiability from the moment you stepped into my *quaint* castle."

I bit my lip.

"Two days late," he added.

"One and a half," I amended. "And surely, you had been apprised of that."

"Surely I had not."

"Papa assured me he had sent word of our delay." Though, even as I said it, I realized how likely it was that he had forgotten to do so. Such details often escaped him in favor of those related to his business.

The way Lord Lismore remained silent, gaze fixed upon me told me that the message truly had not been conveyed. Little wonder he had been irritated upon our arrival. "Perhaps the letter was dropped en route and swallowed up in one of the enormous holes in your roads."

"It is possible." He sighed and regarded me frankly, the hint of a smile in his eyes. "Well, Miss Godfrey, what is to be done now? We are both in disgrace."

I lifted my chin, trying to school my expression into something haughty. "I could never marry a disgraced earl."

"Whereas I am perfectly willing to marry a disgraced heiress."

I laughed alongside him, but his words reverberated in my mind. There truly were no limits to what he would countenance if only he could have Papa's money.

"Will you forgive me for teasing you so abominably when I should have been welcoming you warmly?" he asked.

My mouth twisted to the side as I pretended to consider his plea. "If peat is to be the means of such warmth, I think I would prefer the alternative."

He chuckled. "Do you dislike the smell so very much?"

I hesitated. "No. In fact, I rather like it. But I prefer not to be forced to smell like it at all times."

At that, he leaned in, his breath brushing my ear and neck. My heart skittered as he inhaled softly.

He drew back and met my eye with a teasing glint in his own. "You do not smell of peat, Miss Godfrey."

I didn't respond immediately, taken up with trying to remember whether I had donned perfume this morning. It was the type of silly thought that wasn't to be entertained.

"I am pleased to hear that," I said.

He inclined his head. "And do I indeed smell to you as though I had been six months without a bath?"

I considered doing as he had done, leaning in and smelling the hollow of his neck. The way my pulse raced told me it was a terrible idea. "No. You do not."

"You relieve me."

There was a short silence as we regarded one another,

wondering what to do with this new, more cordial energy between us.

"I am well-aware that this is a business arrangement for both of us," Lord Lismore said, "but I hope we may be friendly rather than antagonistic going forward. What do you say?"

I nodded, feeling strange. What did I think of my intended now that he was not entirely detestable? And perhaps more importantly, how much did it matter what I thought of him? We were participating in a curious exchange of advantages— one that would tie us together for the rest of our lives.

He regarded me through slightly narrowed eyes, as though he feared he had said something to worry me. "I assure you I shan't be a demanding husband."

"Nor I a demanding wife."

He nodded. "You shall have your title, as well as the respect you deserve—"

"—and you shall have your money."

Our gazes held for a moment. "Very good," he said.

I smiled. "I should rejoin my cousin. I assured her I would follow directly after her."

"By all means," he said, moving aside to allow me to pass.

It was only to be expected that Augusta would have something to say for the day's events. Despite her kind but firm words encouraging me to rethink my actions, however, I could not find it in myself to regret anything. I felt more at home at Lochlarren now than I yet had, for I had formed a kinship of sorts with the Duncans. Of course, Magnus had not been present for the race, but given how he had spoken to me at dinner the last two nights, I had reason to think he at least did not despise me anymore.

Dinner was pleasant, even Augusta seeming to unbend a bit, perhaps because she sensed less tension between the family and myself and thus less need to protect me. She was feeling better than she had since our arrival, making me hopeful her cold was to be mild and short-lived.

I went to bed—not in the royal apartments but in my own bedchamber—to the smell of burning wood and with a general sense of well-being. Not only did my impending marriage look to be more bearable, there was the added prospect of a new family. Perhaps, even, future sisters to form bonds with when the earl's brothers married. Until now, I had not realized just how keenly I wished for such things.

Perhaps life at Lochlarren would not be so unbearable after all.

CHAPTER SEVENTEEN

JULIANA

The sword dancing challenge, which Iain and Blair were thrilled to discover would indeed take place, was set for the following afternoon. Magnus spoke little, but when it was suggested that he be the one to judge the sword dancing, he agreed.

"His regiment engaged in the practice regularly," Lord Lismore explained at the breakfast table—the first day all of us had partaken together.

It was admittedly difficult to imagine someone as sullen as Magnus engaging in such an active pastime, but perhaps it was his injured arm which was primarily at fault. Would he have joined in the amusements earlier if not for that?

"Do you anticipate your father's arrival soon, Miss Godfrey?" the earl asked before taking a sip of his tea.

"He assured me he would arrive in time for the party—and certainly for the wedding." It was strange to speak such words, to know that, in a matter of five days, I would be Lady Lismore.

I glanced at the earl as he spoke to one of the footmen in an undervoice. In a matter of four days, I had gone from utter ignorance of my future husband, to indignant dislike, to . . . curiosity? I knew not how else to describe what I felt.

"Well," Augusta said as we took our seats in the parlor, "I am glad to see the family responding to you with less suspicion."

"And I them," I said, taking up some needlework to keep my hands busy. "It is such a relief to be on good terms with them. Even two days ago, I could not have conceived we would be discussing a good-natured competition like sword dancing."

"No, indeed." She looked at me for a moment, then clasped her hands in her lap. "May I say one thing, my dear? I hope you will not take it amiss."

"Of course," I replied. "You may always speak your mind with me."

She nodded. "I feel to give a word of counsel against becoming *too* familiar with the earl or his siblings. These marriages of conveniences can become quite messy if the motivations that brought them into being are forgotten."

My stomach constricted.

Her brows pulled together in sympathy as she looked at me. "I say this only because I so dearly wish for your happiness, Juliana."

"Of course," I said, blinking and smiling at her. "How could I ever doubt such a thing? That is all you have ever sought, and I hope you realize just how much I appreciate it—how glad I am to have you here, for I would not know how to go on without you."

"You are doing very well." She shot me a teasing look. "Even your escapades yesterday and this morning seem not to have done the damage I had feared. And perhaps in this I am being overly cautious as well, but I would rather put you on your guard and be proven wrong than say nothing and see you suffer." The little glistening in her eye was soon veiled when she blinked it away.

No doubt she was right to put me on my guard. I could see how easy it would be to allow the small kinship I had come to feel in such a short time to grow up to something far greater.

Whereas I am perfectly willing to marry a disgraced heiress.

I needed to inscribe those words upon the pages of my mind, for they perfectly encapsulated the motivations Augusta spoke of. I was at Lochlarren for the wealth I brought. And, in turn, I would receive the title of Countess of Lismore. Those were the terms of the arrangement, and they were very suitable ones.

"Both Mr. Iain and Mr. Blair seem quite taken with you," Augusta said.

I smiled and shook my head. "Certainly, more taken than they *were*, but that is not saying much, is it?" I met her gaze and frowned. "Surely, you are not worried I might become *improperly* familiar with either of them."

"You are in a foreign country, my dear, surrounded by people you have never met. It would be understandable to seek friendship wherever it was offered."

I laughed. "Friendship, yes. They are to become my *family*, cousin. Thank you for your concern, though. You need have no fears on my account. My only interest is ensuring my life here at Lochlarren is not entirely miserable." I squeezed her hand. "I am fortunate enough to have you here with me now, but it shan't always be so."

I had no fear of falling in love with Iain or Blair or Magnus. It was the earl himself toward whom I felt the greatest draw.

But I would not admit as much to Augusta. There would be little purpose, for I hardly knew him, and now that we had come to an understanding, I was determined to keep the arrangement amicable but suitably aloof. Papa had worked with many partners in his business over the years, and he had pressed upon me how important it was to keep emotion out of such dealings. That was the sort of relationship I sought with Lord Lismore. Nothing more, nothing less. I was past the age of fancy.

CHAPTER EIGHTEEN

SANDY

I ran a hand through my hair, shuffling through the last couple of letters I had received from creditors—one in particular from Father's tailor and another from the man who supplied us with whisky.

Mr. Godfrey's arrival would help immensely with these charges, but it had been four days since Miss Godfrey's arrival, and her father was nowhere to be found. What would I do if he never arrived? We had agreed upon the terms of the marriage through our correspondence, but little good that would do me if the man absconded, leaving me without money but *with* his daughter and niece to care for.

I didn't anticipate that would be the case, but it was a thought that had pressed itself upon me once or twice. Now that Miss Godfrey was not the wretchedly imperious woman I had first thought her to be, marriage to her seemed more palatable. But palatable was not enough. I absolutely needed to marry money.

If straights became dire, she would have to marry one of my brothers. Both Iain and Blair seemed to have taken a liking to her now, but I doubted that would survive orders to marry her. Neither of them had such a thing on the mind. And even if they agreed, what was to be done with the cousin?

I sincerely trusted such a dilemma would not need solving. Better to hope for the best and expect the arrival of her father at any point—preferably at a sooner point than a later one, for the engagement party was in but two days.

The door burst open as it always did when Iain was the one entering. In each hand, he carried a sword, and I sighed before he even said a word.

I had come to regret the willingness I had expressed to challenge Miss Godfrey in sword dancing. While I had witnessed it, I myself had never sword-danced in my life. I would make a fool of myself. But even more than that, what was the purpose? I was letting my curiosity over Miss Godfrey hold too much sway over me. Curiosity had no place in an arranged marriage. Too much familiarity between us could introduce a host of problems I was not willing to deal with. My experience with Nelly Cochrane had been enough, and I had no wish to relearn that lesson.

"The time has come," Iain said, thrashing the swords around in the air in a way that was likely to result in him losing a limb.

"I had rather hoped she had forgotten," I said, stacking the papers and tapping them on the desk to order them.

"She is not such a poor sport as that," he said, talking somewhat breathlessly after his endeavor with the swords.

"I thought you did not like the woman. You have certainly changed your tune quickly," I replied.

"Haven't you?"

When I didn't reply, he continued. "The moment I saw her fight you with a saber, I suspected we had misjudged her. Now I realize it was your peevish welcome that put her hackles up."

I scoffed, though I agreed with him. I was beginning to suspect, too, that Miss Lowe held a bit of responsibility for putting grand notions into her charge's head.

"The longer you wait," Iain said, "the more practice she has, and the more fool you shall look."

"How can she be practicing when you have escaped with the swords?"

"These are for you. You forget, brother, that there are plenty of swords at Lochlarren to go around." He flashed me a cheeky grin.

"Perhaps we should sell them to pay off a few of these creditors," I murmured as I laid the papers on the desk. "Go on. I shall be but a moment."

Iain hesitated, as though he wasn't entirely sure whether to believe me. "Very well. But you had better hurry. She already shows a great deal of promise. I think she shall win handily. Or footily."

I offered an eye roll and a reluctant smile at his ridiculous pun and watched him leave the room.

I pulled the bell and delivered the correspondence I had composed into the hands of the answering footman. A sigh escaped me, and I made my way to the great hall. I paused just shy of the threshold, listening to the sounds within.

Miss Godfrey and Blair were laughing while Magnus gave instructions in a voice of thinly veiled frustration.

I leaned forward and sneaked a glance into the room. As expected, two swords lay on the floor, crossed together to create four spaces in which to dance. Miss Godfrey was turned away from me, standing in the top right quadrant. She held up the side of her white skirts, displaying a dainty ankle and slipper. A neatly turned arm was raised over her head. Beside her, using his own imagined pair of swords, Blair mirrored her stance.

"Now to second position," Magnus said.

The two dancers hopped not quite simultaneously, shifting one foot to the quadrant next to the one they stood within.

"Hand over the head," Magnus said.

They obeyed, but Blair wobbled woefully. Miss Godfrey kept herself straight, but her slippered foot quaked in the struggle to maintain balance.

Blair laughed at his own inability to stay upright, while Miss Godfrey smiled good-naturedly. She had certainly made inroads with my brothers. Mrs. Boyle's dislike of her had not abated, but instead of outright disapproval and loftiness, she treated my intended with rigid courtesy.

My gaze fixed on Miss Godfrey, who followed politely each of Magnus's clipped instructions. She laughed at her own missteps, but despite them, her movements and bearing were graceful.

I pulled my gaze away. What did it matter whether she was graceful or beautiful or less starched up than I had first thought? Such observations served no purpose. On the contrary, they might lead to places I had no desire to go. My marriage was of necessity entirely wrapped up not in the personality, appearance, or grace of my soon-to-be wife, but in her financial position and my title.

Indeed, my entire life was wrapped up in the earldom. So much so, in fact, that if the entirety of the Scottish nobility was to stand in this room now, I could have lined them up in order of rank. I myself would fall between the Earl of Dunlop, whose earldom was created ten years after the Lismore one, and the Earl of Alyth, whose earldom was created seventy-six years *before* mine.

Were we to include English peers, every single English earl, including those whose earldoms were created after mine, would stand ahead of every single Scottish earl. Such was the way of things. Scotland was considered lesser, and I had no doubt that, if a better option had presented itself to Mr. Godfrey and his daughter in England, they would have taken it.

Our considerable debts—*my* considerable debts, I should say, for they now belonged entirely to me—knocked me down a peg or two in people's estimation. It was the elusive combination of money and title which set one apart, hence the match between Miss Godfrey and myself. Once we were married, Lochlarren would be considerably raised in Society's esteem.

In any case, the important thing was to remember why Miss Godfrey was here, and that was not as an object of my admiration. I merely needed another day to accustom myself to this version of her. No doubt, the contrast between her demeanor today and the day of her arrival was making her seem far more desirable than she was.

"There you are!" Blair said, catching sight of me in the doorway. "You had better set to practicing, Sandy, or Miss Godfrey will trounce you."

"I wouldn't go so far as to say *that*," Magnus muttered.

"Neither would I," Miss Godfrey said, lowering her arm and rubbing her shoulder. "Though I shall certainly endeavor to best you, my lord." Her smile teased me, and I offered my own forced one in return.

But it was nigh on impossible to keep any degree of seriousness about me when I was making a fool of myself dancing between swords. I hadn't Magnus's skill.

My fifth time kicking one of the swords, Magnus shook his head. "You are not jumping high enough, Sandy."

"Easy for you to say," I replied, short of breath, "when you are merely standing there like a post. By all means, demonstrate for us."

His only response was to lift his injured arm slightly.

"You must think elevated thoughts," Miss Godfrey said, sailing with ease over the swords. "But not *too* elevated, or you shall forget to move far enough horizontally and land straight upon the sword as I did earlier."

"Perhaps this is too dangerous an activity," I replied, trying to regain my equilibrium after a higher but less controlled hop.

Miss Godfrey scoffed. "Said by the man with an unfair advantage."

I stopped and turned toward her. "And what advantage is that? Being Scottish?"

"*Two* unfair advantages," she corrected.

"The other being . . ."

"*I* am obliged to take care that my skirts do not disturb the swords. If we were truly attempting fairness, you would be wearing your kilt over those breeches." She looked at me as though delighting in the silly picture her imagination had concocted.

Blair laughed loudly. "The first rule of the *feileadh mor*, Miss Godfrey, is that one wears nothing beneath it at all."

Miss Godfrey's eyebrows raised, and her cheeks infused with color.

"Thank you, Blair," I said ironically. I turned to Miss Godfrey, who wouldn't meet my eye, no doubt thanks to the image Blair had offered up. "If you feel it would be fairer, Miss Godfrey, I will gladly don a kilt over my breeches."

"I shall fetch it," Iain said, already leaving the room.

When he returned with it minutes later, Miss Godfrey watched the folding of the large plaid with interest. She stood just behind me and asked questions as I did my best to perform a quick but worthy pleating of the large swathe of fabric lying on the floor with a belt beneath.

"But now that it is pleated," she said with a frown, "how will you don it without disturbing your hard work?"

I gave a bracing smile. "Like this." I clambered onto the plaid and lay down on the pleats as she watched with curiosity.

Iain shook his head. "You'll have to set yourself higher so that it falls to your ankles. Fair is fair."

Sighing, I repositioned myself, then pulled the fabric on my right so that it covered my waist, followed by the fabric on my left. After securing the belt, I clambered up to a stand, unused to the length of the fabric, which brushed the floor.

"Fascinating," Miss Godfrey said, her eyes fixed on me—no, on the kilt—in wonder.

"Shall we continue now?" Magnus said from his place, leaning against the wall with his arms crossed.

"By all means," Miss Godfrey said. "In fact, if you are ready, my lord, I think we may as well get on with the competition. Unless, that is, you need a bit of time in your skirts."

"Kilt," I corrected.

"Is that not what I said?" Her eyes teased me as she took her place just behind the swords, preparing to dance.

Holding her gaze and trying to suppress a smile, I took my place. *Think elevated thoughts.*

We had no music, but Iain and Blair provided clapping to help us maintain a proper rhythm. That rhythm seemed to pick up speed every few claps. Miss Godfrey looked over at me as she bounced to and fro, and I couldn't resist smiling back as I made my poor attempts at executing a decent imitation of sword dancing.

Her temporary focus on me threw off her equilibrium, however, and she stumbled toward me. I caught her by the arms and, in the process, knocked one of my swords with my foot.

Miss Godfrey looked up at me, her hands on my arms and mine on hers.

"We have a winner!" Iain called out. "Well done, Miss Godfrey!"

"My lord." Mrs. Boyle's voice was loud and clear, almost as though this was not the first time she had addressed me. I looked at her, standing in the doorway. Her face was studiously impassive except for a tightness about her lips. "Mr. Godfrey has arrived."

CHAPTER NINETEEN

JULIANA

Mrs. Boyle stepped aside, revealing Papa, wearing a maroon velvet tailcoat and gold waistcoat, a perfect manifestation of his somewhat eccentric fashion.

Lord Lismore released me and I him, and we stepped apart, both of us unwittingly knocking our swords from their places in a clattering that filled the hall.

"Papa," I said, hurrying over and embracing him. After the last few days of so much that had been strange and new, I melted into his familiar smell and his arms around me. "How happy I am to see you."

"And I you," he said, kissing my hair. "Forgive me for being so late."

"We are pleased to welcome you to Lochlarren, Mr. Godfrey," Lord Lismore said as Papa and I released one another.

"Lord Lismore," Papa said with a bow. "What a pleasure to finally meet you. I hope you will forgive both my tardiness and my arrival in such a state." He looked down at his clothing, which was somewhat wrinkled. "There were issues at the port, and it took far longer to resolve them than I had anticipated."

"I quite understand," the earl replied as they shook hands.

"I seem to have interrupted something," Papa said, looking at the earl's brothers and then to the swords lying on the ground in disarray.

"Not at all," the earl said. "Just a bit of entertainment. Allow me to introduce you to my brothers."

I watched as Lord Lismore performed the introductions, unable to avoid drawing comparisons to my own initial meeting with him and his brothers. Then, the earl had seemed cold, aloof, even vaguely menacing with his unfamiliar way of speaking and dressing. If I had met the man Papa was meeting, I would have reacted quite differently. I hoped.

"You must be fatigued from your long journey," Lord Lismore said after the introductions. "Mrs. Boyle, will you show Mr. Godfrey to his room?"

"Oh, I am happy to do so," I said. I was eager to speak with Papa.

Lord Lismore held my gaze for a moment, the edge of his mouth lifting slightly. "You forfeit our competition, then?"

"She won, Sandy," Iain said. "You knocked a sword."

"In my efforts to save *her* from doing so," he replied with amusement.

"Your chivalry was your downfall," I said with a smile.

"And prevented *yours*," he shot back. "But if that is how you care to win . . ."

I twisted my mouth to the side. "It is not. Perhaps we can finish later."

"Or find another way to settle things," Magnus suggested. "I can't bear to watch another instant of your clumsiness, Sandy."

"Thank heaven the history of Scottish battles did not depend upon his performance," Blair said with a grin.

"We shall discuss it later," Lord Lismore said. "Your father will be staying in the bedchamber just beside yours, Miss Godfrey, if you are certain you need no assistance. I assume your belongings have already been seen to by one of the servants, Mr. Godfrey?"

"By your capable footman, my lord." Papa turned to me. "Shall we, my dear?"

I nodded, and he slipped my hand onto his arm, escorting me from the room.

He closed the door behind us and patted my hand. "I am very pleased, Juliana."

"Are you? And why is that?"

The tower stairwell was too narrow for us to walk abreast, so I led the way, holding up my skirts. The stairs were already uneven and winding; I needed no other impediment to scaling them.

"I shan't try to pretend I have not been worrying over you these past few days," he said. "Only the knowledge of Augusta's presence and capability assuaged my conscience, but even then, I would have liked to be here to ensure a smooth arrival. I have worried you might be homesick or that you and the earl would perhaps not suit so well as I had hoped."

We reached the landing, and I led the way forward, content that he could only see the back of my head.

"We have got on quite well, so you needn't have worried. This is where you shall be staying," I said, turning the knob to his bedchamber. "Just beside me, as Lord Lismore said. Augusta is on the other side. She has been resting this morning. I thought she had a cold, but I begin to think something in the air here does not agree with her. I shall rouse her soon, though, for she will wish to see you." And I wished to warn her against saying anything to give Papa an indication of how things had begun at Lochlarren. Everything was well now. That was all that mattered.

Papa stepped into the room. His valise and portmanteau sat atop the trunk at the base of the four-poster bed. He glanced around with a subtle smile, apparently pleased with his accommodations, then turned back to me, taking both my hands in his.

"I am sorry to hear Augusta is unwell," he said with a frown. It morphed into a smile as he looked at me. "You must imagine my contentment to find you and Lismore on such good terms, though." His eyes were soft and wrinkled at the sides as he looked at me. "It is better than I could have hoped for, my dear. I sought a match that would elevate you and us, but to know you have found someone with whom you may enjoy all those warmer sentiments that may be enjoyed in a marriage? Both love and a title." He squeezed my hands. "Truly, my cup runneth o'er."

I blinked and turned my head away, for my cheeks burned. "I hardly know him, Papa." I bit my tongue rather than add that I had quite despised him until two days ago. But to not despise someone was not at all the same thing as loving him.

"Of course," he said. "But . . . well, suffice it to say, I am much relieved to see you settling in here and getting on with the Duncans so well."

"Thank you, Papa." I kissed him on the cheek. "I feel much more at home, though, with you near."

Augusta agreed there was nothing to be gained from telling Papa about the rougher parts of our arrival—or of those choices which might cast a poor light upon me.

His presence at dinner lent an entirely new tone to things. He was a garrulous man, asking each of the Duncans question after question. As a result, I learned a great deal about each of them. Magnus had served in the 79th Regiment until his injury —which was *not* at the hands of his brother—had obliged him to return home. He hoped to return to service as soon as it was healed.

Both Blair and Iain had completed their education in Edinburgh. The former had not yet decided upon his course in life, while the latter wished to enter into the law.

Discussion soon turned to the engagement party, set to take place in two days, and for which the castle was already bustling with preparations. The mere thought set my heart thrumming in my chest.

Augusta must have recognized it, for she reached over to my hand on my lap and squeezed it. "Never fear, my dear. You cannot help but shine brightly."

I smiled my gratitude, but I wasn't nearly so certain. My initial meeting with the Duncans had been a disaster. Who was to say my presentation to those in the area would be any different? It was entirely possible that gossip—and my reputation—had already traveled to the nearby families.

"Who is to come, by the by?" Iain asked while bringing a napkin to dab at the side of his mouth. The image of him licking his plate clean on the first night presented itself to me, bringing a small smile to my lips. I might have taken offense at the tricks played upon me, but knowing the Duncans a bit better now, I could well see how eager Iain and Blair would have been to run away with my inaccurate ideas of Scotland. I had deserved it, I thought.

Perhaps I could persuade the two of them to remain by my side during the party. They would make me laugh throughout it, if nothing else.

"Appleby is coming, I hope," Blair said.

"Yes, Appleby!" Iain agreed. "Haven't seen him in an age."

"And you shan't see him anytime soon, I fear," Lord Lismore said. "He is engaged."

Silence met this pronouncement. "Engaged?" Blair finally croaked. "Surely not! The man is vehemently against marriage."

"He has undergone a change of opinion, it would seem," Lord Lismore said as he cut his beef. He looked very fine tonight, his hair brushed forward fashionably, his neck hidden amongst the folds of a neatly tied cravat. "In any case, the Fowlies shall be in attendance. Lord Hammell and his wife, Lord and Lady Darroch, the Cochranes, the—"

"The Cochranes?" Iain said, setting his wrists on the edge of the table.

Lord Lismore glanced up at him, his brows rising in a question. "Certainly, the Cochranes."

"It is only that"—Iain glanced at me—"nevermind."

I looked between him and the earl, trying to understand why he might take exception to the Cochranes. Or perhaps they were likely to take exception to *me*. Did they dislike merchants? Augusta had warned me many would look down upon us for the origins of our money and for our lack of the sort of pedigree which made Lord Lismore's family so impressive. She herself had been accepted in Society despite being illegitimate, but that acceptance had not been universal, by any means, and it had ended the moment her father had discontinued his open support of her.

"Who else?" Iain asked. "I understand Orton is in town."

"He is," the earl said, "and he shall receive an invitation, though I anticipate it will be declined. He has far more alluring options than Lochlarren can offer."

The earl rattled off a dozen more unfamiliar names,

bringing back my anxiety at the prospect of being on display to so many strangers. There was to be dinner as well as a bit of dancing, and I prayed I would be equal to the task—that I would present the appearance of a woman worthy to become a countess.

When Augusta and I retired to the drawing room, she prattled on about the merits of my different evening gowns, what sort of coiffure I should wear, whether Dolly would be equal to the task, and the proper etiquette for the evening. Her eyes were still red and glassy, while her nose was pink from having been blown so frequently.

"Shall you feel well enough to attend?" I asked.

"I insist upon feeling well enough," she said with a smile. It was wiped from her face by an enormous sneeze.

"Perhaps you should practice a few songs on the pianoforte, my dear," she said. "It is possible you will be called upon to display your accomplishments to those in attendance tomorrow."

I had not even considered such a likelihood, but she was right. This was an opportunity for everyone to judge how fit a bride I was for the Earl of Lismore. I dearly wanted to come away from it with approval. I hoped the years of practice on the instrument would be sufficient.

I sucked in a deep breath and obeyed, moving to the piano's bench.

When the men joined us fifteen minutes later, I was surprised to find the earl making his way toward me. I pulled my hands from the ivories.

"Forgive me for interrupting," he said.

"Not at all." I turned my knees away from the instrument and closed the lid. "An interruption is precisely what I have been hoping for."

He smiled and flipped out his coattails to sit on the arm of the sofa behind him. "I cannot claim to know you well, Miss Godfrey, so I pray you will forgive any impertinence, for it is unintended."

My muscles tightened, but I nodded with what I hoped was a smile. Was he coming to tell me I had better not play at the pianoforte tomorrow? That I had committed some solecism he wished to warn me against repeating in less forgiving company?

He cleared his throat and met my eyes. "As we spoke of the party, I couldn't help but note you seemed a bit . . . anxious." His dark brow furrowed. "If you dislike the idea of an engagement party, Miss Godfrey, we need not hold one. It is meant to honor, not discomfit, you."

I was momentarily speechless. I had prided myself on masking my anxieties on the subject. Apparently, I had not done so well as I had hoped. "That is very kind of you, my lord. I do not dislike the idea of the party; I am merely anxious to be a credit to your family and mine. Hence your observation of my nerves, which I hope to mask more successfully at the party." I smiled ruefully.

"I have no doubt at all you shall get on very well—though I would advise you not to compliment anyone on the quaintness of their home or title."

I looked down, laughing softly. "I shall endeavor to remember that. Thank you, my lord."

"Sandy," he said. "You may call me Sandy."

My heart fluttered strangely, but I nodded with a small smile. "I suppose that is reasonable given how soon we shall be married." Why did I have the impulse to turn away after saying such a thing? I had never been one for coyness or missish sensibility, and three days before becoming a countess was not the time to become such.

"May I presume to call you Juliana, as well?"

"Of course."

"I shall leave you to your playing then, Juliana." He rose, bowed, and made his way to his brothers.

I sat for a moment, my gaze fixed on the Duncan men, my heart feeling stranger than ever. They were only our Christian names. Surely, we would eventually begin addressing each other with them.

Why, then, did I feel I was going against Augusta's advice of becoming too familiar with my intended?

CHAPTER TWENTY

SANDY

It was a fine day, the sun shining on the loch making its blues all the richer. The window was open, letting a gentle breeze into the study. Looking outside, I felt an unusual restlessness. I had been outside more in this past week than in the few weeks before combined, and I found myself increasingly impatient of my duties. Or perhaps my restlessness was rooted in approaching . . . events.

"Are those terms still satisfactory to you, my lord?"

I turned toward Mr. Godfrey, who was seated in the chair opposite mine at my desk. Sitting in my usual seat was my solicitor, Mr. Rutherford, come for this express purpose. He had a quill in hand, scratching over the paper and, at times, replenishing the ink from the ornate but rusted well before him.

We had been discussing debts and marriage contracts and the like for over an hour, and my mind was losing its focus, particularly now that the weight of debt was beginning to lift. We still had a great deal to see to, however, so I moved away from the window and back to the desk.

"Yes," I replied. "The terms are very generous, sir." Too generous, in some ways. The man was willing to pay a veritable fortune to see his daughter established as Lady Lismore. He could have easily cared for her himself from his large purse, but apparently my title was of that great a value to him.

The door opened again, and Blair's face appeared, retreating slightly at the sight of Mr. Godfrey and Mr. Rutherford with me.

"What is it?" I asked.

"We wished to invite you to come fishing, but I see that you are occupied."

"Fishing?" I repeated.

He nodded, his growing smile telling me he realized how out of the ordinary it was. "Thought you might wish to see whether you can catch more fish than Juliana."

I raised my brows. Apparently, I was not the only one she had given permission to use her Christian name.

"Juliana goes as well?" Mr. Godfrey asked.

"Yes, sir. If that is all well and good with you."

He let out a laugh. "More than well and good. I am happy to know she will be out and about enjoying herself. You should join her, my lord."

"Oh," I said. My gaze traveled to the open window and the abundance of fresh air beyond. Fishing was a far preferable activity to discussing marriage contracts. But with the marriage just two days away, these things could not be put off much longer. Such was my life now. "I had better not. We should finish matters here first, I think."

Mr. Godfrey inclined his head. "As you please."

Blair nodded and closed the door behind him.

"Where were we?" I asked.

My solicitor adjusted his spectacles. "Juliana's pin money, my lord."

"Right," I said.

The solicitor read from the document he had drawn up, according to the correspondence between Mr. Godfrey and me, while I paced the room.

"Do you feel that amount is adequate, Mr. Godfrey?" I asked when the solicitor had finished. "I wish for her to feel amply provided for. Of course, she may speak with me if she has need of more at any point, but I am certain she would rather not be obliged to do so. I confess myself entirely ignorant of what a woman might require over the course of a quarter."

"Juliana is quite independent, my lord," Mr. Godfrey replied. "Perhaps I have given her too free a rein, but she is so capable and, I have preferred to let her manage her own affairs rather than forcing her to apply to me constantly for money. I would not describe her as particularly frugal—indeed, she has not needed to be—but neither is she wasteful. A small increase in the amount would not do any harm, I think."

I nodded and met my solicitor's gaze. "A twenty percent increase, let us say."

"Very good, sir." His quill scratched across the paper, and finding myself at the window again, I rested my arm on the stone sill and looked out over the grounds and loch.

Iain and Blair were pulling two boats from its banks. They were rarely used and, as most things at Lochlarren, in a state of disrepair. Juliana stood at the edge of the loch, her head covered with a straw bonnet and the fishing poles in her hand.

Calf-deep in water, Iain beckoned to Juliana to step into the boat he steadied.

"Fool," I said softly, for he hadn't even offered her his hand.

"What was that, my lord?" Mr. Godfrey asked.

I looked at him and shook my head. "Nothing. Forgive me. What is next?" I glanced again toward Iain, who was taking the fishing poles from Juliana. That was something, at least. She lifted her skirts as the boat wobbled precariously.

Mr. Godfrey came up beside me, following my gaze. He frowned a moment, though a little smile played at the corner of his mouth.

"If it is not too much to ask, my lord," he said, "perhaps you wouldn't be opposed to joining this . . . adventure. I find I am more tired from my journey than I had anticipated and could do with a small rest." He yawned, covering his mouth with a hand.

"Of course." I wasn't certain whether he was truly tired or merely wanted me to watch over his daughter, but frankly, I cared little. It was foolhardy to trust Iain and Blair with Juliana's safety. "Perhaps we can reconvene later? If you are agreeable, that is, Rutherford?"

The solicitor nodded, holding up the paper and inspecting it. "I have plenty of work to do in the meantime if your lordship would grant me the use of the study."

I nodded curtly, distracted by the spectacle of Blair joining in to help stabilize the rocking boat enough for Juliana to step in.

Mr. Godfrey put a hand on my shoulder. "Better not to wait for the inevitable."

I hurried toward the door and down the staircase, hoping I would not arrive at the banks of the loch to find Juliana covered in mud.

Fortune favored me, for the three of them seemed to be reevaluating the situation when I arrived.

"Sandy," Blair said in surprise. "Come to catch a fish or two?"

"Come to set Juliana's father at ease, rather," I replied grimly. "Have you two never been around a woman before?" I strode to the boat and tugged it back from the water so that half of it rested on the dirt and mud. "Hold it steady, Iain."

I offered Juliana my arm, and she took it with a soft, "Thank you," and a hint of amusement lurking in her eyes. She stepped into the boat as I braced her upper arm until she had taken her seat on one of the wide wooden slats.

I put out my hand to Iain.

"I don't need your help," he said, looking at my hand with contempt.

"Give me the poles," I said.

"You are coming?"

I nodded, and after a moment, he gave me one of the three poles he held. I set it in the boat, then hefted the vessel forward until it was just beginning to float. "Steady it," I instructed him again.

Iain scoffed, but Blair obliged me, holding the boat in place as I climbed in with as much grace as I could muster.

"And who shall do that for *us*?" Iain called out as Juliana and I drifted farther from shore.

"You shall find a way," I said.

Juliana watched them with interest over my shoulder, wincing at one point.

When I looked back, Iain was standing in the boat, which listed from side to side, thanks to Blair's purposeful rocking of it. I chuckled and turned back around, shaking my head.

"They were doing their best, you know," Juliana said.

"That is what troubles me most," I said wryly, pulling the oars from the bottom of the boat and taking care not to bump her in the process.

She smiled as I slipped an oar through its ring on the side of the boat. She took the second oar and did the same on the other side.

"Shall I row for a bit?" she asked.

"If I were Iain or Blair, no doubt you would be the one rowing this entire time." I grasped the oar she held. "But I am not, and there is no need for you to row at all."

She considered me for a moment as though trying to decide whether to speak or not.

"What is it?" I asked.

"You forget, I think, that I was not born into a life of luxury, my lord."

"Sandy," I corrected. Her insistence on referring to me by my title bothered me for reasons I had not yet discerned. "Having a man row the boat you are in should not be considered a luxury, Juliana. It is the merest good manners, which my brothers evidently lack."

"I find their personalities refreshing," she said, her gaze flitting to them again for a moment.

I stole a glance at her. What did she think of *me*? I wasn't sure I wanted to know. If she had taken so easily to Iain and Blair, she likely found me dry and boring.

She gazed all around us at the water, the sky, and the forest, blinking in the sun. "I have never seen such blues."

I looked across the water, which was indeed a deeper, more vibrant blue than I had seen anywhere in England. "Enjoy it while you can. Once those clouds cover the sun, everything will become duller."

She took in a deep breath, closing her eyes and tipping up her face so that the sun fell upon it. My gaze rested upon her, noting the curve of her jaw, cheeks, and nose, and the darkness of her lashes against her fair skin.

I cleared my throat and looked around. "Shall we cast a line?"

"Yes. Though, I haven't the first notion how to do so. I assume you know what you are about?"

I tilted my head from side to side. "To an extent, yes."

"Are there truly fish in the loch? I thought Iain and Blair might have been teasing."

"There are, though I couldn't say how many. I believe it was overfished some years ago. We have done little since, however, so perhaps there has been time for replenishment."

Resting the oars in their places, I shifted forward on my seat and took the fishing pole from the floorboards to show her how the mechanism worked—the rod, the line, the reel, the hook, and the bait.

But it was casting the line that required the greatest instruction. I demonstrated the motion a few times, then gave the rod back to her.

"And all this I must do while standing in an unsteady boat?"

I chuckled. "Once you become more practiced, you can cast from a seated position."

"I think it more likely I shall fall overboard and the fish catch *me*." She made an attempt to imitate my demonstration. Apparently pleased with the motion, she looked at me for approval. "Not so terribly bad, was it?"

"Very impressive," I replied with a twitch at the corner of my mouth. "Even without casting the line."

She looked at the end of the rod and followed the line to where it had caught on the edge of the boat behind her. She sent me a sheepish glance and bent to unhook it. "How very mortifying this is."

"Shall I catch the hook on my waistcoat to make you feel better? It would not be the first time I had done it."

"It is such a fine waistcoat," she said. "It would be a shame to ruin it when it complements your eyes so perfectly."

I was momentarily bereft of speech.

She seemed to realize she had said something unexpected,

for she colored up and turned her focus to the fishing rod. "I shall try not to catch it on anything this time. Your waistcoat least of all."

Watching the bait on the end of the line with a wary eye, she pulled back on the rod until the top was at an angle behind her, then she whipped it forward. Her right hand was too near the reel, though, preventing the line from releasing. The bait and hook spun about madly in the air.

Both of us retreated from it, and I reached a hand to still the rod.

"You must show her the way of it, Sandy," Iain called. He and Blair were two dozen yards away, both of their lines cast into the loch, the ends lost in the blue depths.

I shot him a look, though at such a distance, I doubted he could see my annoyance.

"It is not enough to see it," Blair said. "She must be shown properly." He shuffled over to Iain, coming up behind him and wrapping his arms around him to grasp Iain's hands on the rod.

Taking exception to the demonstration, Iain shouldered Blair out of the way. Blair stumbled back and fell over one of the seats. For a moment, the boat pitched dramatically from side to side, and we watched to see their fate. But the rocking eased, and their clothes remained dry.

"It would have served them right if they had fallen overboard," I said.

"Do you find their teasing annoying?"

"Do not you?"

Juliana shook her head, watching them with a wistful smile. "I never had any siblings to enjoy such joviality with. I quite envy you."

I frowned as she fiddled with the reel. I hadn't ever really considered what it might be like to be the only child in a family. My childhood had been full of pranks and laughter and fighting. I couldn't imagine it otherwise.

She did a few practice casts, and I could see where the issue lay.

"*Would* you like me to show you?" I asked, feeling unaccountably nervous all of a sudden.

Her gaze darted to mine, and her mouth broke into a smile. "The mere fact that you are offering tells me I should accept. *Would* you show me?"

I nodded, my mouth going dry. I stepped carefully over the seat separating us as she shifted her feet forward slowly so as not to upset the equilibrium. In order to maintain it, I was obliged to step behind her rather than beside her as reason told me to do. There was only so much room between the two rows of seats, which made for little buffer between us.

"You want to bring the line back slowly," I said, wondering what I would see of her face if her bonnet had not been in the way. "Otherwise, the hook might catch on something again or the bait fall off." Using a gentle finger, I guided the rod back until the line hung well behind her. She leaned toward it, and I set a hand on her back to help preserve her balance, for hers and mine were inextricably connected.

"Now," I continued, ignoring the way my heart pounded at our proximity, "when you whip it forward, you must ensure the arc of the rod is long, or else—"

"Your waistcoat shall be ruined."

I laughed softly. "Not my primary concern, but yes. It is a possibility. Hold it just so." I adjusted her hands slightly to widen the distance between them, letting my hands rest on her gloved ones.

"That's more like it!" Blair called over.

"Ignore them," I said, wishing Juliana's bonnet away. Only because it was obstructing my view of the loch. "We shall cast on three. One, two, *three.*"

The rod and line went sailing forward until the bait plopped in the water and sank down.

"Very good." Despite an inclination to linger, I stepped carefully away before Iain or Blair could accuse me of ulterior motives.

"And now?" Juliana asked.

"And now you let the line out while we wait." I took a seat, and she followed suit, unwinding the reel to release more line as we drifted with the strengthening breeze. The clouds began to mask the sun, making the landscape uneven—bright and colorful on one side of the loch, more subdued and dull on the other. Far in the distance, the clouds took on a deeper gray, portending rain.

Iain and Blair had rowed in the direction of Lochlarren, keeping their distance—a choice I was grateful for. The last thing I needed was for them to be putting ideas in my head or Juliana's. It seemed to be a skill of theirs.

"I have let out the line too far, haven't I?" she said.

We were quickly drifting away from her cast, the growing breeze pushing us toward the west edge of the loch.

I shrugged, though she most certainly *had* let out too much. "Not necessarily. Who is to say all the fish aren't over at that end?"

She laughed. "You may simply tell me I am a bad hand at this, Sandy. I trust fishing is not one of the accomplishments expected of the Countess of Lismore?"

My name on her lips caught my breath for a moment, but I chuckled. "No, indeed."

"What a relief," she said as she reeled in the line. "Perhaps I shall let you have a turn at this—if you dare, that is, after my awe-inspiring attempt." Once the bait dangled above the water, she handed the rod to me.

I cast the line with what I hoped was a great deal of deftness. Juliana clapped as the hook hit the water.

"Bravo," she said. "You make it look like child's play."

"Perhaps because it *was* child's play for us here."

Blair and Iain rowed toward us again, and I stifled a sigh.

"Caught anything?" Blair called over through cupped hands.

We shook our heads.

"Not a fish for miles," he yelled back. "We are going back in now. Iain insists he is starving."

"Typical," I said with a wave. "They have become bored already."

"But not you?"

I glanced at her as I tweaked the reel slightly. "No. And you?"

"Not at all. I have no qualms making a fool of myself."

"We all feel foolish when we begin something new. With enough practice, you would become an accomplished fisherwoman."

"If anyone is to ask, then, let us simply say that it is not my capabilities which are in question but merely a lack of opportunity to refine them."

"Or . . . you could try again." Would she need my assistance? Part of me hoped so.

The reluctant smile she wore was charming. "Very well, then. One more cast."

I reeled in the line, not even caring that we were not leaving it cast long enough to catch anything. I glanced to the shore, which Iain and Blair had just reached. They climbed out of the boat and turned to wave at us before making their way inside.

Juliana stood carefully, and I handed her the rod, waiting for a look or any indication she wished for my help again. But she drew the pole back slowly, her eyes watching the hook.

"A long arc," she said to herself.

I nodded, my eyes fixed on her as she bit her lip in concentration.

She thrust the rod forward, releasing the line. I watched in vain for the bait to plop into the water.

"Oh dear," she said, her eyes searching the surface of the loch. "What have I done wrong this time?"

Frowning, I traced the line with my gaze, but it was too difficult to follow. Rising to my feet, I let the line slip through my fingers, tugging the slack toward me until it became clear where the hook had ended: in the straw of her bonnet.

I smiled slightly. "It is not my waistcoat but your bonnet which has succumbed to the dreaded hook."

She turned, as though she might be able to see where it landed.

"Careful," I said, adopting a wider stance and holding her arm as the boat rocked from her movements. "Allow me." I took the pole from her hands.

She reached a hand to her bonnet to steady it. "Forgive me."

"Gently now. The hook is quite sharp. Will you permit me to extract it?"

She nodded, and I tweaked it slowly from side to side until the straw released it.

"There," I said. "I think the bonnet can be salvaged."

"Thank heaven," she said with a laugh as she turned toward her seat. She lifted a foot to step over it.

"Careful. You are becoming tangled in the line."

But it was too late. She pitched forward, and I grabbed her about the waist. The boat swayed wildly, and I lost my balance, releasing her as I fell into the water.

CHAPTER TWENTY-ONE

JULIANA

Sandy's hands released me as he tipped to the side and over the edge of the boat. With the line wrapped about my legs, I had nothing to counter the sudden shifts in weight, and I tumbled in after him with a splash.

Bone-chilling cold enveloped me from head to toe. I kicked my feet against my heavy skirts, swimming for the surface. I broke through, gasping for air and wiping the water from my eyes. My bonnet pulled on my hair and obstructed my view, and I pulled it off unceremoniously, looking around. My gaze found Sandy, his head bobbing above the water, his breath coming in gasps.

A few feet from us, the boat floated placidly along the silvery water. The oars and fishing pole were strewn about on the water's surface.

Thanking the heavens I had learned to swim as a grubby child, I kicked my legs to keep myself afloat in the frigid water, pushing down on my skirts, which insisted on rising to the top.

"Are you hurt?" Sandy asked, swimming toward me.

I shook my head, clamping my teeth shut to keep them from shattering as I kicked my feet to stay afloat. "Are you?"

"No," he replied. "Merely drowning from the weight of this blasted coat. Let us get you back in the boat."

"We should collect the oars first." I swam toward the nearest one and pulled back to the boat. Lifting it inside, I grasped the boat's edge to permit myself a respite from treading water. Sandy followed shortly after, both the oar and the fishing pole in hand.

"The bucket of bait is at the bottom of the loch by now," he said, hefting the pole and oar over. "I wish joy of it to whatever fish supposedly inhabit this place. Come, I shall assist you back in."

I had never attempted to climb into a boat from the water, and the exercise proved . . . difficult. Even without my water-saturated skirts pulling me down, it was nearly impossible to hoist myself in without letting a deluge of water into the boat. Sandy attempted to lift me in twice, but with nowhere to put his feet, the result was him nearly drowning each time.

"Perhaps we should swim back to shore and leave the boat," I said through chattering teeth. The thought of forcing my limbs to carry me anywhere wasn't enticing, however, when all they wanted to do was nestle tightly into my body to preserve whatever heat might be left in this cold and dreary world.

Sandy looked back toward the shore, his lips pressing together. "I judge it to be about fifty yards. It will feel more like fifty miles in this water, though." He met my gaze, his eyes asking whether I was equal to the task.

A countess would undoubtedly have demanded something be done, though what, I hadn't any notion, for I was not a countess. Not yet, at least, and I was anxious to show Sandy I was capable of more than shrieking and having a fit of the vapors. I doubted I would have been able to shriek even if I had wanted to, for my lungs seemed to have shrunk to a fraction of their normal capacity.

"Whoever reaches shore first wins the bet?" I said with a smile full of chattering teeth.

The concern melted from his brow, and he searched my face for a moment, then nodded. Was I mistaken, or was that a hint of admiration in his eyes?

He swam so that he was even with me, and, treading water and breathing in uneven huffs, we met one another's gaze. Suddenly, he nodded, and both of us dove forward, keeping our heads above water as we swam toward the shore.

Fifty yards had not seemed so far a distance when he had said it, while fifty miles had seemed a gross exaggeration. But I had underestimated the weight of my skirts combined with the difficulty of breathing in icy water.

Sandy quickly pulled ahead, and I fought to meet his pace.

"Once again," I heaved out between breaths, "you are at an advantage due to your lack of skirts."

"If you were wearing this coat," he said over his shoulder, "you would think differently. I can barely move my arms."

"The price of vanity!" I retorted.

He laughed. "Whereas your dress is the picture of frugality?"

"You would prefer your countess wear rags, no doubt?" The delivery of my comment was somewhat ruined by the chattering of my teeth and my uneven breathing. After so many short, shallow gasps, I craved a normal breath, and I sucked in as large a one as I could manage.

Water filled my mouth and throat, and I started coughing uncontrollably, something made more difficult by the fact that I was obliged to tread water while doing so. I sputtered and floundered, trying to clear my lungs of the glacial water I had inhaled.

Sandy was at my side in a moment, his arm around me as he ensured I could hold my head above the surface, his legs and free arm beating the water to keep us both afloat.

It was enough, and my coughing subsided sufficiently for me to take stock of my situation: Sandy's arm around my waist, his face, full of concern, so close that I might bump into it if I was not measured in my attempts to stay afloat.

We bobbed up and down together, our bodies pressed against each other, and all my effort to clear my lungs was for naught. Again, I found myself without enough air to sustain me, though for different reasons this time.

"I suppose that is my reward for taunting you," I said with effort.

His concern transformed into a smile that sapped the last of the air in my lungs. "I see you are fully recovered." And yet he held me still, his eyes fixed on mine while my gaze traced the trail of a drop of water from his dark, wet hair, down his temple and then cheek.

And still he held me. Why? Was he concerned I would swallow another breath of water if he let go? Or was there another reason?

He glanced toward the shore, which was much nearer than when we had at first begun. "I shall swim with you."

"What, and deprive me of my prize?" I said in as rallying a tone as I could manage in my present state. I could only imagine how I must appear, my hair wet and disordered, my face red from coughing.

He laughed and shook his head. "Very well, then. Let us finish what we started." He released me, and the full weight of my clothing and body nearly took my mouth back under. Instantly, he had his arm about me again.

How was I to tell him that his efforts to help me were beginning to be counterproductive, making it more rather than less difficult to breathe? I did not wish to be this helpless creature I appeared to him to be.

Thrusting his arm from around me, I used his body to propel me forward, looking over my shoulder with a mischievous smile.

The splashing that followed told me he was scrambling after me.

In a matter of seconds, he began to pull past me. We were nearing the shore, but I knew only drastic measures would get me there first. I reached over to the dim outline of his tailcoat floating behind him. Grasping the hem, I pulled back hard, using it to push myself forward.

His indignant laughter stretched my lips in a smile just as my knees and feet grazed the bottom of the loch. Letting my hands drop below the water, I crawled forward, then picked up my skirts and pushed myself to my feet, with Sandy just behind me.

I raised my arms in victory, though I had no breath to utter the victorious cry I had hoped for. Once he had pushed himself to his feet, Sandy bowed over, resting his hands on his knees to catch his breath.

"Never did I take you for a cheat, Juliana Godfrey," he said between breaths and airy laughter.

"Cheating?" I protested, my cheeks hurting from smiling. The cold might freeze my face into this expression if it lasted much longer. "I merely used the means available."

He laughed, rising to a full stand and looking toward the castle, attempting to peel the coat from his arms. "Humiliation awaits me, Juliana. I am loath to admit to your father—and to Iain and Blair—that you went overboard under my care."

"They needn't know," I said, my body beginning to tremble

and shake. While the day was fairly warm, the breeze against my wet clothing felt like an arctic wind. I had no wish for Augusta to know of this latest escapade, either. She had been in her bedchamber all day, laid low with more coughing and sneezing and misery. "We might go through the servant entrance and warm up there. Dolly would help us."

Sandy's eyes lit with amusement while his teeth chattered audibly. He pulled his arm out of the sleeve of his coat, then peeled the other one out. His white shirt clung to his arms and body in a way that drew my eyes. "The servant entrance it is. You need a fire and dry clothing as soon as can be managed."

With quick, shaking steps, we made our way to the servant door. My skirts had transformed from pristine white to murky brown, but I cared little.

Dolly was in the corridor with an armful of pressed clothing when we entered. She stopped short, staring in confusion.

"A fire in Mrs. Boyle's parlor, Dolly," Sandy said. "As soon as you can manage it."

"Of course, my lord." She dipped a quick curtsy, then turned back the way she had come.

"Mrs. Boyle's parlor is the closest," Sandy explained. "Best get you warmed up as soon as we can."

We followed her toward the housekeeper's quarters, where she had put down her burden and was already kneeling in front of the fire in the small sitting area. Sandy led me to the sofa, pulling the nearest blanket and setting it on the cushion for me to sit on.

As soon as the fire was lit, Dolly rushed to the corner, where another blanket was folded in a basket. She brought it, draping it over us. "I shall have Cook warm last night's soup."

"Thank you, Dolly," I said, trying to control my shivering and pay no heed to how near Sandy and I were. "If you could have fresh clothes brought down for both of us, it would be much appreciated."

"Preferably bringing as little attention to our predicament as possible," Sandy added, stretching his hands out and rubbing them in the growing warmth of the fire.

"Of course, my lord," she replied, curtsying again, then hurrying from the room.

The fire crackled and grew, and Sandy reached to place an extra log on the fire from the ones Dolly had put on the hearth. His dripping tailcoat hung over a chair by the hearth, while his waterlogged shirtsleeves clung to his arms and chest for dear life.

I looked away, but the room felt suddenly small and intimate. We had been alone on the loch, of course, but then, we had been surrounded by miles of open water and land, in full view of anyone in the castle wishing to watch.

I pulled the blanket toward my chin. If *his* clothing was nearly transparent, mine was too.

"Are you warm enough?" he asked. "I can move the sofa closer if you would like."

"This room is a veritable oven compared to the loch."

He chuckled. "Indeed." His gaze traveled over my face. "I am impressed with your swimming, even if your methods of winning were questionable."

"I would rather say resourceful," I said with a smile.

"Was your fit of coughing genuine or calculated to allow you to pull ahead?"

I laughed, shaking my head. "It was mere clumsiness on my part. Then, I simply took advantage of the circumstances."

"And the tails of my coat."

Dolly entered with clothing draped over one arm and a brush in the other. I ran a hand through my disheveled hair, realizing how bedraggled I must look. Following just behind

Dolly was Sandy's valet, clothing hanging over his arm in a similar manner.

His gaze took in his master, then me.

My cheeks warmed again, while Dolly smiled. "Cook says the soup will be ready by the time I've helped ye inta yer clothin'."

I nodded, and a silence fell as I waited for Sandy to leave us in privacy.

Dolly finally spoke. "Gillies thought yer lordship could change in Kemp's quarters while I . . . assist Miss Godfrey in here."

Gillies cleared his throat meaningfully, and Sandy shot up from his seat. "Of course." He turned to me briefly. "I shall return presently for that soup." Wiping his hands down his wet pantaloons, he led his valet from the room, leaving me to avoid the small smile Dolly was wearing.

CHAPTER TWENTY-TWO

SANDY

I strode quickly toward the butler's quarters, eager to avoid Gillies's penetrating gaze. I hadn't meant to linger next to Juliana once Dolly and Gillies had come, but my mind had been elsewhere. On the small drop of water trailing down her neck, specifically.

The way Gillies looked at me the moment I turned to face him told me that nothing had escaped him.

"Enough of that, Gillies," I said, unbuttoning my waistcoat.

"I said nothin', my lord."

"Your face said it for you." I shrugged out of the wet garment and handed it to him with a grim look.

"I might've said the same thing of you, my lord." There was the veriest quiver at one edge of his mouth, immediately controlled.

"And what does my face say to you now?" I glared at him.

He paused in the act of slipping my waistcoat onto a hanger to take stock of my expression. "That ye resent me for interruptin' ye, my lord."

"You are incorrigible, Gillies."

My pretended irritation with him aside, the clothes he had brought for me—dry as summer dust—were a gift from heaven.

"That blasted cold water has penetrated to the marrow of my bones," I complained.

"Sittin' by the fire with a cup of soup and Miss Godfrey's warmth ought ta see ta that, my lord," Gillies said without even looking at me.

"And ten lashes ought to see to your unruly tongue," I said without venom as I straightened my cravat. Yanking my tailcoat from his hands, I strode from the room, sending him a quick, amused glance before disappearing through the door.

Juliana was not in the parlor when I arrived, and I stopped on the threshold, wondering if she had thought better of eating the soup here. Perhaps she had noticed my thoughts wandering to forbidden paths and decided to take her food in her room. Watching the progress of a droplet of water down her neck was not part of the marriage contracts I had been discussing with Rutherford and Mr. Godfrey. Had I put her off?

A wave of disappointment washed through me just as the door to Mrs. Boyle's bedchamber opened and Juliana stepped out. Her hair had been brushed out and given free rein, spilling over her shoulders and back in damp, brown waves.

"Forgive my state," she said, tucking her hair behind her ear. "If I have any hope of looking decent at dinner, I must allow my hair to dry first."

I swallowed and nodded. "You needn't apologize on my account." Was Dolly smiling at me? She was no better than Gillies or Iain.

"I'll fetch the soup," she said, leaving us alone again with another brief glance at me. I kept my eyes on the doorway for a moment after she had left.

"Feeling warmer?" I put out a hand to Juliana, inviting her to take her prior seat.

She shot me a smile of gratitude as she sat. "I doubt I shall ever be truly warm again."

"Nor I. We shall spend the rest of our days in front of this fire, trying to regain sensation in our fingers and toes."

She stretched out her fingers toward the warmth, then glanced up at me for the briefest of moments. "There are worse fates."

"Warm soup," Dolly said, entering with a tray in hand. She brought it over and rested it upon our laps so that it spanned between us. "I'm afraid the other trays are bein' washed at the moment, so there's just the one. Ye dinna mind, do ye, my lordship?"

I fixed my eyes upon Dolly, but she seemed disinclined to return the favor. "Not at all."

"Is there anythin' else I can get for ye?" she asked as she stoked the fire.

I looked at Juliana, who shook her head.

"That will be all," I said.

Dolly curtsied and left the room, closing the door three-quarters of the way rather than leaving it open as it had been. So that was the way of things, was it? She was attempting to play the matchmaker between her mistress and me. Ironic, that. That the match was already made. Or very near to it.

Juliana seemed not to have noticed Dolly's designs upon us, though, for she was stirring the soup. She filled the spoon and, leaning over the bowl, brought it to her mouth. Her eyes closed as she swallowed.

"Good?" I asked.

Her eyes remained closed, her bow-shaped lashes pressed to the top of her cheeks. "I can feel it warming me as it goes down."

I took a bite for myself and closed my eyes, experiencing the sensation she described, a trail of heat making its way through my mouth, down my throat, and into my stomach. "Perhaps we shan't need to remain here forever, after all."

"That is fortunate, for I imagine you would be missed at tomorrow's party." She cupped the bowl with both hands, warming herself.

"Not nearly as much as *you* would be missed," I countered. "You are the reason people have accepted the invitations, you know." Immediately, I regretted my comment, for she offered a valiant but wry smile.

"Almost you convince me to jump back into the loch." Leaning forward, she took another sip from her spoon. A lock of hair slipped over her shoulder, and I put out a hand to stop it from falling into the soup.

She glanced at me, and I brushed it back over her shoulder until my fingers had trailed through the soft, damp tresses, ensuring it was securely in place.

She tucked her hair behind her ear. "Thank you. I am not accustomed to eating with my hair uncoiffed. Now I can see why Augusta is always so insistent upon it. It is a hazard."

"A beautiful hazard."

Her eyes flicked to me, and I cleared my throat. What was I saying? And why, for that matter, was I saying it? "And what shall your cousin say of your bonnet when she sees it floating on the loch?"

She laughed. "I hope she shan't notice it—and that you shan't tell her."

"And if I do? I assume she is the one you wished to avoid by coming through the servant entrance."

"She is. And if you tell her, I shan't hesitate to tell her and your brothers you fell over the edge of the boat and pulled me down with you."

I threw my head back in a laugh. "Because *you* let out the line too far and tangled yourself in it."

"An insignificant detail."

"Not to me," I teased. "Where *is* your cousin? I have not seen her today, and she is generally not far from you."

She set her spoon against the side of the bowl, her brow furrowing. "She is ill again. Something here seems not to agree with her. She hasn't the strongest constitution to begin with, either."

"Shall I not call the doctor to see to her? I know she has expressed she does not wish for it, but I could insist. I can be a brute when needed."

"I am well aware of that," she said with an arch look. "But I think a call for the doctor would be wise."

"Consider it done."

She smiled at me gratefully.

"Have you always been very close?" I asked. I could not gauge how she felt about her chaperone. Was she a welcome presence in Juliana's life? It usually seemed so, but once or twice, I had wondered if she was eager to shake off that bit of propriety once we married.

"No," she replied. "I quite resented her when I was young, for I saw her as taking away my freedom. But it was only a matter of time until her care and kindness pierced me. She has been the closest thing I've had to a mother. She knows how dearly Papa and I have wished for a match like this, and she does not want me to jeopardize it by my propensity for making rash decisions or my lack of knowledge of the *haut ton*."

I smiled wryly. "You could easily be describing my father."

"The propensity for making rash decisions? Or a lack of knowledge of the *haut ton*?"

"Neither," I said, as amused as she was. "Just as Augusta is to you, my father was the figure in my life afraid I would make a muddle of things. He arranged our marriage out of a fear I should marry a poor aristocrat's daughter and put the nail in the coffin of Lochlarren." I stirred my soup with a frown. "Little did I realize then how he had been jeopardizing the estate himself."

"And now you are charged with bringing it back to its former glory?"

I swallowed a mouthful of soup and shook my head. "I doubt even the entirety of your father's fortune could manage such a thing."

"Then you underestimate his fortune," she said with a teasing smile.

"Or perhaps *you* overestimate the state of Lochlarren."

"What a frightening notion," she said with a laugh.

"Were you terribly disappointed when you arrived?"

She took another sip of soup, then laid down her spoon as though she was finished. "I did not *know* what to expect. Augusta had warned me that my training at her hands might not have prepared me for how things would be in Scotland."

I was right, then. "So, I have her to thank for your . . . interesting attitude upon arrival."

"To an extent, yes. Though, some of the blame lies with you, of course." She met my gaze, her expression provoking.

"Oh it does, does it?"

"Decidedly so. I expected to be greeted by you and your servants, only to a find the audience for my arrival comprising naught but the wind and a hungry squirrel."

"Well," I said as I took the tray and set it on the floor beside me. "I hope the squirrel made his bow."

"He did not. He gave me the cut direct—looked at me for a moment then scampered away."

I covered my amusement with a hand. "If I had received your father's communication warning of your delay and had known you would be arriving at that particular moment, Juliana, I can assure you, we would have welcomed you properly." I hesitated. "Have you been unhappy here?"

"Yes," she said, staring at the fire.

My heart dropped. I shouldn't have been surprised. She had come to a foreign place inhabited entirely by strangers, and I and my household had done our level best to make her feel even more out of place. It had seemed justified then, but now it merely seemed cruel.

"I have been." She turned and met my eyes. "But I am not so now."

I held her gaze, wishing I knew just what she meant by that. Did she mean she was happy now? Or simply not *un*happy? And what was it about this particular moment that was different?

"Have *you* been unhappy having me here?" she asked.

I took a moment to reflect. "I have." I shot her a little smile. "I think we both put our best efforts toward making one another unhappy, did we not?"

She grimaced guiltily.

"But I am not so now." I searched her face, feeling the truth of the words. I might have taken an unexpected swim in the frigid loch after a failed attempt at fishing. I might be sitting in my housekeeper's parlor wrapped in a blanket with the woman who had caused the unplanned dip in the loch.

But all of it had been strangely enjoyable.

What did it mean that I had taken pleasure in the moments with Juliana for the past few days? And what *else* might I enjoy with her?

The hair I had brushed back minutes ago had made its way back to her shoulder. I used my finger to push it to its place, my fingers grazing her shoulder and back again.

Her eyes were fixed on me, a questioning look in them.

Was it the same question I had? My eyes dropped to her lips while my hand lingered on her back.

"Juliana!"

Our heads whipped around to find Miss Lowe staring at us from the doorway.

CHAPTER TWENTY-THREE

JULIANA

Augusta said my name the same way she had when she had found me rifling through Papa's coin purse when I was a child, three shillings already in my fist.

I felt the same shame creep into my cheeks now, only I had done nothing wrong. I had merely eaten soup with the man I was to marry in two days. If she thought she saw the precursor to a kiss, she was entirely wrong.

Well, perhaps not entirely. The thought had flitted across my mind, yes, but only for as long as a bird lights on an unsteady branch. Kissing Sandy would have been imprudent even if he *had* wished for such a thing, which I was uncertain he had. I might have misinterpreted the look in his eyes. His glance down at my lips was undoubtedly because I had a bit of soup lingering at the edge of my mouth. Soup was always a hazard.

Or perhaps I had misread the motivation behind his focus. It made me ever more nervous for when our life would begin together. Naturally, he would expect the degree of intimacy all married couples enjoyed, but that did not mean he felt anything for me. Only yesterday, he had reminded me this was business.

"There you are," Augusta said with relief, stepping into the room. "I have been looking for you this hour and more. Dolly is waiting to discuss your choices for tomorrow's attire."

I glanced at Sandy, who looked faintly amused. Both of us knew Dolly was not doing anything of the sort. She knew precisely where we were, and if I was not mistaken, she had done her best to leave us alone for as long as possible, making quick work of her tasks in the room.

"We would hate to keep *Dolly* waiting," Sandy said.

"No, it would be rude." I rose, letting the blanket slide from my lap. The warmth we had generated beneath left along with it, sending a chill through me.

Sandy rose, too, setting the blanket aside. "Until dinner, then."

I nodded, and he bowed to Augusta and me.

Augusta waited until we had left and entered the servants' corridor to speak.

"How in the world do I come to find you thus, Juliana? Alone with the earl in the servant quarters, your hair entirely undone, and . . . well, let us not say any more on that subject. You might have told me you meant to spend time with him so I could supervise."

"We didn't wish to disturb you," I said, making no mention of the adventures on the loch out of a hope she hadn't heard of it. "You have been so unwell since our arrival."

She sniffed. The edges of her nose were red and raw. "It is no disturbance, my dear. It is my duty to be your chaperone."

"Even when I am to be married in two days?"

"*Especially* when you are to be married in two days," she said as I followed her up the narrow stone staircase. "It would be a great pity to cease observing propriety or to provide food for gossip, particularly amongst the servants, which I fear may already be the case, when the goal is so near. In matches like this one, where there is a disparity in station between the parties, people are quick to believe the worst."

"The worst?"

She stopped at the top of the staircase, pausing on the landing to look at me. "It would grieve both of us if anyone thought you had trapped the earl into marriage, or some such ridiculous thing."

"But the match was decided before we even met," I protested, my cheeks burning at the mere idea that someone could believe such lies.

"That is true, and those who know it will likely disbelieve such rumors. But not everyone is privy to the details of the arrangement, and sowing such seeds cannot be expected to do you credit."

I swallowed, nodding. Would Dolly or Gillies have spoken to the other servants about things? What would they have said?

Whatever the case, Augusta was wise, and her interruption had been fortuitous. It was for the best that I keep a proper distance from Sandy—for my sake as much as anyone's. It would be easy to let a degree of intimacy creep up between us that was unseemly for two people marrying for convenience.

"I shall be late," I said, my heart tapping against my chest as though it might go down to the party without me.

"Fashionably so," Augusta replied in her plugged voice, watching Dolly adjust the white flowers adorning my coiffure. "The earl and his family must be downstairs to greet the guests, of course, but you, my dear . . . you are expected to make an entrance."

I swallowed, regarding myself in the long mirror. I had debated wearing a more dashing color than the cream embroidered dress I now wore. Augusta had assured me, however, that white was the only option. It had been only with a great deal of persuading that she had relented to the cream.

I understood. She wanted my clothing and behavior to be unimpeachable. Well, so did I, and while my behavior was something yet to be tested, I was quite aware that white made me look like a sickly ghost. Mrs. Boyle had already made it clear there were enough ghosts haunting the corridors of Lochlarren; I did not wish to add myself to their numbers. How I longed for the cream dress, which made my skin less pallid and my eyes brighter.

"There," Dolly said, stepping back.

I turned to face Augusta, who was here despite feeling worse than ever. The doctor had asserted she was suffering from summer catarrh, an ailment I had never heard of. She was certainly suffering from something. Her lids were heavy, the eyes beneath an angry pink to match the nose she blew every few minutes.

Despite such misery, her mouth pulled into a smile. "Extraordinary."

I hoped the people downstairs would agree with her, the earl included. I wanted to be a credit to him. That was all. It mattered not if he thought me beautiful or not.

"I shall go inform yer father ye're ready," Dolly said before leaving the room.

"Now," Augusta said, handing me my fan and ushering me slowly toward the door, "you must follow Lord Lismore's lead of how to treat those in attendance. It would not do to show too great a familiarity with those he wishes to keep at a distance."

I nodded, taking in as deep a breath as my lungs would allow. I hadn't been swimming in the loch today, but they seemed nearly as reluctant to draw in breath as they had yesterday.

We stopped at the top of the staircase, and Augusta took my hand in hers, smiling at me with wistfulness in her gaze. "You have done it, Juliana."

"Done what? Left my dear chaperone in the dust while I go to converse and dance and behave prettily?"

She smiled and squeezed my hand. Her hair was uncoiffed and covered in its usual cap. She wore her morning dress rather than something fit for the evening. It was a shame she would not attend tonight's event. "Nevermind me. I would never forgive myself for distracting from you with my ridiculous sneezing." Her speech was congested and strange, and I felt a wave of regret that her time here was so miserable.

"You are too good to me," I said, kissing her on the cheek.

"Nonsense," she said gently. "You deserve every bit of good anyone does for you."

I smiled gratefully as the sounds of chattering downstairs heightened. Taking in a deep breath, I met Augusta's eyes, then nodded and turned toward the stairs.

"Juliana?"

I looked over my shoulder at her, waiting.

"Remember not to—"

"I shan't," I said. I had promised not to hang about Sandy, and I meant to be as good as my word. Better to hang about Iain or Blair or Papa if I needed the security someone's companionship offered. The last thing I wished was to be seen as the overly attached bride.

Footsteps tripped up the stairs, and Dolly appeared, smiling at me. "He's ready, miss."

"Thank you." I closed my hands into fists to keep them from shaking.

Papa embraced me heartily at the bottom of the stairs, complimenting me on my appearance and kissing both my cheeks. "Nearly everyone is here. And every single one awaiting your entrance."

I managed a smile, though my stomach was tied in knots.

He led me toward the door to the drawing room, and I tried to remember Augusta's counsel from our arrival at Lochlarren: *act like a countess*. One would have thought the task would become simpler the nearer the reality drew, but I found myself every bit as unsure now as I had been in the carriage on the journey here. Perhaps this had all been a mistake. How could I have ever thought myself fit to be a countess? It was the greatest presumption imaginable.

But there was no turning back now—not without humiliating Lord Lismore and putting him in an impossible position. All I could do was try to be the best version of myself and hope it wasn't so very different from what a Lady Lismore *should* be.

As the drawing room came into view, the sounds of genial conversation filled the air. There were no frowns or haughty expressions amongst the crowd. Nearly everyone was smiling as they conversed.

I took heart, for they did not seem as though they had come with the express purpose of finding fault with me. There were earls and barons amongst them, but for all their status, they appeared to have come to enjoy themselves, and that was something I could do as well. Had I not prepared precisely for such an occasion?

This evening was the culmination, in many ways, of all Papa's work, Augusta's training, and my own hopes. I was now in a position to be accepted by even the most fastidious of Society.

Papa squeezed my arm as we stepped into the drawing room, and gazes began turning in our direction as the footman announced, "Miss Juliana Godfrey and Mr. Mark Godfrey."

Conversation ceased, and all gazes flitted to us.

If Augusta had been with me now, I imagined she would have instructed me to keep my expression impassive, showing neither exuberance nor disgust, keeping myself above sentiments which were below a countess.

But I was not a countess, and I did the only thing I knew to do when someone took note of me: I smiled.

I caught sight of Sandy on the other side of the room, flanked by two men in their middle age. In contrast to the way his hair had dried tousled and wavy after the incident at the loch, today it was carefully brushed, gleaming with some sort of pomade. His shoulders, so recently—in my memory, at least—peeking through the almost transparent fabric of his wet shirt, were now encased in a dark blue tailcoat.

His eyes fixed on me and mine on him as one of the men addressed a remark to him.

He seemed to excuse himself from their company, and they broke apart to let him through.

"Only look how dashing you are!" Iain came up to me, taking my hand in his and planting a kiss on it so quickly I wasn't even sure his lips had touched my glove.

"You could outshine the women in any London ballroom," Blair agreed, making a spectacularly overdone bow that brought a laugh to my lips. I doubted he had ever been to a London ballroom, but I was grateful for the compliment, all the same.

"And you the men," I replied. They looked very fine, though not so fine as Sandy.

Papa released my arm, winking at me and stepping away to speak with someone.

Magnus gave a curt bow. "You look very well, Miss Godfrey."

"Thank you, Magnus." I tried to keep my focus on the Duncan brothers, but in the edge of my vision, I was ever-aware of Sandy's approach. Some of those in attendance had turned back to their conversations, but a quick glance told me I was not the only one watching Sandy draw nearer. People were curious to see us together.

"Excuse me," Sandy said to his brothers, who stepped aside.

My heartbeat thrummed in my ears as Sandy stood before me, looking every bit the earl. There was no mistaking the glint of admiration in his eye as he met my gaze.

He reached for my hand, which was clasped with the other in front of me. Bowing, he brought my fingers to his lips and pressed a kiss upon the back of my hand. It sent a rush of heat all the way through my body and into my heart. Perhaps it was simply the contrast to Iain's nonchalant kiss, but Sandy's was warm and lingering.

No. It *was* distinctly different from Iain's, as was the way he looked at me as he rose to his full height again.

I curtsied in response, hoping I did justice to the hours Augusta had spent teaching me.

Sandy glanced at his brothers, then leaned in toward me, speaking softly. "It is clear you are none the worse for yesterday's . . . incident. Indeed, perhaps improved by it, even."

Curse these cheeks. They could heat a room better than peat bricks. A moment's hasty consideration put the idea of fanning myself to rest. That would appear coy or perhaps as though I was unequal to conducting the merest conversation with my intended.

"I believe a few of my toes have yet to thaw," I replied.

"Then they shan't mind if I accidentally tread upon them when we dance later."

When we dance. The words brought a flutter to my stomach. Sandy and I had barely spoken to one another since spending the afternoon together in Mrs. Boyle's lodgings yesterday. Dinner had been full of conversation with Papa, and the morning had been taken up by the details both the party and tomorrow's wedding required.

A man came up beside us, and Sandy turned to him. After a quick greeting, he introduced me to Mr. Patton.

"So pleased to make your acquaintance, Miss Godfrey," the man said. He looked out over the people crowding the room. "My daughter is here somewhere, and I am anxious to introduce you to her."

"I would like that very much," I replied, praying she was not the sort to look me over from head to toe and condemn my choice of gown.

The footman's voice rang out across the room. "Lord Cochrane, Lady Cochrane, and Miss Elinor Cochrane."

Sandy turned toward the door as the announced family entered, a silver-haired man and a lace-capped woman flanking their daughter. Miss Cochrane was blonde and elegant, her white crepe dress clinging to her figure as though perhaps she *had* just emerged from the loch—or everything below her head, at least, for her gleaming hair was curled with precision.

Her eyes roamed the room for a moment, then stopped when they found Sandy. Lips curling up in a familiar smile, she leaned in toward her father to whisper something. He searched the room until he found Sandy, then the three of them approached.

I glanced at Sandy, who was smiling in a way that tweaked my heart in a strange way.

"Lord Cochrane," Sandy said, putting out a hand.

Cochrane. That had been the name Iain had protested against when Sandy had mentioned who would be in attendance tonight.

"Lismore," the man responded jovially, grasping his hand in a way that looked to me uncomfortably tight and firm. "How good to see you!"

"And you." Sandy turned his eyes toward Lady Cochrane and her daughter, then bowed. "My lady. Nelly."

They both executed expert curtsies.

If the way they all regarded one another hadn't been enough to tell me the level of familiarity between them, Sandy's use of Miss Cochrane's Christian name put all doubts to rest. Given Iain's cryptic comments at dinner the other night, my stomach felt suddenly uneasy.

Miss Cochrane's eyes flitted to me, curious and discerning. What did she see? Could she tell immediately that I was of common stock? That Papa had toiled and traded whatever he had to his name in order to amass the wealth he now had?

"Nelly," Sandy said, "allow me to introduce you to Miss Juliana Godfrey. Miss Godfrey, this is Miss Elinor Cochrane, and this her father, Lord Cochrane, and her mother, Lady Cochrane."

I dipped into a curtsy appropriate for a baron as they inclined their heads to me. Once I became Lady Lismore, they would be the ones dipping and bowing lower, and I would be the one introduced first. How strange that things would change so quickly and drastically.

"The Cochranes are neighbors to Lochlarren," Sandy said. "Or as near as neighbors can be with a loch between."

"A pleasure to meet you," said Miss Cochrane in her

sweet, elegant voice. She glanced at Sandy with a mischievous smile. "If you ever need aught to use against Sandy—something to persuade him to pay for a new carriage or some trinket, perhaps—you know where to find me, Miss Godfrey."

"Across the loch?" I said with a smile, though my insides turned and turned. It was strange to be marrying a man one didn't know—a man known so much better by those in attendance this evening.

"Precisely," Miss Cochrane replied.

"Happily for me," Sandy said, "I doubt Juliana will be venturing on the loch again for some time." His glance was teasing, and I met it with a mixture of blushing censure and trepidation. I doubted the Cochranes' opinion of me would be improved to know of the mishap.

"Again?" Miss Cochrane asked. "What happened the last time?"

I looked to Sandy, my eyes warning him, pleading with him.

"Just a mishap," he said vaguely.

"Ah, yes," she said. "Mishaps do seem to happen frequently in your company. I hope it wasn't as serious as the time I fell into the river."

Sandy chuckled. "*That* was something very spectacular indeed."

I swallowed, feeling less well by the second. Yesterday's accident had felt like a shared secret between Sandy and me, but now it felt . . . well, I began to wonder how many women he had enjoyed such misadventures with.

Someone tapped me on the shoulder. "Miss Godfrey, forgive me for interrupting, but I have found her."

I turned and found myself confronted with Mr. Patton and his young daughter. She couldn't have been more than seventeen, and she looked at me with trepidation. She looked, in fact, as I *felt*.

I took her hand in mine and smiled broadly at her. "How happy I am to meet you, Miss Patton."

Her expression morphed, relief rushing over it. "And I you."

"I shall leave you two while I speak with Miss Godfrey's father," Mr. Patton said, patting his daughter's shoulder and walking away.

"I told Father not to disturb you," she said apologetically.

"It is no disturbance at all. I was just meeting the Cochranes while I waited for your father to fetch you so that I could make *your* acquaintance."

"I would have thought you would rather speak with the Cochranes than me."

I glanced to where Miss Cochrane and Sandy were conversing. Lord and Lady Cochrane had turned away and were speaking with people I did not yet know. "I was glad to meet them, of course, but I hope you will be my particular friend this evening, for I know not a soul aside from the Duncans."

Miss Patton looked supremely flattered by this and promised to tell me whatever I wished to know about those present. I asked her a few questions about various people within sight, and she gave thorough if somewhat prattling answers. Once I judged it had been long enough to avoid rousing suspicion, I asked the question I really wished for the answer to—and yet somehow feared.

"And the Cochranes are longtime friends of the Duncans?" I asked with as much nonchalance as I could muster.

"Oh, yes," she said. "That and more, for it was always thought that Miss Cochrane and Lord Fortrose—forgive me, Lord Lismore now—would make a match, so well-suited they are. The Cochranes' land borders the loch on the other side, you know, and they haven't any other children but her, so it was thought she could not do better than to marry the heir to an earldom, while *he* could amass more land by the union. And then, of course, they have known one another since infancy."

I strived to maintain my equilibrium as I responded. "And what prevented the match—so well-suited as they are?"

"Money," she replied simply. "When the extent of the late earl's debts became known, it became impractical. Impossible, even, for Lord Cochrane had been concealing debts of his own, they say."

He arranged our marriage out of a fear I should marry a poor aristocrat's daughter. Sandy's words repeated in my mind as I watched Miss Cochrane address a laughing remark to him.

The dinner bell rang out, and a few moments later, Sandy came to retrieve me while Miss Patton's father sought her out. Did he wish he could escort Miss Cochrane?

Every seat at the enormous table in the great hall was filled —thirty in all. Sandy sat at the head, while he asked Lady Cochrane to sit at the foot. I sat to Sandy's right, while Miss Cochrane sat to his left. From all I could tell, we seemed to be observing some strange variation of seating by precedence, for I was seated next to the handsome young man Miss Patton had pointed out as the Earl of Orton. At the other end of the table were the other members of the aristocracy, while Miss Patton and her father were near the middle of the table. Papa and I— and Lady Cochrane at the foot of the table—were the deviations from precedence, for normally, we would have been the ones in the middle.

Miss Cochrane addressed a remark to Sandy, and thus I looked to the partner on my right, for Augusta had ingrained in me that it was my duty to make conversation with those around me.

"We have not been introduced, Miss Godfrey," said Lord

Orton, "but I hope people shall not think too badly of me if I forego that formality."

My eyes widened, for the sound of his voice was like a piece of home. "You are English?"

He smiled widely but put a finger to his lips as though such a thing was best kept a secret. "Tell me, Miss Godfrey, how do you find Scotland?"

I thought for a moment. "Familiar in some ways. Strange in others."

"Very well-put."

"Do you not live here?"

"When I wish to escape, I do. I have an estate a few miles from here, but my primary residence is in Cumbria. And then I am often in London."

Miss Cochrane and Sandy kept up a near-constant conversation over the course of the meal, laughing now and then over some memory or other. Miss Cochrane addressed herself to me three or four times, but inevitably, my response would spark some side conversation between the two of them. Sandy turned to me regularly to serve me or see how I was faring, but his attention was always pulled away again, and mine as well.

I was glad Lord Orton seemed eager to converse with me, for it distracted me from the questions flitting about in my mind about Miss Cochrane and Sandy. Miss Patton had said it was always thought they would make a match. Had they been engaged? Whatever had happened, there seemed to be no unpleasant feelings on either side—quite the contrary, in fact.

Conversing with Lord Orton made me feel as though I was obeying Augusta's direction not to hang on Sandy's sleeve, at least. I would leave that to Miss Cochrane, who seemed to be hanging onto it vigorously.

No. I was being too severe. There was nothing extraordinary about two well-acquainted people enjoying a chat after some time apart, just as there was nothing extraordinary about enjoying becoming acquainted with Lord Orton. Everyone liked familiarity.

I would have my dance with Sandy presently, and then I hoped to be able to better gauge just how much regret he held over the failed match with Miss Cochrane.

CHAPTER TWENTY-FOUR

SANDY

I t was a skill indeed to keep my attention focused in one place when it insisted on veering to Juliana every few seconds. She looked ethereal this evening, with a few small flowers decorating her hair and an embroidered dress that hugged her figure in ways I didn't care for Lord Orton to take note of.

It had been the merest civility to invite Orton once I discovered he was in residence at his nearby estate, but I was coming to regret it with each of his laughs—and particularly with each of Juliana's. Orton was an English earl, though he held an estate and a barony in Scotland. It was generally agreed he retreated here whenever a bit of distance was needed from his latest escapades in London. I had understood these to be money-related, but now it seemed just as likely that they were, in fact, to do with women.

He had a knack for charming people, but I had never been one of them. We had known each other for years and acted toward one another with the civility required of our stations and nothing more.

Between his conversation with Juliana and mine with Nelly, I had hardly strung together ten words to my intended since the meal had begun. Each time I attempted to attend on her by ensuring her plate and glass were full and she was not left without conversation, Orton was before me. Juliana seemed content that it be so.

Not wishing to be aggressively attentive, I focused my attention on Nelly, who seemed eager to reminisce on the past —the time before the weight of the earldom had fallen on my shoulders. The time when we had both thought we would be marrying each other.

Once the meal was over, the women retreated to the drawing room. Orton assisted Juliana from her seat, and given that Lord Fossdale to Nelly's left was seeing to the woman on *his* left, I assisted Nelly.

I knew I could depend upon her and her mother to see to Juliana's comfort in the drawing room, but I still found myself hoping the men wouldn't desire to linger too long over our port. I hadn't forgotten the vulnerability Juliana had shown when we discussed the engagement party. She wanted to be a credit to me, and that thought did something strange to me and my heart.

The formality of dinner gave way to the casual atmosphere port inevitably introduced, and conversation ebbed and flowed as everyone sipped from their glasses at their leisure.

Just when I was about to rise to signal to the company that our segregation from the ladies was at an end, Iain spoke.

"What do you say? Shall we have mercy on Sandy and join the women?"

I frowned. "What have I to say to it?"

Blair smiled devilishly. "The way your foot has been tapping against the table for the last five minutes has said a great deal. You are eager to rejoin your blushing bride."

Were there still laws against murdering one's own brothers? I would have to inquire with Rutherford on the matter.

"Ah," said Fossdale. "A love match, then, Lismore! I had thought it more of a business matter. I stand corrected."

"It is indeed the latter," I said. "Blair and Iain have always had overly active imaginations, as you all know." I made a mental note to suggest clan feuding practice in the morning, if only for the opportunity to wrestle the two of them to the ground until they cried for mercy. Or I could give Juliana a saber and see what happened.

"Perhaps it is business alone on *your* end, Lismore," said Lord Eddleston with a teasing smile, "but it is only natural that a woman would fall for the charms of a man like you."

I chuckled, thankful my collar and cravat would hide the heat creeping into my neck.

The conversation waned, and I found it impossible to stand now that Iain had interfered with his ridiculous comment. My anxiousness to join the women had nothing to do with Juliana—at least not for the reasons he implied. It was the most common decency to wish to see to the comfort of someone amongst strangers in one's home. She had no mother here to stand beside her, and Miss Lowe was absent, as well.

Everyone seemed to have finished their port, and my reluctance to seem overeager was leading to a heavy awkwardness settling over the party. I looked around the table at all the pairs of eyes on me, waiting for my signal.

Resigned, I set down my glass. "Shall we?"

"Cannot bear another moment out of her company!" Eddleston said victoriously.

Stifling an eye roll, I rose along with everyone else, and Mr. Godfrey led the way through the doors to the drawing room.

As I had expected, Nelly and her mother were speaking

with Juliana. Nelly glanced at me as I came through the door, and I smiled gratefully at her.

"What shall we do now?" she asked. "Dance, I hope. Lochlarren has one of the best rooms in the county for dancing."

"I thought you might suggest that," I said. She had always been one for reels and quadrilles. I nodded at the footmen standing near the door, and they left the room to ready the great hall for dancing.

As the preparations were being carried out, a group of both men and women gathered around Juliana and Miss Patton. All my worries for her comfort seemed to have been unnecessary, for she was pink-cheeked and smiling, the center of attention. This was what she had come for, wasn't it? The celebrity a title would bring.

Mr. Godfrey stepped up beside me, following my gaze to his daughter and her admirers. "She was made for this, Lismore, even if she was not born into it." He looked over at me, his eyes still soft and bright with affection for her. "Thank you for making the dream a reality for her."

"No thanks is necessary," I replied, feeling strange. "Heaven knows I am receiving the better end of the bargain."

He clapped a hand on my shoulder. "Saving Lochlarren is a laudable goal."

I nodded, though my eyes flitted to Juliana. I had entered the match to save the estate, without a care for who the bride would be. But now that I knew her, she was becoming an equally desirable aspect of the arrangement.

And *that* was a terrifying thought.

"The hall is ready, my lord," the footman said.

"Very good." I raised my voice over the din in the room. "Shall we dance, then?"

Claps, a few cheers, and a general moving toward the great

hall met my words. A few musicians had been hired to provide music for the evening, and they gathered near the empty fireplace, tuning their instruments.

Juliana entered the room, flocked by two women and three men. She was laughing, and I hesitated to interrupt her with a request to dance. *Were* we expected to dance together first? I had never been engaged before, and I hadn't cared enough to note how things had been done at other such events. Was this a celebration of our union, or an opportunity for Juliana to become acquainted with everyone in attendance? If the latter, dancing together would be counterproductive.

But even as I debated the expectations, the issue was decided for me. Lord Fossdale bowed over Juliana's hand, and she curtsied in acceptance, eliciting playfully distressed reactions from the other two men nearby.

There was no doubt at all Juliana had made a positive impression on those present. She seemed fully capable of managing the attention she was receiving—and to be enjoying it thoroughly. This was her dream, as her father had said. Aside from supplying the title, I had nothing to do with it.

The two disappointed pretenders to her hand turned to other partners, leaving the more obvious choice, Miss Patton, looking very much embarrassed.

Juliana's gaze flitted around the room as though in search for a partner for her. It landed upon me. We were too far apart for words, but her eyes spoke volumes.

"Excuse me," I said, slipping through the people blocking my way.

Miss Patton was looking down, her cheeks aflame with embarrassment.

"Ah, there you are, Miss Patton," I said, as though I had been searching high and low for her.

Her head came up, her wide eyes meeting mine for a

moment before she looked over one shoulder and then the other, as though there was another Miss Patton in attendance I might be speaking to.

"I hoped you would do me the honor of standing up with me for the first set," I said.

She blinked, remaining utterly speechless for so long, I began to wonder if she was, in fact, mute. Mr. Patton had a number of daughters, but I did not think I had ever heard such a thing of any of them.

Juliana took Miss Patton by the arm. "What a splendid idea. Is it not, Emily?"

"Y-y-yes," Miss Patton squeaked out after another nudge from Juliana. "I would be delighted, my lord." She sounded terrified, not delighted, but I put out my hand to her despite that. It hovered in the air, empty, as she stared at me.

Juliana and Lord Fossdale shared an amused glance, and I nearly retracted my offer and told Juliana we were expected to dance the first set together. I refrained, however, as Juliana assisted Miss Patton's hand to mine.

I smiled reassuringly at my partner, and she seemed to relax ever so slightly. "Shall we?"

She nodded, and Juliana took Fossdale's arm, her eyes on me, teeming with gratitude in a way that made me care little for what sort of partner Miss Patton would prove to be. She could use my feet as her personal ballroom floor if she wished.

Thankfully, she seemed to have more skill at dancing than at accepting invitations to dance. Her tendency to look at me to ascertain what I thought of her as a partner was her greatest obstacle to becoming an ideal partner. All she needed was a bit of confidence, so when she made a mistake, I pretended the error was my own.

I recognized the way she was behaving for what it was: awe to be selected as the first partner of the evening by an earl.

It was something I had become accustomed to—the painful awkwardness, the round-eyed furtive glances, the stammering. I preferred it to the alternative, which was fluttering lashes, fawning behavior, and an oppressive need to be recognized.

Juliana had displayed neither of these behaviors upon our first meeting, instead opting for a haughty arrogance that I had since learned was quite foreign to her personality. Thank heaven. She danced well, or perhaps she simply made it look enjoyable. Would she smile so cheerfully when we danced together? *Would* we dance together? And why did it matter to me?

Perhaps now that the financial preoccupations which had consumed me for so many weeks were at an end, my mind was grasping onto whatever problem it could find.

There *was* no problem, though. Tomorrow, I was to be married to Juliana Godfrey, setting in motion all the clauses of the contracts her father and I had spent the past two days cementing and signing. Lochlarren would be saved. Juliana would become countess. Both of us would have what we had set out to achieve.

I returned Miss Patton to her father once the set was over and, just to spite my desire to seek out Juliana, I asked Miss Stewart to join me for the next set.

It became clear by the end of the set, however, that my preoccupation was growing rather than diminishing. The more I considered it, too, the sillier it seemed not to dance with my soon-to-be bride at our own engagement party.

I thanked Miss Stewart, then threaded my way toward Juliana. She was being given a drink by her dance partner on the other side of the room. Nelly and Lord Orton were nearby, having danced the set together. My gaze lingered on them for a moment. Perhaps the two of them would make a match of it. Nelly wished to marry a peer, after all.

Juliana's laugh brought my gaze back to her, and I felt a sliver of hesitation to interrupt her conversation with Mr. Mackay.

What was it that made asking one's own intended to dance so devilishly nerve-racking? I squared my shoulders. I was the Earl of Lismore, for goodness' sake, and it was only natural that Juliana and I dance together before the musicians left us all to take tea.

My heart beat erratically as her and Mr. Mackay's attention turned toward me.

I gave a little nod of acknowledgement to the latter, then directed my attention to Juliana. The sight of her, so near and radiant, tied my tongue in a tight knot. I was no different than Miss Patton, stammering and stuttering as soon as I opened my mouth.

No. I was worse, for I couldn't even manage a sound.

I cleared my throat. "Miss Godfrey, would you do me the honor of—"

"Sandy!" Nelly came up by my side, Orton next to her. "There you are! Surely you do not mean to go the entire night without asking me to dance."

I glanced at her, then back to Juliana, whose eyes had held an almost expectant gleam in them until Nelly's comment.

"On the contrary," I said. "It would be my pleasure to dance with you, Nelly, but I have just asked—"

"It is quite all right," Juliana said with a smile. "You two should dance the next set."

I hesitated. Was she saying so out of politeness or because she wished for a different partner?

"Yes," Orton chimed in, "and I shall escort Miss Godfrey to the ballroom floor—if she will have me." He cocked an eyebrow and looked at her, the smile on his face perfectly communicating how sure he was his suggestion would be welcome. Devil take him.

"I would be delighted," Juliana replied, curtsying.

"You will have her all to yourself soon, Lismore," said Orton. "Let the rest of us enjoy her while we can."

I smiled, gritting my teeth. I cared for Nelly too much to wish to hurt her by insisting on dancing with Juliana, so I made no effort to pursue the subject. "Certainly."

"Shall we, Miss Godfrey?" Orton asked, extending his arm to her.

Juliana's gaze flitted to me briefly as she accepted it.

"Perhaps the next set?" I said.

She nodded with a small smile, and Orton led her toward the dance floor.

CHAPTER TWENTY-FIVE

JULIANA

Thus far, the night had gone better than I could have imagined. Everyone had been kind, attentive, and pleasant to dance and speak with. Lord Orton in particular was quite the most engaging dance partner I had ever had the pleasure of standing up with.

As we danced a reel with a few steps unfamiliar to me, Orton had me laughing at my missteps. He made me feel at ease rather than thinking any less of me for it. I hadn't known him more than two hours, but with his English accent and his sympathy for my lack of experience in Scotland, he felt like a bit of home—a small comfort to me amongst so many strangers.

Lord Orton and I separated to our respective sides of the set while the other couples performed their figures. I watched Sandy and Miss Cochrane, faces both wreathed in smiles as they danced and conversed with ease.

My own smile wavered, but I fortified it, feeling Lord Orton's gaze upon me. I joked and laughed my way through the rest of the dance, but my mind was three couples away—

and my eyes, too, when I couldn't prevent them from wandering there.

"Refreshment?" Lord Orton asked once we left the dance floor after the set.

"Oh," I said, trying to swallow with a parched throat. "I believe I am meant to stand up for the next set with Lord Lismore." Even as I said it, my gaze found Sandy, engaged in conversation with Miss Cochrane on the ballroom floor, as though they had either been too engrossed to realize the dance had ended or meant to remain for the last set of the night.

Would we truly not even dance once together? It seemed wrong. It *felt* wrong. But what did I know of such things? I was not only ignorant of how things were done amongst the aristocracy, I was also ignorant of the customs in Scotland.

"It seems he is otherwise engaged," Lord Orton said.

Sandy *was* engaged. To me. Both to dance and to be married. But perhaps that was not as he truly wished things to be. His circumstances demanded he marry me, but his heart? I was beginning to suspect it belonged to Miss Cochrane.

I allowed Lord Orton to lead me to the refreshments, determined not to allow my eyes to seek out Sandy again. It would be perfectly enjoyable to spend more time with the Earl of Orton, and then I could truthfully report to Augusta I had not hung on Sandy's sleeve all evening. I had barely even seen his sleeve.

"Allow me," said a voice as Lord Orton reached for the nearest tray of drinks.

Appearing out of nowhere, Sandy swiped a tray from the platter and offered it to me.

"I have come for my promised set," he said. "I trust you have enjoyed Miss Godfrey's company for sufficient time, Orton?"

"Impossible," Lord Orton replied genially with a smiling

glance at me. "But, nevertheless, I shall be grateful for the time I had." He took my gloved hand and bowed over it.

Sandy watched him walk off for a moment, then turned to me. "Would you like to dance, or would you prefer to rest?"

"Dance, I think." I took a drink, letting the sweet coolness slip down my throat and, I hoped, steady my beating heart. "If you are agreeable."

He smiled and put out his hand. "More agreeable than when you first met me, I hope."

The spark that traveled up my arm at his touch attested to that fact.

We took our places at the head of the set. Silence reigned between us as the dancing began. I wanted to ask him about Miss Cochrane, but this was neither the place nor the time— and it was none of my business. She and Lord Orton were dancing again, situated just one couple away.

Sandy's eyes traveled in that direction, and he frowned.

And yet, as we came together, his gaze turned to me, making me feel short of breath. We spoke little, but it was not awkwardness which prevailed between us but rather a silent pensiveness, as though both of us were trying to fathom that we would be married on the morrow. How I wished I could see into his mind and know how he felt at the prospect.

But I could hardly explain my own feelings, so jumbled were they. I anticipated and dreaded all at once the ceremony and the thought of being Sandy's wife. Tonight had borne upon me the inequality of the situation, but not because of my station in life.

The music instructed Sandy and I to rejoin hands for a moment, and I searched his eyes. It felt clear to me that our motivations for marriage were quite different. There lay the unfair discrepancy.

Our marriage would grant me a title. It was the vehicle to achieve my and Papa's aspirations.

For Sandy, though, this was a marriage borne of necessity. It was not hopes or dreams which had led him to agree to the match; it was duty—a duty which had apparently taken from him the match he had wanted.

Would he ever be able to look upon me without seeing a reminder of what he had sacrificed for his family's legacy and well-being?

I wanted better than that for him and for myself. I didn't wish to keep him from Miss Cochrane. Not as a dance partner, not as a wife.

Neither could I deny any longer the growing attraction I felt for him. I wanted to call it friendship, but as I curtsied and he bowed at the end of the set, I knew in my heart that it was fast becoming more.

CHAPTER TWENTY-SIX

SANDY

"I shall be obliged to leave an hour or two after the ceremony," Mr. Godfrey said as we sat at the breakfast table. Last night's party had not ended until nearly two, but Mrs. Boyle had informed me that a letter had arrived for Mr. Godfrey by express at the unholy hour of six this morning, since which time he had been awake and busy. The man was indefatigable.

My brothers, on the other hand, had yet to make an appearance for breakfast.

"So soon?" Juliana asked.

Her father grimaced. "I am afraid so. When I left, I thought my business was well enough in hand without me, but it appears otherwise." He held up the letter in his hands. "Never fear, though, my dear. I shall return as soon as I am able."

She nodded. She was looking tired—the same way I felt. She had hardly touched her toast or tea. Was the thought of marrying me in a few hours depriving her of her appetite? "And Augusta?" she asked.

Miss Lowe was not present at the table but abed. The

229

doctor's ministrations had not seemed to improve her situation.

"I would take her with me," her father replied, "but I do not think it would be a kindness to force her to travel in her current state. I hope she will soon turn a corner."

"I hope the same," Juliana agreed. "And I shall be glad to have her with me here."

I frowned. The comment itself was benign, but the way she looked at me afterward . . . less so.

Mr. Godfrey stood. "I had better see to my belongings and dress for the church." He smiled at me, stopping behind Juliana and bending to kiss her on the head. "It is finally here. The day we have been waiting for. My little countess." The words were spoken soft, as though only meant for her, but I heard them all the same.

She looked up at him, grasping his hand and squeezing it. "I shall come see you at your bedchamber shortly."

He patted her hand and left the room.

"I suppose we should ready ourselves as well," I said, watching her expression to try to gauge her feelings as I stood.

"I suppose so." She set her napkin aside. She didn't stand, though, and I wondered if she was waiting for me to assist her. She looked up suddenly. "Might I have a brief word with you first?"

"Of course. In the study, perhaps?"

She nodded, and the way she avoided my gaze set my mind and heart racing as I led the way there.

I opened the creaking door and waited for her to pass through, biting my tongue to keep from asking what it was she wished to speak of. All in due time. I hesitated for a moment, then closed the door behind us. We would be married in the next three hours. Propriety seemed a formality that should not supersede privacy at this point.

Juliana was standing in the middle of the room, her hands clasped in front of her, her gaze on nothing in particular. I walked over to the desk and rested against it, waiting—not terribly patiently—for her to speak.

Finally, she looked up, meeting my gaze. "I do not know how else to say this than to put it frankly, so I pray you will forgive my forthrightness."

"I prefer it," I said calmly, though my heart was anything but.

She nodded. "I simply wish to know, while there is still time, if you truly wish to move forward with this marriage."

My jaw slipped open, though words escaped me.

She gave a grimacing sort of smile. "Do you still prefer my frankness?"

I closed my mouth and cleared my throat. "I do prefer it." I searched her face, wondering what had led to this. Was she wishing to cry off? Had last night's party given her a taste for something better than a Scottish earldom? She had certainly enjoyed Orton's company.

A flicker of panic ignited within me, but I resolved to lighten the situation rather than add to the seriousness of it. "I assure you, I shan't bring sabers to dinner or force you to eat without forks again, Juliana."

The smile she offered was polite but weak.

I let out a breath, giving up my attempt at levity. "The contracts have been drawn up and signed, the ring engraved, our acquaintances informed—and the church expecting us in two hours."

"I know, but . . . I have no wish for you to feel coerced into marriage with me, Sandy."

I frowned, looking at her intently. "There is no coercion."

"Is there not?"

I didn't answer immediately, thinking through my

response. "There is a need for the money the marriage brings —a dire one, even. I cannot deny that, and it would be silly to do so, for you know it, just as I know *your* reasons for entering into this arrangement."

"Yes. But perhaps there is another way to solve your financial troubles without so much sacrifice. Papa esteems you highly. He would happily enter into an alternative arrangement with you, one whereby both of you could benefit without our tying ourselves to one another in this way."

I said nothing, the flicker of panic morphing into a sick feeling in my stomach. *So much sacrifice,* she had said. She had asked me if I wished to proceed with the match, but I was beginning to suspect it was her own sacrifices which were too dear. "Do *you* wish for the marriage to proceed?"

She met my gaze, her eyes troubled, her silence tying knots of anxiousness in my stomach. My mind raced, questions buzzing about what I would do if the match dissolved right here in the study before my very eyes. How would I meet Lochlarren's financial obligations?

"I have no desire for you to feel coerced into marriage with *me*." I studied Juliana, this woman I had so despised upon first meeting but for whom I now felt an unexpectedly strong affection and attraction. The loss of this match would not be solely financial.

"I feel no coercion." She said it slowly, though whether to ensure I believed her or because she was not entirely certain of her words, I couldn't tell. While I wanted to marry her—nay, *needed* to—I had no desire for an unwilling bride. This was a marriage of convenience, but I was no brute. If she truly didn't wish to be married, I would find a way to bring Lochlarren about. I would have to.

I needed to make my wishes clear while ensuring her own were not ignored.

I stepped toward her, and her eyes watched my every move. I reached for her hand, which was clasped with the other in front of her. She did not resist the gesture, allowing me to take it. She wore no gloves, having just breakfasted, and the warmth of her skin on mine sent a wave of courage through me.

"I wish for the marriage to proceed," I said clearly. "But if you have any hesitation, Juliana, now is certainly the time to make it known."

She looked down at the very moment I wished most to see her face. The silence stretched until I felt as though I might snap from the tension. Her thumb gently grazed the palm of my hand, taking my breath.

Just as soon as it had happened, though, it was over. Perhaps I had imagined it.

"I, too, wish for the marriage to proceed." The words were sure, and she looked up, her gaze clear and resolute.

A wave of relief washed over me, but I searched her eyes for a moment, looking for any sign that she was wavering.

I found none, so I nodded. "Good. We had better dress, then."

The intimacy of the wedding ceremony stood in sharp contrast to last night's celebrations. Juliana's father and cousin were there, as were my own brothers, and, of course, the vicar.

Every shuffling of feet, every whisper amongst the scant guests, echoed in the halls of the church as I stood near the vicar, watching Mr. Godfrey escort Juliana toward me. Her dress, a shimmering silver trimmed with Brussels lace, brushed the comparatively dull stone floor.

Every step brought her closer to being my wife. A lace veil, adorned with white flowers, was fastened in her hair, falling all the way to her waist. I yearned to see into her mind and know her thoughts now that the moment had arrived.

She and her father reached the base of the dais, and he kissed her on the cheek before sharing an intimate and significant look. He shook hands with me, then took his seat in the pew beside Miss Lowe. She was looking better than when I had last seen her, but her eyes were red and glassy.

The vicar began to read from *The Book of Common Prayer*, outlining the varied purposes of marriage. Juliana's cheeks pinked at the mention of the procreation of children, and my own thoughts strayed to the events that would follow the ceremony—to this evening.

Anticipation and nerves flooded me. It was curiosity as much as anything—a desire to examine the flickers and flashes of feeling I had experienced for Juliana, to see whether there was enough kindling there to produce something more. The prospect of the potential flame both excited and frightened me. It was territory I had promised myself not to enter. But I wanted to. Did Juliana?

As no one produced any objection to the marriage, the ceremony continued, and the vicar caused us to join right hands. In the damp of the kirk, Juliana's hand felt cold, and I pressed it between the two of mine for a moment, hoping to share some of my own warmth.

She smiled gratefully as the vicar said the words for me to repeat. "I, Alexander Daniel MacLeod Duncan, take thee, Juliana Godfrey, to be my wedded wife, to have and to hold from this day forward, for better for worse, for richer for poorer, in sickness and in health, to love and to cherish, till death us do part, according to God's holy ordinance; and thereto I plight thee my troth."

To have and to hold. To love and to cherish. Those were not the words of a marriage of convenience, and yet I was charged to repeat them, to make them my vows. Looking at Juliana, I couldn't find it in myself to regret it.

Juliana repeated the vows given to her, and the minister charged me to produce the ring. I took it from the inner pocket of my tailcoat and set it on the book the minister held. It was a plain band of silver, with our initials and the day's date engraved inside. The minister returned the ring and spoke the words for me to repeat as I slid the ring onto Juliana's fourth finger.

"With this ring I thee wed, with my body I thee worship." My body infused with heat, and Juliana's lashes fluttered as she glanced quickly away. I wanted to set her at her ease, so I added my own emphasis to the next words. "And with *all* my worldly goods I thee endow." Her gaze flitted to mine, and I smiled. She was the one endowing *me* with worldly goods, and though the minister cleared his throat disapprovingly at my emphasis, I didn't regret it a jot. Her smile and the way her shoulders relaxed was well worth it.

I hoped I would be able to elicit such reactions from her as time went on, that she would know she had nothing to fear from me. I would respect her wishes, whatever they were, whatever I personally felt.

There was silence at the end of the ceremony, and the vicar's eyes shifted to the congregation, fixing somewhere in particular. His lips pressed together, an almost annoyed expression passing over his face. I followed the path of his gaze and found Iain and Blair nodding at the vicar in encouragement.

I frowned, wondering what they were up to.

The vicar sighed. "You may kiss your bride."

Ah. So, *that* was the game. My brothers had convinced the vicar to add that last bit. My heart thudded as the pastor waited along with the guests. Iain grinned and raised a provoking brow.

Juliana watched me intently, her brown eyes wide and earnest. There was no fear there. Or perhaps I was merely seeing what I wished to see—not that my preferred circumstances for our first kiss would have been with an audience.

But there would be time for more later. I hoped.

I questioned her with my eyes, and she gave the slightest of nods.

Her hand still in mine, I stepped toward her. Who knew that a brief kiss in the damp church, two feet away from the somber vicar, could set my heart knocking as it now was?

I lowered my head toward hers and closed my eyes, feeling her warmth before my lips found hers. They were soft and inviting, and her hand grasped mine tightly—almost drawing me closer, I thought—before she pulled away and the vicar finished the ceremony.

I was a married man. I had a wife, sitting beside me at the dining table amongst my family—*our* family—and she was somehow more beautiful now than before the ceremony.

I didn't know how to feel. Lochlarren was effectively saved. Barring some atrocious management on my part, the estate and title would pass on to my heir in a better state than they had been in for several generations.

My heir. The two words sat strangely in my mind, carrying a new weight. My heir would be as much Juliana as me. Juliana would not only be my wife but the mother of my children. Somehow, amidst all the turmoil of the past weeks—Father's death, the discovery of the true state of his debts, and welcoming Juliana to the castle—I had never truly considered that.

As she leaned over to speak to Blair, I pictured her with a babe in her arms, throwing rocks into the loch while holding the hand of a toddler, playing at hide and seek on the castle grounds. The images stirred something deep within me.

Mr. Godfrey pushed his chair out from the table. "What a joyous day this has been! And how reluctant I am to leave the celebrations so prematurely." He grimaced apologetically at his daughter, who rose to say goodbye.

Watching them take farewell of one another inspired me with an even greater determination to ensure Juliana's happiness and comfort. She had come to Lochlarren a week and a half ago—a strange place in a new country with unfamiliar faces—and was expected to make it her home, to say goodbye to her father and settle in with her new family. My conscience pinched with regret at how difficult I had made her arrival.

Of course, she had been unbearable then, but if I had taken a moment to think on her situation, perhaps I would have responded differently, and then *she* would have responded differently.

Well, there was no changing the past. The present and future were what remained to be determined. I resolved to do whatever was in my power to ensure they were happy for her.

I rose to shake hands with my father-in-law.

"It was kind of you to hold an early dinner on my account, Lismore," he said, gripping my hand firmly.

"It was no trouble at all," I replied. "I hope you will not stay away too long."

"I shall return before you are ready for me, no doubt. I will just take my leave of Augusta and be on my way." Miss Lowe had returned to her room amidst a chorus of sneezing and sniffling shortly after the ceremony.

"I shall accompany you," Juliana said, excusing herself from the table.

Once Juliana returned from seeing her father off, the only ones remaining at the table were my brothers and me.

Iain and Blair had both been imbibing freely of the whisky I had ordered to be brought up from the cellar, making them particularly talkative and easily diverted. Magnus, too, had been drinking, but its effect was to make him even more somber than usual.

I pulled out Juliana's chair when she returned. She looked at her plate for a moment, as though deciding whether she wished to finish the food there. A glance around the table told her the rest of us had finished our meals.

"I shall leave you to your port," she said with a smile.

"There is no need to hurry yourself," I replied. "Eat your fill. Unless you are put off by Iain and Blair, in which case, I cannot blame you for wishing to retire. Indeed, I am tempted to join you."

"No, no," Iain said, his words slurring slightly. "You shan't avoid us. This is your wedding day. There are traditions to be observed!" He raised his glass, and the liquid inside threatened to come out.

"Traditions," Blair agreed, tapping his glass against Magnus's on the table.

"Oh," Juliana said, lowering herself back into her chair. "What traditions?"

Blair and Iain shared an impish glance, while Juliana's brows drew together.

"Enough," I said, sensing danger. "I think a glass of port the last thing either of you need, so perhaps *you* should excuse yourselves."

"Sandy," Juliana said softly to me, "if there are traditions that should be observed, I would not wish to deprive you of that."

Blair snorted with laughter.

"Thank you," I said, pointedly ignoring my brothers. "But this particular tradition is not one which needs to be observed."

"What is it?"

"The bedding," Iain said in an overloud voice. "We accompany you to your bedchamber and wait outside to ensure things are..."

"Official," Blair offered, raising his glass before the two of them burst into laughter.

Juliana blanched, and I nearly throttled my brothers on the spot.

Instead, I clenched my teeth and directed my attention to my wife. "As I said, it is a not a tradition which needs to be observed, neither *has* it been for some time."

She glanced at my brothers, who were laughing at something together, then returned her gaze to me. Her cheeks, which had gone white, were now full of color. "Thank you. I very much appreciate that. I had been thinking they meant a tradition like clan feuding practice."

I chuckled, though my mind whirred with questions about what *her* expectations and hopes were for this evening. "I doubt that particular tradition was *ever* observed."

"A new tradition for future generations, then," she responded, her coloring evening out.

"I will take any excuse to teach those two a lesson," I said, casting a long-suffering eye toward my brothers, who were conversing in what they no doubt assumed were whispers.

"You are fortunate to have them." She looked at them with indulgent affection.

"Wait until you have known them as long as I have. You may see them differently in twenty years."

She didn't respond immediately. "I think I should check on Augusta. I shall see you. . . later," she said, not meeting my eye.

I nodded, cursing myself for my comment. Twenty years must seem like an eternity to her just now. I needed to tread carefully as we began our married life together, or I would overwhelm her. Slow and steady was the way forward.

CHAPTER TWENTY-SEVEN

JULIANA

I stayed with Augusta far longer than needed. It wasn't that I was dreading what was to come. I was simply nervous. Nervously eager.

"Ye're still here, my lady?" Dolly said as she came through the door with a bowl of gruel for Augusta.

"She is keeping me company," Augusta said from her place lying in the bed. Her eyelids drooped over red, watery eyes. Every few minutes a tear would slip down toward her ear, unsolicited but unstoppable. She claimed she was well enough, but she looked miserable.

Dolly brought the tray over and set it on the bedside table. Then, both of us assisted Augusta to a position from which she could more easily eat.

"She is kindness itself," Dolly agreed, setting the tray on her lap. "And I hope this gruel will bring a bit of relief. But a lady mustna make her husband wait on his weddin' night."

I tried to maintain an appearance of nonchalance, busying myself with scooping some gruel onto the spoon and praying my cheeks were not betraying me. As they could have warmed the great hall, however, I doubted my success.

"That is true," Augusta said. "I keep forgetting you are a married woman now, Juliana. I feel a wretch for being so absent."

"It is *because* you feel wretchedly that you need to rest, cousin," I said. "I will stay to feed you if you wish."

"It is not necessary," she replied, taking the spoon from me. "I am not so ill as that."

"In that case," Dolly said, "perhaps ye'll excuse me ta tend ta Lady Lismore while ye eat?"

I frowned for a moment until realization dawned. She was speaking of me. I was Lady Lismore now. A countess. And yet I felt no different than I had this morning when I was nothing but plain Miss Godfrey.

Augusta nodded, and I hesitated for a moment before rising, unsure whether I wished to delay longer or hurry. How could one feel such contrary emotions at the same time?

I led the way from the room, Dolly following closely behind me.

"Where are ye goin', my lady?"

I stopped, frowning. "To change in my bedchamber."

She smiled slightly. "But 'tis yer bedchamber no longer. I moved yer things over this mornin' ta the one ye share with his lordship."

"Oh."

Her face fell. "Did I do wrong, my lady?"

"No. You did no wrong." I paused, looking toward the door that led to Sandy's bedchamber. *Our* bedchamber.

I swallowed. "Is he there already?"

"Nay, my lady. He told me when I saw him below that he'd be a quarter of an hour or so seeing to correspondence."

A quarter of an hour. Was that enough time to prepare myself for what was to come? It would have to be. The fact that he was seeing to correspondence on the night of his wedding was . . . well, it was either a testament to how busy he was or evidence that he was not overly eager for what came next. He had not seemed any keener than I to observe the bedding tradition Iain and Blair had mentioned.

Would tonight be merely another duty for him?

Dolly assisted me out of my dress, undoing my stays and pulling the stockings from my feet. I tried to focus on the details of our task rather than letting my mind wander a quarter of an hour ahead or letting my eyes wander to the bed.

Once I had my wrapper over my shift, Dolly set to my coiffure, undoing the pins and pulling out whatever flowers had held on all day. She was quiet as she brushed through my hair, and my mind revisited the events of the morning. Sandy's hand holding mine. His fingers slipping the ring over mine. *With my body I thee worship. Obey, love, serve, honor. Keep thee only unto him.*

Saying such words had blurred the boundaries more than ever, confusing me about what precisely it meant to be Sandy's wife. Which wifely duties *were* expected of me? Was I to serve and honor but not love? He was marrying me for the sake of his estate, but there had been moments, glances, glimmers of more. Or perhaps the words of the ceremony had played tricks upon my mind, making me see things that were not there.

And yet. . .

I felt the hope of more as surely as I felt the cold metal of the ring upon my finger.

Sandy had assured me he did not feel coerced, and I wanted to believe him. I wanted to believe he held me in friendly affection at least, that he was not secretly despondent that it was I rather than Nelly standing across from him at the kirk.

Perhaps, just perhaps, he might come to care for me as he cared for her.

"There, my lady." Dolly set the brush down on the dressing table. "Is there anythin' more I can do for ye?"

I shook my head, eager to be alone. "I would rather you see to Augusta. Her need is far greater."

"Sleep well, my lady." She curtsied, the ghost of a knowing smile on her face. She paused in the doorway and looked back at me, the smile stronger than ever. "Or perhaps no' at all."

The door clicked closed, and I pressed a hand to my burning cheeks.

Staring at myself in the mirror, I took in a long, deep breath. Dolly had brushed my hair until it gleamed, falling down my back and over my shoulders. I had never worn my hair so free in front of a man as I had twice now in front of Sandy. Though it covered more of me than usual, it somehow made me feel bare. What would he think when he saw me?

I reached for the perfume on the table. I wanted to smell and look my best, so I applied it to my wrists and neck, then stilled. Would Sandy like the scent of jasmine?

I put the stopper back in the bottle and rose, fanning myself as though that might disperse the smell and make it less potent. It was useless, though. I hurried over to the water basin and took the cloth there, dipping it into the tepid water and rubbing it on my wrists and neck, glancing at the door every few seconds and straining my ears for the sound of Sandy's footsteps.

The scent lingered on me, but it had dissipated. I looked around the room, unsure what to do now. My gaze lighted on the bed. It was my bed now. No, ours. A bed I had never slept in and would now share with Sandy.

I tried to picture myself under the covers beside him. How would I ever manage even a wink of sleep?

Sleep well. Or perhaps not at all.

The mere thought of Dolly's words—impertinent as they were—lit the flame in my face again. I reached for the tassels draping from the bed-hangings to distract me. All I could think of, however, was the short kiss Sandy and I had shared in the church. What would it be like to kiss him again, this time without an audience? Without being instructed to do so by the vicar?

The door opened, and Sandy appeared, stopping short at the sight of me.

I suppressed the desire to smooth my hair. His gaze took me in from head to foot, and he took a step toward me, his brow knitting with concern.

"You look warm," he said. "Are you well?"

If anything was needed to add fire ravishing my skin, it was those words. He had caught me red-handed—or red-faced—imagining kissing him. And now he thought I looked ill.

"Augusta's room was warm," I lied.

"Oh," he said, frowning even more deeply. "That will not do. I shall call one of the servants to see to it." He strode over to the bell cord.

"No," I said hurriedly.

He paused, looking a question at me.

"She prefers it that way." More lying, and all to cover my own mortification at the thought of kissing my husband.

He came away from the bell pull. "How is she faring?"

"The same as ever, I fear," I replied, eager for a change of subject. "Mornings are generally worse, I think."

He smiled slightly. "She sneezed eight times during the ceremony."

"Did she?"

He nodded, shrugging out of his tailcoat. If he was counting Augusta's sneezes, perhaps I *had* imagined the affection in his eyes. A man saying matrimonial vows to a woman he cared for simply did not count sneezes.

There was silence as he lay his coat over the chair at the writing desk by the window, and the air crackled with tension. I fiddled with the tassels more, unsure what to do with myself. Would he undress right here before me? Should I sit on the bed and draw the hangings to give him privacy?

How very awkward it was to be married for the first time.

He ran a hand over his folded tailcoat distractedly. "I wished to speak with you."

"Oh?" My voice cracked on the word.

He nodded and turned toward me, searching my face until his gaze flicked to my hands.

I pulled them away from the tassel and clasped them before me.

He let out a large breath. "We needn't . . . *do* anything tonight, Juliana."

My mouth slipped open, utterly silent.

"Both of us are tired," he continued. "It has been a long day, as I am certain you will agree. And there is no urgency to . . . producing an heir."

I stood stock-still, speechless. Sandy did not wish to take the final step of the wedding. He did not wish to share his bed with me. Indeed, for his part, the only apparent reason for such a thing would have been to produce an heir. It was duty.

The tingling of oncoming tears pricked my eyes, and I let out a bursting, shaky laugh, turning back to my trusted tassel. "What a relief it is to hear you say that," I said as my throat thickened. "It is precisely what I was hoping for. I *am* so very tired." I forced a yawn, but my body, full of energy from nerves and excitement, refused to produce one. I was certain Sandy was unconvinced by it.

"I shall just return to my bedchamber, then," I said. It occurred to me that all my possessions were now here, though. Would Sandy think I had ordered it to be thus? "Dolly brought my things here—you know she can be a bit overeager—but she can collect them in the morning."

Sandy frowned and looked down at the floor.

"What is it?" I asked.

He didn't respond immediately. "You must do whatever makes you most comfortable."

I stayed where I was, wondering what I had said to bring such a reaction from him. He wanted me elsewhere, did he not? "I have said something to displease you."

He shook his head. "You have not. It is only that. . ." He shook his head again. "It needn't concern us."

"What needn't concern us?"

He let out a sigh, then cleared his throat. "If we do not sleep in the same bedchamber, it may occasion talk amongst the servants—the sort of gossip I would rather avoid."

I swallowed. He was right. I didn't wish for the Duncan servants to be whispering about how their master couldn't even bring himself to share a bed with his new wife. My humiliation was enough without that added weight.

"I shan't regard it, though, Juliana. Not if you prefer to sleep in a different bedchamber."

I shook my head, my heart like lead in my chest. "No, I agree with you."

We stared at one another, wondering what came next.

"I shall just . . ." I went over to the bed, then paused. "Do you prefer the right or left side?"

"I am content to let you choose."

I tried for a grateful smile and pulled back the covers on the right side. I still wore my wrapper, however. With a quick glance at Sandy, I turned my back to him and untied the ribbon, letting the light garment slip off my shoulders. Normally, I would set it on the dressing table chair for Dolly to put away in the morning, but tonight I let it drop to the floor in my urgency to slip under the covers.

I blew out the candle on the bedside table, then turned my back to the side of the bed Sandy would sleep on, taking a deep breath as silently as I could to fend off the threatening tears. There would be no kissing Sandy tonight—and certainly nothing more than that. He had counted Augusta's sneezes during our wedding. He had probably counted the minutes of the celebrations. And now he must be counting himself fortunate to have avoided unwanted intimacy with his new wife.

I clenched my teeth until my jaw ached. I would do anything but let him hear me cry.

The room was silent except for the sound of Sandy removing his garments. I could hear when he removed his waistcoat, then his cravat. His boots, his stockings.

I shut my eyes, wishing I could plug my ears without him noticing. I didn't want my mind trying to conjure images of how he looked without such garments. It was the very last thing I needed.

The covers on my back lifted gently, and the mattress shifted under me as he climbed into bed. It was large, but not so large that two bodies could share it without some contact.

I shifted toward the edge of the bed as inconspicuously as possible until my space was my own. My feet hung over the edge of the mattress, but I didn't regard it. I would sleep on the floor to save Sandy from having to touch me.

Whatever I had thought might occur between us, that was at an end. I would be a wife to Sandy in name, and I would be a proper countess, but that was all. How could I complain? That was what I had come for. And now I had it.

Why, then, did I feel so very despondent?

"Good night, Juliana," his soft voice cut through the silence.

I swallowed the lump in my throat. "Good night."

And then the room was dark.

CHAPTER TWENTY-EIGHT

SANDY

I had slept ill. How restful could sleep be when you were in bed with a woman who wished herself anywhere but there? It was only the threat of servant gossip that had kept her from fleeing the room the moment I told her we needn't let custom force us into doing anything she would rather wait to do.

What a relief it is to hear you say that.

How long had she been dreading our wedding night? That was what I wanted to know. When I had slipped under the covers, she had shifted away until there was space between us, until no part of me was touching her.

With my back to her, I listened to her breathing, for any sign of stirring, but she was peaceful. Taking care, I turned onto my back, wincing when my arm brushed hers, but aside from a deep breath, she remained as she was.

I turned my head, allowing myself a glimpse of her. She was turned toward me, her cheek resting on her hands. She was beautiful and serene and so quiet I almost worried she might not be breathing. A few tendrils fell over the blanket, and I thought to the day we had fallen in the loch, how I had kept her hair from dropping into her soup. I could have sworn then there was something between us.

I had been wrong. But then, that wasn't terribly surprising; I had been wrong about her from the start.

With a little sigh, I slowly slipped out of bed, careful not to wake her. I didn't call for Gillies, doing my best to dress myself. I had a great deal of work ahead of me. Finally, I had the finances at my disposal to bring all our accounts current. There were repairs to tenant properties waiting as well as farming equipment needing to be replaced and modernized. Perhaps it would be enough to keep my mind from Juliana.

I partook of breakfast alone, committing the unpardonable sin of doing so with one of the account books. Cairnie would never forgive me if I spilled on it, but I was desperate for something, anything to distract me.

All three of my brothers stepped into the room just as I was finishing. Iain and Blair looked heavy-lidded and sluggish, and I gathered my cutlery and plates, making as great a din as possible. They had terrified Juliana with their talk of bedding, and I had no sympathy for them.

Iain put a hand to his head and cringed as I let my spoon drop onto my plate. "For heaven's sake, Sandy. Must you make such an infernal racket?"

"Ah, forgive me," I said. "Imbibed a little too freely yesterday, did we?"

He shot me an irritable look as he took a plate from the sideboard. "Didn't think to find *you* here. Thought you would take breakfast abed."

My jaw tightened. "If I had known I would find you here, perhaps I would have."

"Only *you* could manage to be so irritable the morning after your wedding," Blair said as he put a piece of toast on his plate. "Isn't it a bit early in the morning for a newly married man?"

I made no response, ignoring the way Magnus's gaze studied me as he waited for his brothers to pile their plates with food. Underneath my cravat, my neck was warm, mortification coursing through my veins.

"I, for one," said Iain, "am looking forward to having little Sandys running about the castle, so long as they have Juliana's temperament rather than yours."

I slammed the account book shut and rose. "You may be left waiting for quite some time, then." I strode toward the door, but Blair hurried over and stood in front of it, blocking my way.

He looked at me under brows that bunched together in concern. "What does that mean?"

"It means if you do not get out of my way," I said testily, "I will be obliged to throw you and that plate of food into the fireplace."

Ignoring my threat, Iain joined Blair at the door. "You don't intend to give us any nephews and nieces? Not very obliging of you, is it? Not to mention it making no sense. An heir must be produced."

I forced a smile through gritted teeth. "If it was up to me, I would produce fifty heirs to avoid the estate having any chance of descending upon *you*, but, alas, it is not."

They glanced at each other as though trying to interpret my meaning. Blair looked at me again, any trace of humor gone. "Is Juliana . . . is there trouble between you?"

I looked away, though I could feel all three sets of eyes fixed upon me. "Perhaps it slipped your minds—I imagine it is not easy to remember anything else when they are filled with such important matters as how much money to lose at the gaming table or what scrape to get into next—but I was obliged to marry an heiress to save this estate and your futures. I married for money; Juliana married for a title."

There was silence.

"Do you mean she does not wish to . . . produce an heir?" Iain asked.

I forced a large grin. "Why would she be when she has reason to fear they might turn out like you?"

His brows snapped together. "No need to be a cad about it." He stepped away from the door, as did Blair, and guilt swam in my stomach.

I shut my eyes and let out a large sigh. I *was* being a cad. My pride was hurt, and I was taking it out on my brothers. "Forgive me." I turned to face them. "I should not have said that. If Juliana fears an heir following in anyone's footsteps in this room, it would obviously be mine."

Blair came over and put a hand on my shoulder. "That is not true, Sandy. If she is hesitant to . . . well, you know"—he cleared his throat—"it is likely because you gave her reason to be so."

"Is this your idea of reassuring someone?" I asked wryly.

"What I mean is that perhaps she thinks *you* do not wish for that. One couldn't blame her after the way you acted when we mentioned the bedding yesterday."

I turned toward him, forcing his hand from my shoulder. "You mean when you terrified her by threatening to make yourself a participant in the marriage bed?"

He couldn't help a small smile. "It was only in jest, Sandy."

I shook my head. "It hardly matters. I have too many things on my plate to worry over such things now."

"Don't be daft," Iain said, stabbing his fork full of meat. "She's your wife, Sandy, and it's obvious you fancy her."

I scoffed. "You would have me force myself on her, no doubt?"

"No," he said, shoving the food into his mouth and chewing. He didn't wait until he had swallowed to speak again. "Start small. Don't overwhelm her, but for heaven's sake, do *something* to ensure she knows you welcome that sort of thing." He shrugged. "Kiss her."

My heart sped, but I gave a little snort. As though it was so easy to kiss one's wife!

"He is right," Magnus said. "You've already done it once—"

Iain and Blair shared a victorious, conspiratorial look.

"—so, it won't take her off her guard."

"We were ordered to by the vicar last time." I pointed at Iain and Blair. "And don't think I don't know you put him up to it."

"That is precisely why it is the perfect step to take," Blair said, "but this time of your own accord. A simple but effective message to send—and a perfect way to gauge *her* interest."

I wanted to believe them. I wanted to do what they said, but the thought terrified me. What if Juliana was disgusted? And how, for that matter, was I to kiss her in the first place? Simply go up to her right now and do so? Wait for the perfect moment, supposing there was such a thing? I hadn't the slightest idea how to go about kissing my wife.

"Go on," Iain said, shooing me with his hands. "You can report back to us in the morning. Then we can plan the next steps."

"Very tempting," I said, pulling the door open, "but I think I shall pass, as none of you are qualified to offer any advice on this matter."

All they had done was fill my mind with thoughts of kissing my wife—as though it hadn't been already.

CHAPTER TWENTY-NINE

JULIANA

The left side of the bed was empty. Sandy must have risen early and left the bedchamber.

I, on the other hand, remained under the covers, staring up at the ceiling until I knew not what time. Dolly, who had made a habit of coming in at the same time every morning, did not do so today. She would wait to be summoned, and I knew why.

I sighed. She needn't have waited, but I was glad for the time to myself. The bed smelled like Sandy—his pillow even more so—and I wasn't yet ready to leave my thoughts or the imprint in the bed where he had lain.

I would drive myself mad, though, thinking of him and wishing things had been different last night, so I smoothed the sheets where he had slept, turned his pillow over, and threw the covers off, yanking on the nearest bell pull.

I could languish and regret and dwell, or I could put myself to good use and act like Lady Lismore.

I braced myself for Dolly's comments, laced with heavy implication as they would be. But perhaps she sensed my mood, for she confined her comments to questions about my attire and hair.

Once she had left, I went to my dressing table and took the vial of jasmine perfume, dabbing it on my wrists and neck. A countess should smell good, no matter how her husband felt about her—or didn't feel about her.

During the long, restless night, it had occurred to me that his reasons for not wishing to do more than sleep next to one another might be centered around Nelly. He had believed for so long that he would be marrying her, perhaps he found it difficult to face marriage to *me*. Our betrothal had been so abrupt and short. Did he feel as though he was betraying her or himself by showing me affection he didn't feel?

It was a lowering thought, but there was a glimmer of hope in it. He, though a man of duty, desired love. If he had come to love her, perhaps he might come to care for me in time. That was what I held onto as I left my bedchamber and walked to the stairwell.

I took the narrow, winding steps quickly. Whoever had built the castle might have given more serious consideration to making three normal stairwells rather than two small ones and one enormous one. The stairs were uneven, too, requiring me to concentrate on my foot placement to prevent myself from falling.

"Oh—"

The voice came just as I collided with Sandy's solid form on his way up the stairs.

I put a hand to my head where it had collided with his chin, which he rubbed.

"Forgive me," I said. "I was watching my footing."

"Are you hurt?" he asked, trying to peer at my head in the dim light afforded by the slim window nearby.

"As much as you, I imagine," I said with an attempt at a laugh.

"I congratulate you on the sturdiness of your head."

"And I you on that of your chin."

He gave a little bow, a half-smile pulling at one side of his mouth.

"I was just on my way to speak with you," I said.

"Oh?"

I nodded. "I hoped we might discuss a few renovations to the castle—and see whether you would let me manage them."

His eyes searched mine. "I am happy to discuss anything you wish. Perhaps we could meet in the study? I just need to fetch something in my bedchamber."

"Certainly."

"I shall come presently," he said.

I smiled my agreement, and both of us hesitated.

"I shall just . . ." I tried to slip past him, but the stairwell was narrow, and my body was pressed against his before I realized my error. I had admired his broad chest enough times that it shouldn't have come as a surprise to find we could not easily fit past one another in the space.

"My apologies," I said, trying to ignore the way my mind insisted on detailing every point of contact between our bodies.

"It is quite all right, I assure you."

My eyes flew to his, which widened.

"That is," he clarified, "you needn't apologize."

I couldn't tell whether it was my heart or his I felt thudding against our chests, but I sucked in and, back grating against the wall, tried to slide past him as quickly as possible. The bodice of my dress resisted, and I looked down to find one of the buttons of his waistcoat had snagged on the trim of my dress.

"Oh dear," I said, wondering why I had ever left the safety of the bed.

"Ah," he said, noting the problem. "Allow me to just . . ." He put his hands to the button, his hands grazing my body as he worked to untangle us. I looked down to watch his progress, and our heads knocked together again.

He winced but kept at his work. "Again, a very sturdy head."

"Thank you," I said in a strangled voice, leaning my head back and looking up at the ceiling to prevent any other mishap. His fingers worked, brushing against my ribs, which seemed to close in on my lungs. Would we be stuck in this stairwell forever?

"There," he said as the tug of tension on my dress released.

I shifted to the side to put distance between us, letting out a breath and thanking him.

"It was my pleasure," he said. His eyes widened. "That is . . . I am pleased to have been a help."

I nodded, my nerves fraying like an old rope. "The study, then?"

"The study," he confirmed.

"Very good."

"Very good."

With one final meeting of gazes, we both turned and continued on our ways.

I had managed to regain most of my composure once Sandy entered the study a few minutes later. He, too, seemed calm and unruffled, and the subject was left alone while we discussed the more urgent needs of the castle interior.

"Perhaps we could begin with the great hall," I suggested. "I imagine the plasterwork was its most eye-catching feature at one time."

He moved one sketch of the castle's architectural plans in

favor of another. "A time long past, but yes. There is a painting in one of the upstairs bedchambers that shows it in all its glory."

"That is fortunate," I said. "Shall we attempt to recreate it, then?"

"It was certainly beautiful," he said, "but this is your home now, too, Juliana. You may decorate as you see fit."

I nodded, somewhat breathless.

His mouth pulled up on one side, displaying the half-smile I was coming to love so much. "First, though, I think we had better get that ladder in the library."

I laughed. "Naturally."

"And a new billiards table, I think."

I adopted a deep frown. "Oh, it would be a shame to do anything that takes away from the quaintness of the castle."

His lips pulled into a wide smile, and I swallowed.

It wasn't good for my health to make Sandy smile, I decided. "I should go see how Augusta is getting on today, I think."

He nodded. "I have a number of things to see to, as well. I shall be occupied most of the week with surveying the tenant lands, but we can speak in the mornings or evenings about whatever issues you find."

My cheeks heated at the mention of evenings, and I offered a quick smile, then left.

Augusta was sitting by the window in her room, a few used handkerchiefs sitting on the sill beside her. I felt a wave of guilt looking at her. She had been so confined, so miserable since our arrival, and our only real venture out of doors had only aggravated her ill health, it had seemed.

Now that I was married, there was no real reason to keep her here. I no longer required a companion, and though I could hardly bear the thought of her leaving me, I could not be selfish.

"How are you, cousin?" I asked as I shut the door.

She sniffed and smiled at me. "Well enough, my dear. More importantly, how are *you*?" She blinked rapidly and wiped one of the tears escaping her eyes with a handkerchief.

"Oh, Augusta," I said, hurrying over to her. "What is it?"

She laughed. "I am not crying. Do not be deceived. It is merely part of this summer catarrh, the doctor says. My eyes *and* nose leak."

I sighed, putting a hand on her arm. "Cousin, I think the time has come."

"The time for what?"

"For you to go," I said. "To rejoin Papa."

She turned, looking at me with a furrowed brow.

"You will get along so much better there. I cannot bear seeing you in such misery here, and I have no need of a chaperone anymore."

"Nonsense," she said, folding her handkerchief. "I shall be right in a trifle."

I pressed my lips together. Her eyes had been pink and heavy-lidded since our arrival. Her symptoms seemed worse rather than better. With each day, her nose became rawer, her lids droopier. I would write Papa to see if he could come to Lochlarren and take her back to Newcastle with him, or Edinburgh, even.

So much had changed since the wedding yesterday, and yet nothing at all. I was "my lady" now, no matter how strange it sounded to my ear. I was consulted about the menu for the

---

week and about employing Mrs. Boyle's niece as a maid to replace Dolly.

The housekeeper seemed to have relented to me a bit. Perhaps it was because she realized I had the power to deny her niece—or herself—a place at Lochlarren, or perhaps it was because the wedding had occurred and she realized it was a useless fight. Whatever the reason, I was grateful for it. I had no desire to exhaust myself with challenging her or vying for power. I felt enough of an imposter as it was.

I dreaded when bedtime would inevitably arrive and kept myself busy with plans for renovation all through the afternoon and even in the drawing room after dinner. All my efforts were for naught, however. My mind *would* insist on wondering whether Sandy would bring up the subject of an heir. He had said there was no rush to it, but what did that mean?

Frustrated with my stubborn thoughts, I retired before the men had finished their port, summoning Dolly to prepare me for bed.

Sandy arrived just as Dolly was leaving, and my heart raced as he smiled at her and closed the door behind her.

"How was your day, Juliana?" he asked.

"Good," I replied, ignoring all the moments of despair that had punctuated the hours. I took a seat on my side of the bed. "Productive, I think. What of yours?"

"The same," he said with a smile. "I have my work cut out for me at the tenant properties, of course." He untied his cravat and pulled it from his neck. "We only made it through perhaps a quarter of the surveyal today. So much has been neglected for so long. It is little wonder the tenants are wary of me." He looked down, working at the buttons of his waistcoat. My gaze fixed on them, thinking of the way one of them had caught on my dress earlier and how being so near him had taken the air straight from my lungs.

"You shall prove them wrong soon enough," I said vacantly, my thoughts still occupied.

He started with the buttons on his shirt, undoing them more quickly than I would have thought possible. "I shall. Underneath their frustrations, they are all curious about you, of course."

I nodded, my eyes flitting to the skin of his chest visible as he undid the top buttons, and then his stomach as he made his way down the line. He untucked the bottom of his shirt from his pantaloons, then pulled the shirt off over his head and tossed it over the nearest chair. His upper half was entirely visible now, revealing every line and crest his wet shirt had teased me with the day of the incident on the loch.

A second or two had passed when I realized his gaze had flitted to me.

I cleared my throat and slipped into bed, turning my eyes to the wall. "I hope I shan't disappoint them."

"Impossible," he said.

I stole a quick glance at him as he pulled a nightshirt over his head, quickly covering the view of his body. Before his head was through the neck hole, I averted my gaze again.

How long would we be required to share a bedchamber before it became acceptable for us to sleep separately? I knew there *was* a bedchamber for the mistress, for Mrs. Boyle had shown it to me on the tour. I wasn't certain how my composure would survive many nights of sharing a bedchamber with my husband.

I pulled the covers up, and shortly after, he joined me in the bed. I scooted toward the edge again to make room for him, until my knees hung over the edge.

"Juliana," he said with a hint of a smile in his voice, "this is your bed too. You needn't fall off trying to accommodate me."

I laughed shakily and slid back in so that my knees were

supported. It put my back against him. At least I didn't disgust him so much he couldn't bear to touch me.

The bed shifted under me as he rose onto his elbow, looking down at me. There was a moment's pause with nothing but the beating of my heart to break the silence, then he leaned over and placed a kiss upon my cheek. "Sleep well, Juliana."

He blew out his candle, and I blew out mine, wondering if I would sleep a wink with my cheek tingling with heat the way it was.

It had been at least an hour, perhaps a year, when he turned from his back to his side, facing me as he breathed in slow, rhythmic deep sleep. I looked over my shoulder at him, his face so near mine, yet unconsciously so. In the dark, I could just make out some of his features and the hair that hovered over his brow.

Slowly, I turned toward him, allowing myself the luxury of watching him sleep for a short time, to note the rise and fall of his chest, the contrast of his lashes against his skin, and the hair tickling his forehead with each exhale. Slowly, carefully, I reached my finger to it and moved it out of his face, holding my breath in case the gesture woke him.

He was still as ever, though, and I sighed, wondering how many women like me had unintentionally begun to fall in love with their husbands.

CHAPTER THIRTY

SANDY

"Well?" Iain looked at me expectantly, arms folded across his chest as I gathered a few papers from the study.

"There is a reason I did not breakfast at the same time as you, Iain."

"Did you kiss her?" he asked, ignoring my roundabout way of informing him I did not plan to discuss the subject with him. I needed *someone* to help me know how to approach things with Juliana, but Iain was not my first choice, or even my tenth.

"If you must know," I said, tapping the papers on the desk to organize them, "I did."

"And?" he asked. "How did she respond? Did she kiss you back?"

I set the papers in the portfolio to take with me to the tenant properties, not meeting his gaze. "As it was a kiss on the cheek, she couldn't very well have."

Iain threw a hand at me. "A kiss on the cheek? What rubbish! One kisses one's mother on the cheek, Sandy."

"I am treading carefully," I said in annoyance.

"No, Sandy," he said. "You are being a coward. Take the woman's face in your hands and kiss her properly!"

I wanted to. And I had nearly kissed her on the lips last night, only she was turned away. It would have been awkward and clumsy and cumbersome, and I was a coward. There. I admitted it. I had been too scared to try it—in the stairwell or in the study or in bed. What would happen if she rejected me?

On the other hand, she *had* watched me undress. I had thought it was admiration in her eyes, but perhaps she had been so transfixed out of fear of what I might be expecting afterward. She had certainly turned away in a hurry.

But when I had teased her about falling over the edge of the bed, she had listened, hadn't she? She hadn't recoiled, either, when I had kissed her cheek. *That* was something.

Barely.

There was a knock on the door.

"Come in," I said, preparing myself to defend my cowardice to Blair as well. But it was Juliana who entered. She peeked inside, glancing at me, then Iain.

"Oh, forgive me," she said. "I wasn't aware you were with anyone."

"No, no," I hurried to say before she closed the door. "It is only Iain."

He scowled at me.

"Is there something I can assist with?" I asked her.

"Only if it isn't an inconvenience," she replied.

"Not in the least." I set down my portfolio and waited as she entered, a frame in hand.

"It is nothing terribly pressing," Juliana said, walking toward me. "I have just been thinking about the ceiling of the great hall, you know, and I found the painting you mentioned. I thought I would try to match the look from it, including the paint colors—preserve the history as much as possible." She looked at me, uncertainty in her eyes. "If, that is, you are agreeable?"

I didn't respond immediately, finding my throat strangely thick and unwilling to carry sound. The great hall had been fine in its heyday, but it was certainly not what one would call *in modern style*. Most people redecorating would be glad for the opportunity to start afresh and follow the newer trends—to make it into something to awe and to draw admiration. I had given Juliana free reign so that she could make this castle into a place she could love. She was choosing to bring it to its former glory, and that meant a great deal to me.

"Of course, I am open to other ideas," she said when I didn't reply.

I cleared my throat. "No, no. I am very much in agreement with you on this. Besides which, I trust your judgment implicitly."

She hesitated, and I realized my comment might have given her to believe I didn't wish for her to seek my advice on such topics. That couldn't have been further from the truth.

I cleared my throat. "Though, I should perhaps see the painting again to be sure." I could hardly have been more contradictory if I had tried, but Juliana seemed not to mind.

She came behind the desk and set the framed painting in the space I created. "The painting itself is a bit faded," she said, resting a hand on the desk and leaning over it, "but I thought you might know whether this is more of a scarlet or a crimson." She pointed at the walls in the painting.

I stole a glance at her profile beside me. Her hair was becomingly pulled into a bun at the nape of her neck. I couldn't help remembering her hair on our wedding night, falling over her shoulders so freely. I hadn't seen it thus since and wasn't certain I would.

"It is difficult to say," I said. It wasn't. It was scarlet. But I liked having Juliana near me, to have her shoulder touch mine and for her not to retract.

"I rather think," I said slowly, "that it is scarlet."

She stood straight. "That was my thought, as well. I shall try to match it as nearly as is possible."

She smiled, and I smiled back, and for a moment, we looked at one another. I could accustom myself very easily to working with Juliana on projects. Too easily.

"Working on improvements to the castle, are you?" Iain asked. "Perhaps you could see to the stuffing in my mattress next."

"I think that is a low priority on her list," I replied.

"That will depend entirely upon your behavior toward me, Iain," she said in a rallying tone.

"Or," he said significantly, "perhaps my behavior toward *you* would be improved by better sleep."

She laughed and picked up the paper. "We are agreed upon the scarlet, then?"

"The scarlet," I verified, almost wishing she would argue for the crimson, but she was gone as soon as she had come—a woman with a mission to accomplish.

She shut the door, and Iain stared at me slyly.

I shot him a look and picked up my portfolio.

"That is a woman needing a proper kissing, Sandy," he said as I walked toward the door.

He didn't need to tell me. Juliana had her mission, and I had mine: garner the courage to do just as Iain said.

I looked forward to dinner, for it was there I could rely on discovering more about my wife. I learned of her life in

Newcastle, I listened to her laugh, I watched her draw Magnus out of his shell with questions about his time in the army. In short, I felt more drawn to her than ever—and more uncertain what to do with my growing feelings, with my ever-increasing wish to be near her.

When the time came to retire for the evening, I did as I had done the night before: gave her time to prepare for bed before coming in to do so myself. Gillies often helped me undress in the evenings, but I had given him the night off, just as I had the night prior. I was anxious for the time alone with Juliana—and I intended to put my plan into play.

She was seated at the dressing table on her side of the bed, wearing her dressing gown, the plait of brown hair hanging down her back. Her eyes met mine in the mirror. She had been so relaxed at dinner, but there was a tightness in her bearing now that made me wonder if I was a fool to even consider kissing her.

I had a feeling, though, that the longer I waited, the harder it would become. We were still in the infancy of our marriage, which meant we had not yet established patterns and habits. If I did not make kissing her one of those, it would make it more significant and riskier when I *did*.

I sat on the edge of the bed to remove my boots, my heart hammering far more quickly than was natural for such an innocuous activity.

"How are things with the tenants?" she asked.

I chuckled wryly and stood. "In a state. But we will come about, thanks to you." I wanted her to know how much I appreciated what she had made possible by marrying me. "What of your plans for improvements to the castle?"

"Tomorrow we should have paint for the great hall, though the plaster must be seen to before some of the painting can happen."

I tugged on the sleeve of my tailcoat, cursing my choice to wear my most tightly fitting one when I didn't have Gillies to assist me out of it. It had been quite a chore to put it on this morning. Perhaps that was why his eye twinkled when I gave him the evening off—he knew what a task I would have peeling it from my body.

Glancing at the mirror to ensure Juliana was not looking, I turned my back to her and yanked on my left sleeve. The fabric was unyielding, as though it had been sewn to the fabric of the shirt beneath. I tried the other one, to no avail. Rolling my shoulders back, I shook them subtly, hoping to dislodge the coat.

A sound from Juliana's direction made me still. I turned enough to glance over at her. She was trying and failing to mask a smile as she watched me in the mirror.

"Would you care for some assistance?" she asked.

My mouth twitched at the corner. "If you would not mind, that would be very helpful."

She rose and came over to me. "Perhaps I should have waited. It would have been fascinating to see what other methods you attempted."

"Thank you for *not* prolonging my torture," I said as she stood in front of me.

She slid her hands up into the coat and over my shoulders, pushing on the fabric. My heart thumped, and I wondered if perhaps I should dismiss Gillies and instead ask Juliana for help every day. The coat resisted her efforts, though.

"I quite see the problem now," she said, pushing more forcefully. "If only your shoulders were not so broad . . . you must roll them back."

I did as instructed, forcing my mind away from noticing how close she was to me or the feeling of her palms on my shoulders.

Little by little, the coat yielded, finally slipping over my shoulders. She pulled at the edge of one coat sleeve, then the other, until I was free from my cage.

"There," she said, slightly breathless as she laid the coat over a nearby chair.

I shook out my shoulders. "I think it is time I gave that coat to Blair or Iain."

"Oh, don't do that," she said, smoothing its fabric. "It looks so well on you."

My eyes flicked to hers, but her focus was on the coat. I put my hands to my cravat and worked at its knot. It was not the usual one, however, and my fingers struggled to find their way.

Juliana looked over at me, watching me for a time, a growing smile on her face. She raised her brows.

I dropped my hands and sighed. "Evidently, I made the wrong choice to give Gillies the night off."

She walked over, and I lifted my chin to give her the space to work. Each brush of her skin on my neck made my lungs constrict.

"Good heavens," she said. "Is your valet a sailor? Wherever did he learn to tie such a complicated knot?"

I chuckled as I felt the fabric finally give way and reached my hands to finish the job. They tangled with Juliana's, and our eyes caught and held.

This. This was the time to kiss her. I felt it in my bones. I could almost hear Iain whispering in my ear, "Don't be a coward. Kiss your wife, Sandy. Kiss her properly." I looked into Juliana's eyes, which gazed up at me, wide and questioning. What *was* the question, though? Was it, "What are you waiting for?" or "Why are you looking at me that way?"

Perhaps I should ask her which it was.

Her gaze suddenly broke from mine, and her hands dropped. "That should be enough to help you get the rest undone." She walked toward the bed and pulled her covers back.

Unmoving, I watched her for a moment. I had missed my chance, but I wasn't certain whether it was because I had taken too long or because she hadn't wanted what she had seen coming.

There was no veering of her gaze in my direction as there had been last night while I finished undressing, and I sighed as I set everything on the chair for Gillies to see to in the morning.

I blew out my candle and climbed into bed beside her. The only bit of reassurance I found was in the way she didn't move when our bodies came in contact. Maybe tomorrow. I would not be such a coward tomorrow.

CHAPTER THIRTY-ONE

JULIANA

Papa's letter arrived the next day. As Augusta showed no signs of improving, he agreed she should leave Lochlarren and join him in Edinburgh, where he would be spending a week on business matters before returning to Newcastle. His letter made me smile, for he was full of good news about investors and buyers. My marriage to Sandy was doing precisely as we had hoped it would do.

And yet, I wanted more. I had thought Sandy might kiss me last night. I could have sworn he was considering it. And yet, the moment had stretched on so long—too long for a man who wanted to do such a thing.

"Papa shall arrive in a few days," I said to Augusta as we walked on the lawn outside. We never came outdoors without Augusta's symptoms worsening, but she had insisted, and I couldn't blame her. She had been cooped up far too long. "He wishes for you to join him in Edinburgh and then back in Newcastle."

She stopped walking, and I followed suit. There was a

crease to her brow as she looked at me. "But . . . but what of you? How can I leave you?"

I lifted my shoulders and looked up at the towering castle. "I shall remain here. This is my new home."

She swallowed, and there was a pause.

I pulled her hands into mine. "I wish for you to feel well again, cousin. It has been terribly selfish of me to keep you here even this long."

She looked down at our hands. "I should remain here, Juliana. Perhaps you will wish for someone at your side when the time comes for your confinement. You may need care even before then—perhaps quite soon."

The heat rose in my cheeks like a fiery sunset, and I looked down. She took it for granted there would be a pregnancy— and soon. Of course she did, because that was what normally occurred. It was the prescribed course of events.

"I do not anticipate such a thing will be necessary," I said, trying to keep my voice even.

I felt her eyes on me as she replied, "You cannot know that, Juliana. Many women feel gravely ill in the early months."

"I do know it." I looked up at her, and her eyes searched mine.

"What do you mean, my dear?"

I hesitated before responding. Augusta had never been married. She had no experience in this, and yet I craved for someone to reassure me, to tell me there was nothing wrong with me. "Lord Lismore is not in haste to produce an heir."

Her brows furrowed, and silence took over yet again. "I do not understand. Do you mean to say . . . you have not . . .?"

I shook my head and looked out toward the loch, forcing a smile. "It is his title, so he must decide how to go about securing its future."

"But, Juliana," she said, leaving the thought unfinished as a sneeze took over.

I began walking again. "Let us talk of something else. And perhaps return indoors. Your eyes are looking puffier than ever."

She stopped me with a hand on my arm. "Juliana, have you any idea why the earl wishes to delay securing an heir to the title?"

I shook my head. Far from reassuring me, this conversation was making me feel my inadequacy even more fully. "To tell you the truth, I have wondered if perhaps his heart is still engaged to Miss Cochrane. This all happened so suddenly, Augusta, and they were intended for one another from a young age. I cannot imagine it has been easy for him to accept so many changes to his future, all at the same time."

She sighed, and we continued our walk. "No, I am sure it has not been easy. But . . . well, we must hope his sense of duty will prevail."

I said nothing, for duty was the last thing I wished to motivate Sandy toward me.

Augusta returned to her bedchamber, while I asked one of the maids to take tea to her. I felt restless, needing something to occupy my mind to keep it from avenues I didn't dare let it explore. It seemed to veer toward a melancholy sort of despair on the one hand or a vibrant, overenthusiastic hope on the other.

Work was the best solution—I had seen it carry Papa through his grief over my mother's death. I sometimes wondered if that was why he *still* worked so hard. My plans for the great hall were in my bedchamber, and I hurried up the stairs to retrieve them. Today, I hoped to discover who we could employ to see to the plasterwork on the ceiling.

"Juliana."

I stopped in the stairwell at the sound of Sandy's voice coming from below.

I descended a few steps, meeting him near the bottom. He had on a riding coat and boots, and he held his top hat in one hand. Perhaps it would have been simpler to keep my mind on a reasonable path if he didn't manage to look so very handsome all the time.

"I only thought I would ask if you are in need of anything," he said, standing on the step just below mine. It made us nearly the same height, giving me a perspective into his eyes I hadn't before enjoyed. And I *did* enjoy it, even in the dim light of the stairwell. "I am on my way out with Cairnie for more surveying."

"It is kind of you to ask," I said. Part of me wished to invent a need if only to keep him here with me. But he had his own matters to see to, and I did not wish to force him. I wanted him to seek me out of his own accord. "I think things are well in hand, though."

He nodded, his gaze fixed on me in a strange way, as though he had something more to say. His eyes searched mine for a moment. "Then I shall see you later."

I smiled softly at him, and he hesitated still. He took one of my hands in his, then leaned in to press his lips against mine.

I sucked in a surprised breath as our mouths met. The kiss was gentle and soft, our lips pressed together while my heart pounded hard and fast.

He pulled back, my hand still clasped between his fingers. "Until this afternoon."

"Until this afternoon," I managed to croak out as his hand dropped mine, and he turned and left.

I stayed in the stairwell long after the large wooden door had closed behind him, trying to understand what had just occurred.

Sandy had kissed me goodbye. That was all. We were husband and wife, and he had said farewell for the day in a way natural to two married people. And then he had rushed off.

I tried to convince myself that the kiss meant little. Yet, my mind insisted on traversing the glittering path of hope, demanding I relive every second—all two of them—and look for any hint or sign that it might have been motivated by more.

By the time dinner arrived, I had worked myself up into an embarrassing state, looking through the windows of the great hall every five minutes for sign of his return. Would he kiss me then, as well? It seemed only fitting that a departure kiss would be met with a return one. It was a matter of reason and sense, really. My feelings for Sandy had nothing to do with it.

A visit from Augusta to see my renovation progress, however, must have made me miss his arrival. Dolly informed me Gillies was already assisting his lord in dressing for dinner. I told her I wished to do the same, swallowing the disappointment I felt at the lost kiss.

By the time we went upstairs, Sandy was already in his tailcoat—the same one I had helped him out of last night. My gaze tripped to his cravat, and I noted with a flutter of hope that it was the same knot as last night's. Would he need my assistance this evening, as well?

He smiled at me. "Good evening."

"Good evening," I replied as Dolly went to retrieve a dress for me. I glanced at Gillies, who was taking care of the clothing Sandy had been wearing earlier. I could not kiss my husband in front of his valet and my maid.

Could I?

I hesitated, as Sandy fiddled with his collar.

"Here, my lady," Dolly said, laying a yellow dress on the bed.

"I must speak with Iain for a moment," Sandy said. "I shall see you at dinner, though."

"Of course," I said, smiling.

He nodded, sending me one more glance before Gillies opened the door for him and he disappeared.

I suppressed a sigh and turned to look at the dress Dolly had taken out for me. I had only worn it once before, but I remembered the line of buttons up the back. What would happen if I gave Dolly the evening off?

My insides warmed at the thought of Sandy undoing the buttons for me, and I shut my eyes tightly. What woman in her right mind schemed to force her husband to be close to her? And yet . . .

Had Sandy not worn the impossibly tight tailcoat again? And adopted the same complicated knot in his cravat?

"Dolly," I said as she helped me shed my day dress, "would you like to take this evening off?"

She paused draping the dress over her arm to look at me. "My lady?"

"You have been working so hard, and I would like you to have an evening to yourself."

She smiled gratefully. "'Tis too kind of ye, my lady!"

"Nonsense. It is well-deserved." The look of hesitation on her face gave me pause. "What is it?"

"'Tis only . . . well, if it suits ye, of course, my lady, perhaps I could have tomorrow evenin' instead? There's a wee party at my uncle's house and . . ."

"Of course, of course," I said. "That suits me quite well."

She grinned widely, and I stifled a sigh. My scheming would have to wait.

CHAPTER THIRTY-TWO

SANDY

As it turned out, kissing one's wife goodbye was a different matter than kissing her good night. There was note of finality and the safety of departure in the first, while the second was rife with possibility and uncertainty. What would happen *after* I kissed her good night?

I considered telling Juliana I wished to discuss the matter of an heir, but it had only been a few days since the wedding. Besides, it wasn't the truth. An heir was not on my mind. Juliana was on my mind. It was our marriage I wished to discuss, but just as Iain had said, I was a coward. I was too afraid to tell Juliana I had begun to desire more from our marriage than simple convenience or a business arrangement. It seemed the height of presumption to do so. What if she did not share my feelings? It would create an unbearable awkwardness, possibly ruining the terms we were now upon.

And how could I expect her to share my feelings? I had explicitly assured her I would not be a demanding husband. Telling her I wanted not just her money and her hand in marriage but her heart also was surely as much as it was possible to demand of a woman.

So, instead, I watched her, looking for signs my wishes were shared to some degree or another—or might be shared in the future. I could wait if that was all that was required. I had kissed her earlier today, an act of selfish bravery immediately followed by a cowardly retreat. She had pulled away the slightest bit at first, enough to make me wonder whether it was surprise or distaste which had caused it. But then she had seemed to settle into it, perhaps even kissing me back?

Cairnie had been obliged to repeat himself on five different occasions due to my head being in the clouds afterward. I didn't miss the irony of the situation. After so many weeks of preoccupation with my inability to see to all the problems facing the estate, now that I had the capital to do so, I could not focus on them.

Juliana had a restless energy about her as she helped me out of my tailcoat and cravat, and I wondered whether it was due to our kiss earlier. Was I moving too quickly, making her uneasy? I wanted to kiss her again and again, but I reigned in my selfish instincts and merely thanked her for her assistance, hoping the fact that I had allowed her to help me when Gillies might have done so would send her the message that I craved her near me.

When I woke in the middle of the night to find her arm draped across my chest and her face turned toward me, I barely breathed for fear she might wake and pull it away. I prayed it was a sign of things to come. I could be patient until then. I would not rush her or assume she felt the way I did.

"Are you going out again? To the tenant farms?"

I stopped with my fingers around the handle of the front door, turning to see Juliana at the bottom of the main staircase. "I am," I said. And I was late doing so, for I had spent no less than twenty minutes pacing in the study, trying to decide whether to kiss Juliana goodbye again. My steward, Cairnie, would already be there, waiting. "Do you need something?" The hope in my voice was so obvious, it was embarrassing.

"We found two men to work on the plaster," she said. "The great hall will look quite different when you return later today, I think."

I smiled. "I shall look forward to seeing your hard work in progress."

"I would like to see yours, as well. Perhaps I can come along with you one of these days."

It was entirely possible I was grinning from ear to ear. I couldn't help myself. I was an utter and complete fool, feeling like a king because my wife had given an indication she would like to spend more time with me. "I would like that very much, Juliana."

"I would too."

We looked at each other for a moment and, without letting myself think for another moment, I strode over to her, took her hand in mine just as I had done yesterday, and kissed her. She didn't pull back this time, almost as though she had been expecting it. Dare I hope she had come for it?

I wanted to linger there, I wanted to explore, to say with my lips what I had not yet managed to voice to her. But I would not push my good fortune.

I pulled back and forced myself to look at her this time. "Until this afternoon."

"Until this afternoon," she repeated, looking at me in a way that nearly made me send one of the footmen to tell the steward I would not, in fact, be coming today.

I released her hand, allowing myself one quick glance at her as I closed the door behind me. How did she manage to look more beautiful with every day that passed?

I took in a deep breath as I made my way toward the stables. Juliana would be here when I returned. There was plenty of time.

I had my foot in the stirrup, ready to mount my horse, when I noticed a carriage approaching over the stone bridge that led to Lochlarren. I recognized it at once as the Cochranes' chaise.

I led my horse from the stables toward the courtyard, wondering if I would have to inform my steward I would not be there after all.

The postilion opened the door, and Nelly descended, smiling at me. He shut the door behind her, making it clear she was alone.

"Good morning," she said, walking over to me and offering me her hand. "I thought to come pay a visit. I have been wanting to, but Mama has been ill, and I decided I would rather not wait any longer."

"I am very sorry to hear she is ill," I replied, kissing the back of her glove.

"Are you leaving or arriving?" she asked, noting my attire.

"Leaving, I am afraid," I replied.

"That is quite all right. I came primarily to visit Lady Lismore. Do you have time for a quick stroll around the castle, though?"

"Of course," I said, looping the reins of my horse around the nearby wooden post.

She took my arm and led the way to the path that circled Lochlarren. "How are you faring?"

"Well," I replied. "Occupied with all manner of business, of course. Tenant and castle improvements, for the most part."

She nodded. "I imagine so. It must be a relief to be setting such things in motion."

"It *is*. They are desperately needed, as you know."

"I do know," she replied, "for they are the precise reasons you are married now, but not to me."

I glanced over at her, and she smiled ruefully. "If only you could have waited a bit longer."

I frowned. "I do not understand."

She stopped and faced me. "My situation has changed, Sandy. Aunt Georgie died a few days ago." Her gaze became more intent. "She left me her fortune."

I took in a long, slow breath. I wasn't certain what to say. What *was* there to say? "It was not I who ended things, Nelly," I reminded her softly.

She nodded, looking down. "I know. But it wasn't *I* who arranged so swiftly for an alternative."

I grimaced, but inside, my hackles were rising. "Straits were dire, Nelly. More dire than you know. I did what duty required of me."

She looked at me for a long moment, then nodded and turned to walk again. "And how *is* Lady Lismore?"

"She is well," I said, aware I was smiling at the mention of her. "Busy with plans for Lochlarren. The great hall will be the first room transformed."

"I hope not *too* much transformed," she replied.

"No, she hopes to restore it to its original splendor even though I gave her free reign to do as she pleases."

"It is good she has something to occupy her time. It cannot be easy to trade a life in town for one here. I imagine she misses it greatly."

I only nodded. I didn't want to think Juliana was discontent at Lochlarren, but perhaps it was more difficult for her than I realized. When I was in town, I craved the fresh air and simplicity of life at Lochlarren. It was entirely possible she felt the opposite. I hated the thought that she might dislike it here.

"I shouldn't keep Cairnie waiting any longer," I said as we reached the front of the castle again. "Shall I escort you inside to Juliana?"

Nelly regarded me thoughtfully for a moment, then shook her head. "I can find my way."

It was true. She knew Lochlarren well.

"Very well, then." I took her hand in mine. "You will make a brilliant match, Nelly. I am certain of it."

She tried for a smile. "Perhaps so. I simply cannot help thinking what might have been." She took her hand from mine and walked toward the castle.

I let out a long breath as I watched her make her way to the front door. I hated to see her unhappy, but I couldn't find it in myself to regret how things had happened. I had been angry at first, of course. To have so much happen in quick succession—Father's death, the title and debts descending upon me, Lord Cochrane informing me a match between Nelly and me would no longer be possible, and the arranging of a marriage to Juliana—had produced a bitterness in me for a time.

But no longer.

Father had saddled me with a great number of things I hadn't wanted, but my marriage to Juliana was no longer one of them.

CHAPTER THIRTY-THREE

JULIANA

The sound of chipping plaster and the dust it generated surrounded me as I stared through the window, watching my husband as he watched Nelly Cochrane walk to the castle doors. The expression on his face —the wistfulness, the small smile—intensified the heavy feeling in my stomach that had long been growing..

The feeling began as I watched them together. They had walked the castle grounds—something Sandy and I had yet to do—talking with the ease of people who had known each other for a very long time. The lightness in me after Sandy's kiss goodbye had been eclipsed the moment I'd spotted them through the window.

"My lady?"

I turned and found one of the footmen in the doorway to the Great Hall.

"Miss Cochrane is here to see ye. I've left her in the drawin' room."

I blinked swiftly. I had been too busy watching Sandy stare

after her to realize her reason for approaching the castle. She was here to see me.

"I will come directly," I said.

He bowed and closed the door. I looked at my bodice and skirts, both generously sprinkled with plaster dust, and brushed at them, managing to rid them of the largest offending pieces. I would have liked to look my best to visit with Miss Cochrane, but this would have to do. I would not keep a guest waiting.

Miss Cochrane was not seated when I arrived at the drawing room. She was walking around the room as someone accustomed to having free rein. She wore a blue pelisse that set off her matching eyes and blonde hair admirably, drat her, and her greeting to me was perfectly amiable and kind. Why could she not be easy to dislike?

"I am so pleased you have come," I said, wishing I felt the words. I should be happy to become better friends with Sandy's friends.

"I am glad to hear it, my lady," she said. "I should have written to inform you of my intention, no doubt, but I am not accustomed to standing upon ceremony with the Duncans, and I find it difficult to change now."

I smiled, wondering if her words were merely offhand or if she meant for me to realize I was the one in unfamiliar territory here. "Well, you needn't do so on my account, surely." I pulled the bell to call for tea. "Shall I inform Iain, Blair, and Magnus of your visit?"

"That is kind of you, but no. I came to see you and Sandy."

I ignored the annoyance I felt hearing his name upon her lips. Now that he was married, should she not be calling him Lord Lismore?

"He tells me you have many improvements planned for Lochlarren," she said.

"I suppose time will tell if they truly are *improvements*," I said.

She looked around the room. "I hope you shan't change too much. I have so many happy memories within these walls. I always envied Sandy's castle and fancied living in one just like it one day."

My teeth gritted together. *Fancied living in this very one, more like.* There was nothing pointed in her tone, but her words bothered me despite it. As she spent a good part of the next quarter of an hour conveying her intimate knowledge of all the castle's nooks and crannies, my temper became somewhat frayed. I was left to wonder whether I would do better to ask *her* what improvements should be made to mirror the castle's original state.

"I have been rambling," she said, setting her teacup down, "I hope you will forgive me. You must be bored to death here after being accustomed to life in town."

I knew I was being unreasonable. She was not purposely trying to make me feel this way. In my secret disappointment over my relationship with Sandy, I was too quick to see what was not there. Her comments were not intended as a way to cast herself as a better, more familiar mistress. She was merely trying to establish a connection between us and show her affection for the castle.

"It is an adjustment, certainly," I said, "but there is much to love here."

She searched my face, as if wondering if there was a hidden meaning in my words. I hadn't said it with that intent, but it was true. Was her love of Lochlarren purely nostalgic, or was it centered around Sandy's presence here?

"And I hope Sandy's brothers have been keeping you company," she said. "Sandy has been occupied, as I understand it."

"He has been seeing to improvements beyond the castle walls. I confess I know little more than that."

She smiled and tilted her head to regard me. "That is no wonder. A woman of the town cannot be expected to know the issues which present themselves in a place like this. It is something that must be experienced firsthand."

"Which you have done, no doubt," I said, feeling smaller by the moment.

She laughed. "Since I was a child."

"I hope to experience it, as well," I said. "In fact, Sandy just expressed his wish that I come along with him one of these days."

She raised her brows. "Ah. Is that right?"

I smiled. It wasn't the full truth, for I had been the one to suggest it, but Sandy *had* seemed to like the idea. "Yes, in fact, before you came, I was preparing to meet him there." Also not the full truth. I had considered meeting him today and decided against it. But now, I felt a renewed determination. If I meant to be an exemplary Countess of Lismore, I needed to understand the things Miss Cochrane referred to.

"Well," she said, rising, "in that case, I shan't keep you any longer."

I followed suit, setting down my tea saucer and standing. "You are welcome to stay."

She shook her head with a smile, then stopped as a thought occurred to her. "Do you mean to ride there? Or take the carriage?"

My mouth opened wordlessly. I hadn't arranged anything, of course.

"I have my carriage," she said. "I can let you down at the crossroads. The tenant housing is a short walk from there."

"That is very kind of you," I replied, sincerely grateful. "Let me fetch my bonnet."

After a quick stop in my bedchamber for a bonnet and gloves, I peeked in on Augusta to inform her I was leaving. I was relieved to find her asleep—I didn't think she would approve of me going out to trudge about with Sandy.

I climbed up into the carriage beside Miss Cochrane a few minutes later, hoping Sandy had been genuine when he had welcomed my presence. He would have it sooner than he knew.

It was my first time leaving the castle grounds since my arrival, and I was reminded of the state of the roads as we rumbled over the bridge. As I looked over my shoulder when we reached the end of the bridge, the view of the castle in the back window made me smile. It was truly feeling like home now, becoming more beautiful to me by the day.

It was only a few minutes before we reached the place Miss Cochrane had mentioned.

"Look," she pointed through the open door and across a field. "I can see Sandy just there."

She was right. I recognized him easily, and the man beside him too, even from this distance. They had their heads over a paper.

"Thank you very much for conveying me," I said, stepping down and turning back toward her.

"Of course. The remainder of your journey should be quick enough."

We said our farewells, and the equipage continued on its way. I turned my gaze toward Sandy again, wondering if I should walk back to Lochlarren rather than show up unannounced in this way.

No. I would take my chances. Hadn't Miss Cochrane said experience was key in coming to an understanding of estate matters?

I looked around, trying to determine the fastest way to

arrive at my destination. The road curved around and passed through the village, but there was a sort of path through the field before me—a much shorter route. If I took the road through the village, I would lose sight of Sandy and perhaps not be able to find him again.

The path it was.

I lifted my skirts and stepped into the expanse of green rows. It looked to be a farming field of some sort. Hopefully, I would soon be able to identify the different crops grown on all the tenant farms.

I followed the dirt path for a few minutes, but once I had traversed three-quarters of the distance to Sandy, it nearly disappeared, and the plants changed. I came to a stop in front of the less forgiving plants. I had come this far, though. Going back would mean tracing my steps and then being obliged to take the road into the village.

Sandy's head turned toward me and his steward's, too. Sandy shaded his eyes with a hand as though trying to determine my identity.

I gave a hesitant wave and again lifted my skirts, stepping into the greenery. The plants brushed against my skirts and stockings, their tips clinging to the fabric. I tugged and continued on my way, glancing up to find Sandy coming toward me, his hand waving.

I winced as something poked my ankle, but there were less than a hundred feet left. It wasn't until I had gone ten or twelve more steps that the burning began to take hold. It was centered in my ankles, but my legs and arms began to sting, as well, with every brush against the plants surrounding me.

As the pain built, I stopped and looked around, but at this point, the way forward was just as short as the way back to the crop field.

"Juliana!" Sandy was hurrying toward me, pushing the brush out of the way. "What are you doing?"

I winced again, trying for a smile. It was not quite the greeting I had hoped for. "I came to join you." I sucked in a breath as one particularly strong sting pierced my wrist. "What fiendish plants are these?"

He reached me and took the hand I was inspecting. "Nettle." He showed me his hands, which had raised, angry red bumps where he had pushed aside the plants.

I pressed my eyes shut as the burning intensified. "Is nettle your name for the devil's own garden?"

He grimaced as he pulled back the edge of my glove and looked at my arm and wrist. There were raised areas of red all over, just as he had on his hand.

"You needn't have come to me," I said, feeling guilty even as my ankles throbbed.

"Nonsense. I have boots and a sturdy coat." He looked at me for a moment. "I shall carry you the rest of the way."

I shifted, trying to move my ankle away from one of the leaves poking it. "That is not necessar—" I sucked in a breath as my movement brought my foot up against an even sharper sting.

Sandy stepped toward me, put one arm around my back and the other under my legs, scooping me into his arms. And then he trudged through the nettle toward the village.

As I wrapped my arms around his neck to hold on, my face burned almost as intensely as my legs and arms. Nelly Cochrane would never have got into a scrape like this. She would have sensed innately that nettle was nearby.

"See if Mrs. Lorne has any chamomile, Cairnie," Sandy said breathlessly as we reached the edge of the nettle.

The steward nodded and disappeared as Sandy set me down gently so that my back rested against the stone wall of a thatched cottage. I tried not to wince at the throbbing sensation all over my arms and legs, but Sandy's brow furrowed as he watched me. "Where is it the worst?"

"My legs and ankles," I said, closing my eyes to concentrate on the pain.

He nodded and took my wrist again, inspecting it. "You are developing hives."

"As are you," I said through clenched teeth.

"Not nearly as bad as yours." He showed his own wrist, comparing it to mine. It was true. His was covered in small red dots, while mine had patches of raised, stretched skin, pink in the center, and white on the edges.

Mr. Cairnie came around the corner, holding a jar in his hand. "Here, my lord."

Sandy took it from him with quick thanks, then instructed him to return to Lochlarren to see Mrs. Boyle was informed of my state. "She will know what to do."

Mr. Cairnie nodded and soon disappeared again.

Sandy crouched down, kneeling before me as he opened the bottle. "Let me see your leg."

The pain was intense enough that he might have been a stranger from a brothel and I would have obeyed his instructions—anything to have the cool ointment he held relieve my pain.

I pulled up on my skirts, revealing my white stockings, which had been pulled and frayed from the constant pricks of nettle. Sandy set aside the bottle, reached just above my knee, and set to untying my stockings.

Somewhere within, I was conscious of the intimacy of the gesture, but instead of dwelling on it, I untied the other one. He dipped his fingers in the ointment and rubbed it against the largest hive on my right leg. It hurt at first, but the pain was followed by sweet relief. He submerged his fingers into the jar again and again, rubbing the balm between his fingers, then gently applying it to my skin.

"There is not enough to cover it all," he said as he reached the end of the jar's contents.

"No matter," I said. "It is helping enough." The more stabbing pains had subsided to something duller, but my skin was still on fire in places.

"Let us get you back to the castle," he said, scooping me up into his arms as though I was a feather rather than a fully grown woman.

"You cannot carry me all the way, Sandy," I protested. "I can walk."

"We shall ride," he said as his horse appeared ahead, chomping at the grass near the ring it was tied to.

"Can it carry us both?" I asked doubtfully.

"For the short distance to Lochlarren, yes. We shan't be able to use the saddle, though." He set me down gently and worked at the buckles and straps, setting it on the ground. "Here," he said, showing me to the mounting block. I climbed it, and Sandy helped situate me far forward on the horse's back before he followed, sitting behind me.

He took hold of the reins with one hand and wrapped the other arm around me to secure me to him. "I shan't let you fall," he said in my ear.

I swallowed and nodded, for I believed him.

"So stupid of me," I said as he led us out of the village. "I should not have taken the shortcut."

He chuckled, his breath warm on my neck. "Let us say it was the enterprising and efficient road, rather."

"Efficient to have forced an early end to your work?"

"I was more than ready to go home," he replied. "And very happy to see you."

My heart raced, and I barely noted the continued pricking

sensation on my skin. All I could feel was Sandy's arm around me, holding me to him in the way I had dreamed of the last two nights, his chest against my back.

When we reached the castle, Sandy assisted me from the horse, and I was ushered away by Mrs. Boyle and her newly employed and anxious niece. I frowned slightly, looking for Dolly, only to remember I had given her the afternoon and evening off. Mrs. Boyle and her niece escorted me to my bedchamber, where a number of medicines awaited me.

They ministered to me with the housekeeper's balms and herbs, Mrs. Boyle instructing her niece while my mind wandered to Sandy again and again, heartened by the way he had reacted to my poor choices, hopeful by the way he had held me and spoken to me.

CHAPTER THIRTY-FOUR

SANDY

"For heaven's sake, Sandy," Iain said as poured himself more port, "go see to your wife. Your leg-shaking has nearly spilled my glass twice already."

I stilled. I hadn't even realized my restlessness or that it had been moving the table.

When I had gone to change for dinner, Mrs. Boyle and her niece had been in the room. I had instructed Gillies to take my clothing to my old bedchamber for me to change into, but I might have spared myself the trouble. Mrs. Boyle had been so occupied with tending to Juliana, they would not have even noticed me.

I glanced at Magnus and Blair.

"Go on, then," Blair teased.

Magnus nodded, a little smile playing at the corner of his lips.

"Very well." I emptied my glass and left the room, ignoring Iain's knowing eye.

In truth, I wasn't entirely at ease. Nelly's words from earlier had been bothering me ever since, and the incident with the nettle had only underlined to me the realization that Juliana might not be enjoying her time at Lochlarren as much as I had hoped. The restless energy she had exhibited for the past few days made more sense in that light.

When I reached the corridor at the top of the stairs, I found Miss Lowe leaving the room.

"How is she faring?" I asked.

"Well enough," Miss Lowe replied, not looking terribly well herself. "The salve Mrs. Boyle made has helped a great deal, and the stinging has lessened, I think. The hives are still present but becoming less pronounced."

I nodded. The skin on my hands prickled faintly, but that was the only residual effect I faced. I still wasn't certain why Juliana had taken it into her head to come when she had. I was glad for it, of course, but why not wait until tomorrow when I could have accompanied her?

My interactions with the woman had been limited, partly due to her indisposition, partly due to the suspicion she didn't particularly care for me. But if anyone could tell me more of Juliana, it was her.

"I am glad she is improving," I said. "I am terribly sorry it happened at all."

She sighed. "I as well. Juliana is a creature of town, my lord. There is no nettle there, so she has no experience dealing with such things." Miss Lowe gave me a tired smile and moved to leave.

"Miss Lowe?"

She stopped and looked at me, waiting.

I fiddled with the hem of my coat. "She has seemed a bit . . . restless the past few days. Tell me truthfully, if you will . . . do you think she misses town? That she would prefer being there?" I wanted Juliana to be happy. I did not want her to feel like a prisoner at Lochlarren.

Miss Lowe looked at me intently. "I think, my lord," she said slowly, "that she is unaccustomed to a life so far from town, which may well be contributing to her restlessness."

I nodded as my heart twisted.

"She has greatly looked forward to becoming a countess, as you know," Miss Lowe continued, "but many of the perquisites of that position are not available to her here."

She was right. While I was busy putting the money the match had granted me to good use, Juliana had gained a title and none of its advantages. She was living in an old, dilapidated castle when she had likely dreamed of entertaining and being admired.

I smiled at Miss Lowe, an expression entirely opposite what I was feeling. "Thank you for your honesty. I am grateful for your perspective."

"Of course, my lord," she curtsied, then made her way to her own bedchamber.

I stepped up to the door of my and Juliana's bedchamber but paused with my hand on the knob. Should I allow Juliana to go to town? Should I go with her?

I grimaced. I could not. There was too much that needed seeing to here. But the thought of her leaving made my stomach fill with lead.

Taking a deep breath, I entered.

She was in bed, propped up by a few pillows, the blankets covering her. She offered me a kind smile, then lifted her chin. "Have you come to pay your respects? People seem to think I am on my deathbed."

I laughed softly and sat on the edge of the bed beside her. "Let me have a look, then, if you want my official opinion." I reached for her hand, resting on the covers. Taking it between mine, I inspected it. The color was more even than before, though I could still see where the nettle had stung. "Much better, certainly."

"I should hope so. If there is an ounce of chamomile or vinegar or marigold left in all of Scotland, I shall be extremely surprised."

I smiled and regarded her, thinking of Nelly's and Miss Lowe's words. She did not look miserable, despite her encounter with nettle. Perhaps they were wrong.

"I am now intimately familiar with the temperature of the loch, the way the roads jar one's very skull, and the aggressiveness of your plants. Tell me, if you please, what other painful surprises I have in store for me at Lochlarren."

I chuckled, wondering how much truth there was behind her humor. That was the saying, was it not—that every pleasantry had its roots in truth?

"Ah," she said before I could respond, "I meant to tell you. Papa shall be here in two days. He shall only stay one night, then take Augusta with him to Edinburgh, where he has meetings with a few investors and bankers. He quite likes it there, as I understand it. If I am not mistaken, he favors the port at Leith to the one in Newcastle."

"He would do well there. Edinburgh has grown immensely, and I only see it continuing to expand."

"I admit I was quite taken with it," she replied, rubbing absently at a spot on the back of her hand. "There is nothing like Princes Street in Newcastle."

"Edinburgh is a town full of history and character, surely," I replied, feeling more than ever that Miss Lowe and Nelly had been right after all. I sighed. "I should change for bed."

"I am quite exhausted myself." She turned and pulled one of the numerous pillows from behind her, resting it on the floor as I began undressing. "Being tended to so fastidiously is a tiresome business. It was all I could do to convince Augusta I did not need to be taken to the nearest town for a doctor. She has forgotten, I think, how far the nearest one is. Do you need assistance with your coat?"

"No, no," I hurried to say. "Stay there. You need rest, Juliana. I can manage on my own this evening." Gillies had insisted the coat I had worn for the past two dinners needed to be laundered, so I had been obliged to wear a less form-fitting coat that was easy enough to shrug out of.

Juliana situated herself in the bed, blowing out her candle just as I pulled my nightshirt on. As I climbed into bed and extinguished the one on my side table, I had an impulse to turn and wrap my arm around her, just as I had done on our ride back to Lochlarren.

I suppressed it, aware how shocking that would be to her. So far, I had been the one to initiate all of our more intimate contact—namely, one kiss on the cheek and two goodbye kisses. I desperately wanted Juliana to be the one to do so next, to give me reason to believe she welcomed anything at all from me.

I lay on my back, staring up at the dark ceiling.

"Sandy?"

"Hm?"

There was a pause. "I know you said there is no rush for an heir . . ."

My heart raced.

"I simply wish to be certain you do not delay your duty on my account."

I didn't respond immediately, for my thoughts had scattered. It was thoughtful of her, but how was I to respond? Duty was not what urged me to wrap my arms around her or to kiss her every time I was within sight of her. It was not duty which made me reluctant to leave the castle each day, knowing I would not see her for hours at a time.

And I didn't wish for duty to motivate *her*, either. I wanted so much more.

"Thank you," I said with genuine feeling.

"You may simply inform me when"—she cleared her throat —"you feel it is time."

"Very well," I managed to croak.

The air was still and quiet. Was she waiting for me to tell her it was time? Or was she going to sleep? Part of me wanted to do just that—tell her I wished for an heir. Perhaps if I had the chance to hold her and kiss her the way I wanted to, it would change things between us.

"Good night, Sandy," she said, turning her back toward me.

I let out a sigh. "Good night, Juliana."

I stared up at the darkness for I knew not how long, willing my eyes to feel heavy, for sleep to take over. But anytime I lay beside her, my mind and body hummed. I craved sleep, but I feared it too. I had come to dream of her often enough that waking to reality ached.

I looked at her back, at the loose braid that fell over it and onto the pillow. Did she long for home, for the clamor of town? I wanted so deeply for her to find happiness at Lochlarren. To find happiness with me. I wanted her to know how valued she was, how deeply I cared for her and wished for her contentedness.

I wasn't certain what time my mind finally gave way to sleep; I only knew I dreamed of her again. I dreamed I held her against me, smelling her hair as she rested her hands against my chest. I dreamed of staying like that for hours in all-encompassing bliss.

She stirred, and I opened my eyes slowly, reluctant to wake from the dream.

My every muscle stilled.

In the darkness, I could feel my lips resting against

Juliana's hair and my arms wrapped around her, while her hands pressed softly against my nightshirt. One of her fingertips rested against the skin of my chest, laid partially bare from my open collar.

I had not been dreaming.

She shifted, her lids slowly opening until her eyes settled upon me.

My heart pounded against my chest as I waited for her to recoil.

Instead, she smiled sleepily, sliding her hands up my chest until they wrapped around my neck.

I shut my eyes and let out a shuddering breath of relief, tightening my hold around her. She nestled her head into the hollow of my neck, her breath warming my skin. I pressed a fervent kiss to the top of her head, then ran my hand down her braid, eager for anything to assure me I was indeed awake. The thrumming of my heart was evidence enough, though.

She moved her head from its place at my neck, tipping it up to look at me through sleepy eyes and a soft smile. The pressure of her hands at my neck grew more insistent, pulling me toward her.

I needed no pulling. I needed no guidance. Countless dreams had taught me where to find her lips.

I brushed mine against hers, testing their softness and warmth, weighing reality against fantasy. Despite a hundred imagined kisses, it was not reality that fell short.

She drew me even nearer, cupping my jaw with her hand and running her thumb along the roughness of my stubble as her mouth proved the smoothness of my lips. Her body shifted, the skin of her foot sending a shock of cold where it touched my ankles as it threaded through, tangling our legs together.

She kissed me more deeply, and I wondered how much longer I could survive such bliss.

And then suddenly, she froze, our lips pressed against each other, unmoving.

Gently, I pulled back to look at her. Gone was the sleepiness in her eyes, the drowsiness of her smile. Her eyes were open, wide with shock as her gaze moved to her hand around my neck, then to the one holding my jaw, then to my lips.

And then I understood.

I hadn't been dreaming. But she had.

I released her in an instant, going cold with embarrassment and shame. "Forgive me. I thought you were . . ." I left the sentence unfinished. There was no way to give a satisfying explanation of what had just happened. "I am sorry, Juliana."

She shook her head, blinking rapidly. "No, it is my fault."

I didn't respond. *Her fault.* What did that mean? That she saw it as a mistake? That she regretted it?

My head swam trying to understand the situation. She *had* pulled me down to kiss her, perhaps unconsciously so, but what was I to make of that? Had she been dreaming of it as I had?

Both of us lay staring up at the ceiling, the air thick with confusing tension and questions about what would happen now.

I couldn't say how long had passed when Juliana's breathing became slower and deeper, but I was awake long after, wondering what to expect and hope for next.

CHAPTER THIRTY-FIVE

JULIANA

My hives had disappeared in the morning. The prickling I felt upon awakening was due to something else entirely. It was wisps of memory, pressing themselves upon my consciousness with urgency.

Sandy and I had kissed during the night. The entire thing felt like a dream—and what a dream! Only in the refuge of my sleeping mind had I allowed myself to explore what might have been between Sandy and me. In my half-sleeping state, though, I had turned dream into reality.

And he had kissed me back. Had he also been half-asleep? He had seemed less surprised than I when I realized I was not dreaming but well and truly kissing my husband. Had he merely capitalized on what had been offered him? Or, heaven forbid, had he been afraid of humiliating me by rejecting me?

I touched a finger to my lips. It had not felt like a perfunctory kiss. It had been earnest and warm. I shut my eyes, trying to remember every second of it, of the feel of our legs tangled together. Sadly, though, specific recollection evaded me, much like a dream.

I glanced beside me at Sandy, still fast asleep, and my heart swelled at the sight of him. Was it possible he wished for more, just as I did? I had given him the opportunity last night when I had told him he needn't delay the matter of an heir on my account. When he had not done so, I had begun to despair, any hope that the goodbye kisses had been invitations for more dashed.

But then . . . the way he had held me.

My arms itched to wrap around him, to see what would happen if I did. But he had been working so hard, and he looked so peaceful. I wouldn't disturb him now.

Gently, I slipped out of the bed and went to my old bedchamber, where I pulled the chord to summon Dolly. After dressing, I took the time to respond to Papa's letter, though I couldn't be certain it would reach him before he left for Lochlarren.

My entire body was full of pent-up energy as I waited to see what would happen when I saw Sandy next. Rather than twiddle my thumbs as I now was, I determined to see whether the laborers working on the great hall had yet arrived.

They were already chipping away at the most spoiled bits of plaster, filling the room once again with chips and puffs of white as it fell to the floor below. I watched for a time, then discussed with them which parts were salvageable now that they had taken stock of things from a closer perspective.

When I left the hall, I met Magnus on the stairwell, on his way out of the castle.

"Have you seen his lordship yet this morning?" I asked with as much nonchalance as I could muster.

"He is in the study, I believe," he replied.

"Thank you, Magnus," I said before making my way there. Perhaps I could accompany Sandy today—if my incompetence yesterday hadn't made him despair of my usefulness, that was.

I wanted so much to be a proper countess. I didn't wish to be compared to Miss Cochrane and come up short.

I reached the door to the study, which had been left slightly ajar and put my hand on it to push it open when the sound of voices within reached me—Mr. Cairnie's in particular.

" . . . said Miss Cochrane shall receive her aunt's entire inheritance. Was he mistaken?"

I paused.

"He was not," Sandy replied. "She told me as much yesterday. Of course, when exactly she receives it will depend upon the efficiency of the estate's executor."

"It seems a terrible shame, my lord, that things should happen this way—a matter of weeks all that stood between the two of you being able to marry. From the sounds of it, her inheritance would have been sufficient to allow for that."

"I gather so," Sandy replied. "But what's done is done."

The steward sighed. "I suppose so."

There was a long silence. "Shall we look at the improvements we were discussing yesterday?" Sandy asked.

"Yes, my lord."

I stepped back from the door, my heart squeezing. I tried to swallow and found my throat thick as I tried to understand what I had just heard. Miss Cochrane had received a sudden inheritance. She and Sandy might have married after all if not for . . . me.

What's done is done, he had said.

I thought on Miss Cochrane's visit, about the misty look in Sandy's eye as he had watched her walk away from him. Now I knew why.

And what had he said last night when he had pulled back to look at me? *Forgive me. I had thought you were . . .*

In his partially conscious state, had he believed himself to be kissing Miss Cochrane?

I turned and hurried down the stairs and through the castle doors, gulping in the fresh air. How had I allowed myself to believe he might have begun sharing my feelings, wishing for more than a marriage of convenience? I grasped my hand at my chest as though I could massage away the hurt in my heart.

I should have listened to Augusta. I should not have allowed myself to draw close to Sandy, to the Duncans. I was not of their world, and in my naivety, in my desire to be accepted by them, I had allowed myself to hope for too much. My money had been the only factor in Sandy's decision to marry me, and now, he would live forever regretting his haste in that decision when he could have had Miss Cochrane instead.

"Juliana?" I dashed at the tear on my cheek, took in a large breath, and turned to face Augusta.

"I thought you still abed, my dear," she said, coming toward me swiftly. "Are your hives bet—" She stopped, her eyes searching my face. "What is amiss?"

I shook my head and tried for a smile. "Nothing, cousin." My voice trembled on the words, betraying me.

"Oh, Juliana," she said, scooping up my hands and pulling me toward the bench that overlooked the loch. "Come tell me all about it."

I fought back the tears that tried to escape as we settled onto the bench. "It is nothing. Only my own silliness, as usual."

She squeezed my hand between hers. "You are not silly, Juliana, and no one knows that better than I."

I took in slow, deep breaths, trying to decide how much to tell her. I couldn't bear to admit I had fallen in love with my husband, against all her advice, all her teaching and preparation. But I could tell her one truth that made my heart ache. "I miss home."

She nodded. "I do as well."

We stared out at the loch for a moment, our minds both on home, on the time before things had become so complicated. Somehow, I had truly believed myself sensible enough to marry for a title and nothing more. Life had been so much simpler when I had inhabited a world I understood and knew how to navigate. Here, I felt as though I was on that rickety, unstable boat Sandy and I had rowed. I was constantly trying to regain my balance, only for my heart to be plunged into the frigid water. I was not nearly as reasonable or steady as I had believed myself. I had merely never met Sandy Duncan before.

It was not Newcastle I missed. I missed the time before I had despaired of him coming to love me as I loved him.

"My dear," Augusta finally said. "Why not come with your father and me to Edinburgh? I think you would find life more familiar and to your taste there. You are a countess, but I imagine it hardly feels that way when you have not tasted of the privileges and benefits it brings. Such things are best experienced in town."

I looked down at my hands, thinking what it would be like to go to Edinburgh. Would Sandy come, as well?

I clenched my eyes shut. Why must I always be so concerned with what Sandy was doing? It was becoming an obsession. Time and space might benefit both of us. I would have the opportunity to meet new people and focus less on Sandy's every move and every touch, while he . . . well, he could spend time with Miss Cochrane if he wished.

The very thought gripped my heart, evidence of just how attached I had become.

"What say you?" Augusta asked.

I hesitated. Could I leave Lochlarren, could I leave my husband after such a short time married? I didn't want to, but that was precisely why I *should*. I needed time to clear my head and my heart—better now than in weeks when it would be irrevocably his.

"I will think on it," I replied.

She smiled sadly at me and pulled me into her arms. "Shall we go inside for some tea?" she asked.

"Thank you, cousin," I replied. "I think I will stay out here a little longer. I shall join you presently."

CHAPTER THIRTY-SIX

SANDY

I could not find Juliana when the time came for me to leave with Cairnie. I could have left without speaking with her, but I knew how interminable the day would seem if I did that. I hadn't seen her since last night's incident, and I burned with curiosity to see what, if anything would be different today as a result.

The laborers in the great hall had spoken with her betimes but had not seen her since. Dolly could not tell me where she was, either, and neither could any of my brothers. Only an enquiry with Miss Lowe yielded fruit, though reluctantly given. I had not been mistaken: Miss Lowe was not fond of me, though I did not know the reason.

With a bit of coaxing, she informed me that Juliana could be found outside. I decided against asking her precise location and determined to find her myself. There were only so many places she could be, after all. Lochlarren as a castle was tall and imposing, but its grounds were not extensive.

The sky was gray and the ground wet from the night's rain, and I followed the path around the castle until I caught sight of

Juliana, standing at the edge of the loch, not far from where we had emerged the day we had fallen in.

She had removed her bonnet, holding it in her hand as the ribbons fluttered in the breeze. She seemed in a pensive mood, and I wondered if that was why Miss Lowe had been reluctant to tell me her whereabouts.

I was too curious to leave her to her thoughts, though, particularly because part of me hoped those thoughts might be centered on me. I could only hope they were happy ones.

I walked up beside her without speaking, and she glanced over at me. The guarded look in her eyes made my heart pinch.

"You are leaving with Cairnie?" she asked.

I nodded. "After tomorrow, the surveying should be done. You are welcome to accompany us if you wish. I shan't let you venture into any nettle today."

Her laugh seemed void of true amusement. "Thank you, but I think I shall stay behind today. There is a great deal to arrange for now that work is progressing on the great hall."

I ignored the flash of disappointment within me. "Certainly. You seem to be managing it admirably."

"I hope that is true," she replied, her gaze still focused somewhere out on the loch. A moment of silence passed, then she turned to me. "I have been pondering, my lord, and I think I shall accompany Augusta and Papa to Edinburgh."

My heart plummeted into my boots. "Oh?" It was all I could manage.

She nodded and gave a smiling grimace. "I wish to ensure Augusta's health improves, and there is a great deal of work I can assist Papa with there."

I swallowed, then cleared my throat. "How long shall you be away?" Did I sound like the disconsolate puppy I was?

She lifted her shoulders and smiled slightly. "Augusta is insistent I shall be the recipient of a stack of invitations the moment I arrive. I am less optimistic, but assuming she is in good enough health, I imagine we will attend a few parties, perhaps go to the opera. She very much enjoys such entertainments, and now that she does not have to concern herself with my chaperonage, I wish for her to enjoy herself as she otherwise would. She has been so miserable here."

I kicked at a rock on the ground, wondering if Juliana too had been miserable. "That is very kind of you." I felt her eyes on me.

"Of course, if you dislike it, I shan't go," she hurried to say, "I only thought, you have been so occupied with estate matters, you would hardly notice my absence—you might well accomplish more without having to rescue me from drowning or venturing into noxious weeds."

I laughed quietly and shook my head. "The first instance was no one's fault but my own."

"I agree," she said.

I glanced at her and found that playful glint in her eyes I had come to love. I would miss it, however long she was gone.

I took in a large breath and let it out in a gush. "Very well, then. Perhaps I shall join you in Edinburgh at some point."

"I would like that," she said.

I held her gaze for a moment, trying to understand this incomprehensible woman who had become my wife. If she wished for me to join her in town, why was she leaving? Did she miss the hustle and bustle so very much? Had last night's kiss given her a distaste for my company? Perhaps she hoped a bit of time away would cool my feelings for her.

"I should be going," I said.

"And I should go inside."

We walked toward the castle in silence, where the stable hand stood at my horse's head. Juliana stopped and turned toward me once we reached him. There was a pause as our gazes held and I debated whether to kiss her goodbye again. Three days in a row would certainly solidify it into a habit, but I was afraid I had already gone too far after last night. What would she think, though, if I didn't? Would it seem pointed, or that—

Suddenly, she rose on her tiptoes and pressed her lips to mine.

It was over as soon as it had begun.

"Until this afternoon?" she asked.

"Until then," I said dazedly.

She smiled and turned toward the castle, soon disappearing through the door.

Mr. Godfrey arrived the next day, grinning and gregarious as he had been the last time he had come to Lochlarren. This time, however, he did not arrive to find Juliana and me stumbling into one another's arms over swords. I wished he had.

Despite her continuing ill health, Miss Lowe's spirits were higher than ever at the prospect of leaving Lochlarren. For her part, Juliana kept busy arranging things for the improvements she had planned. The great hall would be well on its way, but the others would wait until her return.

Whenever that was.

I tried not to dwell on it, and when Mr. Godfrey's comment at dinner informed my brothers that Juliana would be leaving, I avoided their eyes, directing a business remark to him instead.

"Half the country is in town right now," Iain said, derailing my attempts to redirect the conversation. "Orton left to go there just the other day." He set his gaze on me, his cocked brow full of meaning.

I clenched my jaw. I hated the thought of Juliana being courted by other men, for she certainly would be, but Orton . . . that was a bitter cup indeed.

I slipped into bed that night with a heavy heart, knowing it was my last night with her beside me for heaven only knew how long. I lay on my side, facing her, and she turned to face me as well, our faces only inches apart.

We looked at one another for a few moments, and I wished I had the courage to ask her what was in her mind. "You leave first thing in the morning?"

She nodded against the hands she was using as a pillow. "After breakfast. Papa believes in a hearty meal before traveling."

I smiled. "A wise man." I let out a sigh, wishing I could capture this image in my memory forever. "You will enjoy Edinburgh, I think."

Her forehead pulled together slightly as she looked at me intently. "Will I?"

I could have sworn there was more to the question than it seemed, as though she truly doubted it.

"It is more of what you are accustomed to than Lochlarren," I replied. "And Miss Lowe is right. You will have invitations of all kinds the moment your presence in town is known."

"And you will come visit," she said. "When you are able."

I swallowed, wondering how soon would be too soon. "I shall."

She gazed at me a moment longer, then let her eyelids fall closed, and soon, she was asleep.

CHAPTER THIRTY-SEVEN

JULIANA

The carriage was loaded with Papa's, Augusta's, and my trunks, and the horses pawed impatiently at the ground, eager to be off, to take us away from Lochlarren.

I looked up at the castle, letting my gaze travel over its stony exterior, at the vines that crept along the east tower, and out to the vividly blue loch. My heart ached at the thought of leaving it. It had become home to me, each room full of memories with Sandy—from our initial meeting in the drawing room and enjoying soup in Mrs. Boyle's quarters to the time his button had caught on my dress in the stairwell.

I didn't know when I would see it next. Only time would tell. My heart dithered between two hopes: the first, that I would manage to put my feelings for Sandy behind me, the second, that my absence might stir something in him, something that might lead him to think of me as more than the wife he was obliged to marry—the wife who had deprived him of the marriage he had truly wished for.

Papa led Augusta outside on his arm, and behind them

followed Iain, Blair, and Magnus. I looked in vain for Sandy. The brothers came up to me one by one to say their farewells.

"I am quite angry with you for leaving us, you know," Iain said after a quick embrace. "Sandy will be unbearable."

"He's right," Blair said. "Don't stay away too long, or we shall be obliged to come after you."

"You are being nonsensical," I said, wishing I had the courage to ask them what they meant. Why would Sandy be anything but happier with me gone? He could spend the money from our marriage in peace—and take as many walks around the castle as he liked with Miss Cochrane.

Magnus took his turn to embrace me. I expected a quick, formal one, but he held onto me longer than usual. "We shall miss you, Juliana. Sandy especially. Come back soon."

I swallowed hurriedly as we broke apart, hoping my emotions were well-masked.

Sandy emerged from the castle doors, wearing the tailcoat I most loved him in. I would not be assisting him out of it tonight. I would sleep alone and explain to everyone who asked why Lord Lismore was not in town with me. Why had I agreed to do this? Did I truly think I could return here at some point, as I would be obliged to do, and be unaffected by him?

I was far from certain of it.

"Juliana?" Sandy called to me. He hadn't come over but rather waited near the doors.

I picked up my skirts and walked over to him there, wondering if something was amiss—almost hoping it was, if only it meant I could stay.

Sandy held a small box in his hands, and he extended it toward me. "A very belated wedding gift."

Keeping my gaze on him, I took the box. Our gazes held for a moment, then I wiggled the box until the top gave way and came off. Within was a simple gold chain with an amethyst pendant. I touched a finger to it gently as it sparkled in the sun.

"I hope you will be able to use it in Edinburgh."

I looked up at him. His face was more somber than usual, his eyes subdued.

"It is beautiful, Sandy," I said. "But I fear I have nothing for *you*."

"It is no matter," he said, a small smile tugging at the corner of his mouth. "You have been gift enough."

I searched his face, trying to discern his meaning. Was he referring to the money I had brought to the marriage? Or did he mean what I hoped he meant?

"The horses are restless, Juliana," Papa said. "We should go."

I nodded, and he shook hands with Sandy, who then bowed to Augusta. Papa guided her toward the carriage and saw to helping her in.

I faced my husband. I had kissed him yesterday upon our parting. What of today?

He took my hands in his and stared down into my eyes intently. "Be safe, Juliana."

"I shall." I smiled slightly. "There is no nettle nor any lochs in town."

He gave a soft laugh, but the smile faded quickly as he gazed at me. He brought a hand and set it upon my cheek, sending a thrill through me. His thumb grazed my skin as our eyes locked. He shut his, then brought his lips to mine, securing us together with the gentle pressure of his hand on my cheek.

I moved my hand to his chest, taking the opportunity to express to him, however briefly and inadequately, that I cared for him in the way I had promised myself I would not. I kissed him as though it would be my only opportunity ever again.

We pulled apart, and his hand dropped to mine as I stepped back.

"I shall write when we arrive," I said.

He squeezed my hand. "Only tell me when you wish for me to join you."

Now. I wish for you to join me now.

I nodded and turned, going to where Papa waited to hand me into the carriage.

Minutes later, the view of Sandy and Lochlarren grew smaller and was swallowed up by the trees.

CHAPTER THIRTY-EIGHT

SANDY

I watched the carriage take my wife away from our home and toward town, toward Orton and heaven only knew who else.

Iain approached, stopped just before me, and clapped a hand on my shoulder. "You're a fool." He squeezed my arm, then continued toward the castle.

Blair grimaced in a way that said, "I agree."

Magnus, at least, I could rely upon not to criticize me for a lack of romanticism. But I was wrong. He frowned and shook his head at me as he passed.

I gritted my teeth and turned to watch them walk toward the doors. "She *wanted* to leave!"

But none of them heeded me.

Lochlarren felt empty without Juliana. I was not the only one to feel so. Dinner was vapid, everyone in a more subdued humor than usual.

"Well," Iain said after a long silence at the table, "at least we may comfort ourselves that Orton will look after her in Edinburgh."

I sawed roughly at the meat on my plate.

"Don't like that, do you, Sandy?" Iain said. "He seemed *very* anxious to know her better at the party."

And she didn't seem to mind it, I nearly said.

"You can be a real dolt sometimes," Blair said, his eyes fixed on me.

"A family trait," I replied.

"Did you ever even kiss her?" Iain asked.

"I did," I said, setting down my knife with unnecessary violence. "I did, Iain. And as you see, this is where it has led. My wife has left me for town. So, thank you for your *invaluable* advice."

"What did she say when you told her you wanted her to stay?" Blair asked.

I frowned and took up my knife again. "I didn't. She wished to leave, and I have no wish to keep her as prisoner here."

Silence greeted my response, and I reluctantly looked up to find my brothers sharing glances. I slammed my knife down again. "What? Out with it."

Blair reared back, as though I might throw my knife at him at any moment. "You're sulkier than a toddler with a broken toy."

"A broken heart, I think," Iain said.

I didn't counter him.

"We all care for her, Sandy," Magnus said. "Perhaps it is time you made that clear to her."

I stared at my plate, my heart telling me he was right while my mind insisted it was both too soon and too late. She was gone now. "And if she does not return my regard?" The mere thought of such rejection struck my heart with a flash of pain. I had been valued primarily for my title my entire life. What reason had I to assume Juliana would see me any differently? She had married me for that very title.

"Then at least you will know," Magnus said with a shrug. Iain and Blair nodded their agreement.

I sat silent, staring at the tablecloth, trying to decide whether I could bear continuing as I now was when the alternative might give me hope—or irrefutable proof that my wife did not care for me the way I cared for her.

Then at least you will know.

There was something to be said for that, certainly. Juliana had kissed me back outside. She had kissed me until it had been all I could do not to scoop her into my arms and take her back into the castle. When I had told her she would enjoy Edinburgh, she had asked, "Will I?"

I looked up. All three of my brothers were watching me, their food forgotten.

"They are breaking the journey in Fort William," Iain offered.

I fixed my eyes on him, my brain working. If I left now, I could reach them tonight. Late tonight, but tonight nonetheless.

"Well?" Blair said. "What are you waiting for?"

I hesitated one more second, then threw my napkin on the table, and rose to get my coat.

CHAPTER THIRTY-NINE

JULIANA

Augusta seemed to grow more well by the minute, as though Lochlarren had been her illness. She prattled away about the different people we might meet in Edinburgh, detailing all of the Scottish peers she had met when she had been young.

I participated when called upon, but otherwise, I stared through the window, counting each mile that took me away from Sandy and Lochlarren, wondering when I would return and what circumstances it would be to.

Would Sandy be with me then?

Only tell me when you wish for me to join you.

Those words had been haunting me.

They followed me like an insistent spectre into the inn Papa had chosen, pestering me while we ate and for the hour afterward. Papa looked at me more than once with a troubled expression, but he forbore asking me the reason for my soberness.

I was going mad wondering when I could reasonably send

Sandy a letter telling him I wished for him to join me. A week? Two weeks? Had they been idle words of his? Perhaps he had business to conduct in Edinburgh and that was his motivation for wishing to come.

But the way he had looked at me when he said it made me think otherwise.

Now that I was a married woman, I was not obliged to share a room at the inn with Augusta. I bid goodnight to both her and Papa, then closed myself in my room, embracing the solitude—while wishing I could have shared it with Sandy.

I laughed aloud at the sight and smell of peat in the fireplace. As if I needed another reminder of him.

I donned my shift and dressing gown, then took out the box Sandy had given me, removed the necklace, and clasped it around my neck. It was a beautiful piece of jewelry and a unique one. I loved its simplicity, but even more, I loved that Sandy had given it to me.

Only tell me when you wish me to join you.

I shut my eyes tightly, as though I could shut out the words. But they repeated again and again, refusing to leave me alone.

Finally, I surrendered and asked the inn for a quill and paper and wrote the words: *I wish you were with me now.* I let the ink dry, considering whether I should have it sent to Lochlarren in the morning.

I was going mad.

I folded the paper and left it on my desk, hoping the thoughts would leave me be for the night at least. When I did write Sandy, I would find a less ridiculous way to ask him to join us in Edinburgh.

After the quiet of Lochlarren, the bustle of an inn was strange. There were calls from the ostlers, carriage wheels grinding on rocks and dirt, horse whinnies, creaking stairs as travelers came and left. I yearned for the calm of my castle in the middle of the loch. I ached to have Sandy beside me, his heart beating nearby.

I took in a deep breath and closed my eyes, willing myself to accept my life as it was. It was the life I had dreamed for myself, but it felt hollow now.

The stairs creaked as yet another traveler ascended to find whatever sleep he could achieve in these damp sheets.

A knock on my door had me shooting up, pulling the covers to my chest as my heart hammered.

"This bedchamber is occupied," I called out.

"May I come in?"

I stilled at the voice.

No. I was imagining things, trying to make reality out of a dream, just as I had done when I had kissed Sandy in bed.

"Juliana?" the voice repeated when I didn't reply. "It is Sandy."

I threw the covers off and hurried over to the door, lifting the latch and pulling the heavy door open the slightest bit.

My heart stuttered at the sight of him. I stared and stared until his mouth pulled up at the edge. "I take it you do not mean to let me in?"

Blinking, I pulled open the door. The room was dark, for I had already extinguished the candle. It must have been nigh midnight.

"Sandy, what are you doing here?" I asked. "Is something amiss?" My heart galloped at the thought of one of his brothers being injured.

"No," he said. "That is, yes."

"What is it?"

His gaze dropped to my neck, and his eyes narrowed slightly. "You are wearing the necklace."

I grasped it, embarrassed he had noticed. It was not normal

to wear a necklace to sleep. "Sandy, for heaven's sake, tell me what is amiss."

He took in a large breath and met my eyes. The seconds dragged on until finally, he spoke. "I am. Without you, I am amiss, Juliana."

Every muscle in my body froze. Perhaps this *was* a dream. What had roused me last time? I needed someone to throw a jug of cold water over my head. Loch water, perhaps.

"I know it is not what we agreed upon," he continued, taking my hands in his, "and I know I have no right to ask any more of you than I have, but . . ." His throat bobbed. "I do not wish for you to go to Edinburgh, Juliana. I want you to stay." He swallowed. "With me."

My breath came quickly, the suddenness, the unexpectedness of his appearance miles from Lochlarren making my brain slow to understand.

He squeezed my hands more tightly. "I promise you, I will do everything in my power to make your life a happy one there. We can host balls and dinner parties—whatever you wish—so long as I have you with me."

Tears burned my eyes. "Sandy . . ."

"I know. I know it is overwhelming, and you needn't answer me tonight, but I—"

"Sandy." I squeezed his hands until he stopped talking, then pulled one of my hands from his and dashed at a tear. "You said when I left Lochlarren that I should tell you when I wished for you to join me."

He nodded, his face becoming more subdued. "I did. I am sorry I could not wait. But if it is what you wish, I *will*. I will wait for you, Juliana, if it means there is any chance at all you could come to love me the way I love you."

I pulled my other hand from his and turned away, fetching

the folded paper on the desk. Without saying a word, I handed it to him.

He looked at me for a moment, his eyes wary. He unfolded it, his gaze fixing on the words. His eyes flicked to me.

I lifted my shoulders. "I spent the majority of the carriage ride wondering when I could reasonably ask you to come to Edinburgh—how soon would seem too soon to you. That is what I wanted to say. I wrote it down hoping when the time came, I could write something more reasonable."

He looked at me, his eyes full of warmth. "Reason may go to the devil for all I care."

The paper dropped to the floor, forgotten, as he scooped me into his arms. His lips pressed to mine, and I wrapped my arms around his neck, threading my hands into his hair as he held me against him.

Mouths still pressed together, he took me to the bed and laid me gently down. He drew back long enough to smile down at me in a way that made my heart race, then climbed onto the bed and caged me in with his arms on either side.

In the dark, his eyes searched my face and mine his, and I pulled him down to me again, wanting him nearer, needing more evidence he was truly here—that he had wanted me enough to ride all the way to Fort William.

We broke apart, and he lay beside me, looking at me tenderly as he brushed a lock of hair from my face.

"Can I hold you?" he asked in a whisper. "Can I hold you the way I have wished to hold you?"

I nodded breathlessly, and he pulled me toward him so that my head nestled in the hollow beneath his chin. We stayed that way, our breath slowing and our arms around one another, for an age, it seemed, and yet not long enough.

"Why did you leave?" he asked softly, stroking my hair.

I sighed, my hands tracing lines on the back of his shirt. "I heard you speaking with Cairnie the other day. He mentioned Miss Cochrane's inheritance and what a shame it was that it had come too late. *What's done is done*, you said." I pulled back and met his gaze, swallowing at the memory of how those words had made me feel, of the despair they had inspired. "I was certain you regretted marrying me, that you would never feel for me what you felt for her."

He pulled me into his chest, burying his face in my hair. "I never cared for her in that way, Juliana," he whispered.

I tried to breathe in his words as he pulled back to look at me again. "I knew before we even married that I was receiving the far better end of this arrangement, Juliana, and not because of the money. Because of *you*. If we could turn back time and do it all over again, I would choose you, no matter your circumstances. I would rather have you than all the money and prestige in the world."

"And I you," I replied.

"Will you come home with me in the morning, then? Back to Lochlarren?"

I nodded, unable to stop a smile at the thought of returning there together.

"We can hold another party as soon as the great hall is finished."

I gripped the lapels of his coat and looked up at him. "I don't care for parties and balls, Sandy. I was lonely at Lochlarren for *you* and you alone. I only came to Edinburgh to set aside my feelings for you—or perhaps inspire you with feelings for me."

"Well, you have certainly accomplished the latter," he said, resituating me in his arms and tangling our legs together. "And I mean to make certain you cannot accomplish the former."

"It was a mission doomed to fail." I gazed into his eyes. "I love you, Sandy."

His mouth quirked up at the edge. "And I you, lass."

Taking his shirt in my hands, I pulled him down to me again, kissing and holding my husband until light crept through the curtains.

EPILOGUE

SANDY

The boat listed dangerously, and I grabbed Juliana's arm as though it was us on the loch rather than Iain, Blair, Magnus, and our son, Alexander.

"For heaven's sake," I hissed as the boat settled.

Alexander's giggle rang out over the loch, and I glanced at my wife, who smiled. "He is in his element," she said.

"Unfortunate that *his* element is *my* idea of torture," I replied, though I couldn't stop a smile at the sight of my three-year-old son's grin. "Do you truly trust thos three with his safety?"

Juliana went up on her toes and pressed a kiss to my cheek. "I do. They promised to stay within twenty feet of shore, and besides, you know they would never let anything befall him. Magnus, at the very least, may be counted upon to ensure nothing goes awry."

I nodded. Alexander was not only the pride of Juliana and me, but of all three of my brothers, as well as his grandfather and Aunt Augusta. My brothers had offered to spend the day and night with him to offer us a little respite, with plans to sleep in one of the castle's tower rooms—a favorite haunt of Alexander's. None of my brothers would hesitate to sacrifice themselves for their nephew's safety.

"You are right." I took her hand in mine, and she shot me a teasing glance.

"I usually am." She threaded her fingers through mine as a splash brought our heads around.

One of the oars, previously in the boat, now floated atop the water beside it.

Iain waved genially at us. "Not to worry!" he called out as he grabbed Alexander's arm to keep him from trying to reach the oar. "Everything is well under control!"

Juliana waved in acknowledgement, and I let out a long, measured breath through rounded lips.

"Come," she said to me. "Shall we go inside?"

"I think that would be for the best." We walked toward the castle, both of us looking up at its heights. The exterior had changed little in the last three years, but inside was another story entirely. Together, Juliana and I had overseen the restoration of the great hall, the drawing room, the parlors and study, and all the main bedchambers. The kitchens had been refreshed and modernized last year, and the stables would soon receive the same treatment.

The state of the interior reflected the entire estate—flourishing and ever-changing. Not for over a hundred years had Lochlarren thrived as it did now. I glanced once more at my son, content that he would receive a boon rather than a burden when he inherited.

"A letter for you, my lady," said the footman when we entered, holding out the silver salver toward her.

She smiled and thanked him, and he bowed himself out. "It is from Augusta," Juliana said, pausing in the entry hall as she broke the wafer. "Ah. She and Mrs. Paterson have found lodgings in New Town, not far from Papa's offices. Large enough for fifteen girls."

"An ideal situation," I replied. During her time in town with Mr. Godfrey, Augusta had become reacquainted with an old friend, Mrs. Paterson, now a widow. Together, they had begun a finishing school. It had taken a year or two, but it was well-known and respected amongst Edinburgh society— enough that it now required a larger residence to house the teachers and girls.

"She spoke with Lady Orton," Juliana continued after reading a few more lines. "She and Lord Orton have plans to travel to London for the Season."

"Excellent," I replied. Once Nelly had come into her aunt's inheritance, she and Orton had made a match of it. They were rarely in Scotland, and almost never in the High-lands, as both seemed to enjoy the pace of town life far more.

Juliana flipped the page, which was filled—and crossed— with more news. "Good gracious, Augusta has a great deal to say!"

I snatched the letter from her hands and folded it up. "It will keep. Right now, I wish to spend time with my wife."

Juliana made no move to resist as I tucked the letter into my waistcoat, smiling as I pulled her into my arms. "What did you have in mind?"

I cocked a brow, and secured her to me. "Wouldn't you like to know? It is a surprise."

"A surprise? However did you manage that? Nothing goes on in this castle without my knowledge."

It was true. Mostly. It had required the greatest care—and the trust of a few deserving servants, chief among them Mrs. Boyle—to ensure Juliana remained ignorant of my plans. I pressed a kiss to her lips, then took hold of her hand and pulled her with me toward the stairs. "I still have an ace or two up my sleeve, you know."

We took the wide, central staircase, then passed through a corridor to one of the narrow tower staircases. It was the least direct route to our destination, but that was necessary to retain the element of surprise.

"Where in the world are you taking me?" Juliana asked as our steps pattered on the cold stone.

I looked over my shoulder at her and smiled but said nothing.

Finally, we reached a landing and stopped. I pushed the door open, moving aside so Juliana could see.

She sucked in a breath and stilled. Daylight, shining through the open curtains, illuminated the royal apartments. The old silk bed-hangings had been replaced with new ones, a new carpet set across the floorboards, the furniture polished and gleaming, and a fire crackled in the grate.

Juliana turned to me. "How did ... when did you...?"

"Over the last two months. With a great deal of help from Mrs. Boyle."

"So *that* is why the door has been locked." Her gaze returned to the room, full of awe. "It is breathtaking, Sandy—and it was beautiful even before."

"I am glad you think so. We are to receive a royal visit, so a few changes seemed in order."

Her brows shot up. "A royal visit? From who?"

I shook my head and pulled her by the hand into the room, closing the door behind us. "From a queen."

Her brows drew together as I stepped toward her and wrapped my free arm about her waist, grasping her other hand to my chest.

"Queen Charlotte?" she asked.

I shook my head again and stared down into her eyes, eyes

that held everything dear to me—things I never imagined I would have. I was immensely fortunate, unaccountably blessed, with a prosperous estate and a healthy son who drove me mad with both aggravation and love. But Juliana was prized above all that.

"I do not understand," she said, full of adorable confusion.

"These are our apartments now, Juliana," I said softly, brushing a curl away from her forehead. "You are the Countess of Lismore—and a more perfect one than I could ever have envisioned—but you are *my* queen."

Her hand grasped mine more tightly as she gazed into my eyes, hers intent and shimmering.

"You deserve the best Lochlarren has to offer," I said, "for you are the heart of it."

She raised up on her toes and pressed her lips to mine. I let go of her hand and scooped her into my arms, our mouths still fast together as I carried her to the bed and laid her upon it gently, just as I had done in Fort William years ago.

Our lips broke apart as I climbed in beside her amongst the voluptuous blankets and pillows.

She smiled widely as she stared up at me, then looked around at the polished wood and gleaming bedcovers.

"How very quaint," she said with a twinkle in her eye.

Before I could respond, she pulled me to her for another kiss.

THE END

AUTHOR NOTE

In *A Suitable Arrangement*, Augusta suffers from what we know as seasonal allergies. Allergies were understood in the early 19th century. The symptoms of hay fever were recognized as early as the 16th century, when they were referred to as *rose catarrh*, since they seemed to be connected to the presence of roses. Later on, the affliction was called *summer asthma* or *summer catarrh*.

These symptoms were largely considered to be an aristocratic disease, as that was the class who most sought treatment and was most afflicted.

In 1819, John Bostock wrote a paper about "JB" (himself) and his symptoms, which he called "hay fever." He tried various treatments: self-induced vomiting, bleeding, and opium. None of them worked. However, he and others found their symptoms lessened when they took trips to the seaside. They were certainly onto something, since pollen counts are generally lower on the coast.

It wasn't until 1859 when Charles Blackley had a violent

reaction after sniffing a bouquet of bluegrass that a connection was made to pollen.

The term "allergy" wasn't coined until the beginning of the 20th century.

As for the horse racing scene in Lochlarren, that was inspired by true historical events. At Fyvie Castle in Aberdeenshire, Scotland, the Gordon family sons rode their horses up the large stairwell as part of a wager. I loved this little tidbit so much, I had to include it in the story!

THE CASTLES & COURTSHIP SERIES

An Amiable Foe by Jennie Goutet

To Know Miss May by Deborah M. Hathaway

A Heart to Keep by Ashtyn Newbold

A Noble Inheritance by Kasey Stockton

The Rules of Matchmaking by Rebecca Connolly

A Suitable Arrangement by Martha Keyes

An Engagement with the Enemy by Sally Britton

Charming the Recluse by Mindy Burbidge Strunk

OTHER TITLES BY MARTHA KEYES

Standalone Titles

Host for the Holidays (Christmas Escape Series)

A Suitable Arrangement (Castles & Courtship Series)

Goodwill for the Gentleman (Belles of Christmas Book 2)

The Christmas Foundling (Belles of Christmas: Frost Fair Book 5)

The Highwayman's Letter (Sons of Somerset Book 5)

Of Lands High and Low

Mishaps & Memories (Timeless Regency Collection)

The Road through Rushbury (Seasons of Change Book 1)

Eleanor: A Regency Romance

ACKNOWLEDGMENTS

As always, I owe so much to so many for the support they've offered me through the writing of this book.

My husband is affected most nearly and dearly, constantly helping me think through issues. His insight into human emotion is excellent, and I'm so grateful to have him by my side through everything.

Jess, Deborah, and Kasey are not only dear friends but valued and talented authors who help me with both the craft and the ups and downs of the trade. I love them so much!

To my fellow series authors—Jennie, Deborah, Ashtyn, Kasey, Becky, Mindy, and Sally—thank you for talking through things with me and just generally being amazing women to work with.

To my beta readers, thank you for reading the first version of this and for making it better than it ever would have been without your feedback. To Brooke Losee especially, who read the first AND second versions of the book and helped me immensely with ironing out kinks.

Thank you to my editor, Molly Rice, for her wonderful work and for cleaning up the messes I made.

Thank you to my Review Team for your help and support in an often nervewracking business.

And thank you, finally and most importantly, to God, for blessing me with all I have.

ABOUT THE AUTHOR

Whitney Award-winning Martha Keyes was born, raised, and educated in Utah—a home she loves dearly but also dearly loves to escape to travel the world. She received a BA in French Studies and a Master of Public Health, both from Brigham Young University.

Her route to becoming an author was full of twists and turns, but she's finally settled into something she loves. Research, daydreaming, and snacking have become full-time jobs, and she couldn't be happier about it. When she isn't writing, she is honing her photography skills, looking for travel deals, and spending time with her family. She lives with her husband and twin boys in Vineyard, Utah.